Anthony Price was bor... was educated at King's ... studied history at Mert... from some temporary pe... has been a journalist all h... reviewer of historical boo... ...g on to become the *Oxford Mail's* crime reviewer, then Deputy Editor and then Editor of the *Oxford Times*.

He won the Crime Writers' Association's Silver Dagger award for his first novel *The Labyrinth Makers* and their Gold Dagger award for the best crime novel of 1974 for *Other Paths to Glory*.

Also by Anthony Price:

Anthony Price

War Game

Futura
Macdonald & Co
London & Sydney

A Futura Book

First published in Great Britain by
Victor Gollacz Limited in 1976

First Futura Publications edition 1979
Reprinted 1982

ISBN: 0 7088 1621 5

Made and printed in Great Britain by
Hunt Barnard Printing Ltd., Aylesbury, Bucks.

Futura Publications
A Division of
MacDonald & Co (Publishers) Ltd
Maxwell House
74 Worship Street
London EC2A 2 EN

For
Margaret and Brian Aldiss

PROLOGUE:

The Battle of Swine Brook Field

From *Perfect Occurrences of Parliament and Chief Collections of Letters from the Armie*, 9th to 16th May 1645:

Friday, May the 9.—I shall this day in the first place present you with a May-game; but such a one as is not usuall, and deserves to be taken notice of, and it is an action of Warre too, and therefore the more sutable to the times.

In Kent the countrey people (no where more) love old customes, and to do every yeer what they have done in others before, and much pastimes, and drinking matches, and May-Poles, and dancing and idle wayes, and sin hath been acted on former May dayes.

Therefore Colonell *Blunt* considering what course might be taken to prevent so much sin this yeer, did wisely order them, the rather to keep them from giving the Malignants occasion to mutinie by such publique meetings, there having been so many warnings by severall insurrections, without such an opportunity.

Colonell *Blunt* summoned in two Regiments of his foot Souldiers to appear the last May-Day, May the 1, at Blackheath, to be trained and exercised that day, and the ground was raised, and places provided to pitch in, for the Souldiers to meet in two bodies, which promised the Countrey much content, in some pretty expressions, and accordingly their expectations were satisfied.

For on May day when they met, Colonell *Blunt* divided them into two parts, and the one was as Roundheads, and the other as Cavaliers, who did both of them act their parts exceeding well, and many people, men and women, young and old, were present to see the same.

The Roundheads they carried it on with care and love, temperance and order, and as much gravity as might be, every one party carefull in his action, which was so well performed, that it was much commended.

But the Cavaliers they minded drinking and roaring, and disorder, and would bee still playing with the women, and compasse them in, and quarrell, and were exceedingly disorderly.

And these had severall skirmishes one with the other, and took divers prisoners one from the other, and gave content to the Countrey people, and satisfied them as well as if they had done a maying in another way, which might have occasioned much evill after many wayes as is before declared . . .

(Appendix F from Sir Charles Firth's *Cromwell's Army: A History of the English Soldier during the Civil Wars, the Commonwealth and the Protectorate*, being the Ford Lectures delivered in the University of Oxford, 1900–1.)

THE SWINE BROOK was running red again, with the wounded and dying laid out along its banks under the dappled shadow of the willows.

Mostly they were quiet now, engrossed in the final act of the tragedy which was about to take place in the bright sunshine of the water-meadow where the London pikemen and the wreckage of their brother regiments were huddled, waiting for the last great Royalist assault.

Bathed in sweat under their buff-coats and breastplates, unnerved by the suddenness of the fall of their general, the footmen had nevertheless fought like lions. Twice already they had repelled enemy attacks at push of pike; once—ill-advisedly—they had even tried to follow their retreating attackers up the ridge; galled by the fire of the two sakers up the hillside when their own cannon had fallen silent they had closed up and stood firm, so that the original extent of their line was now marked by their dead to the left and right of them. 'Steadfast' had been their field-word and they had lived up to it: now they were about to die by it. The lions had become bullocks waiting for the arrival of the butcher.

The moment had come. The sakers banged out for the last time, the trumpets on the hillside shrilled and were drowned by the rising tide of Royalist cheers.

God and the King!

The answering cry from the water-meadow, *God our strength*, rang hollow. This day God was a Cavalier, and both sides knew it.

Even so, the Parliamentary ranks held firm for one shouting, grunting, groaning minute after the rival pikemen met. Then the lie of the land and superior numbers—and history itself—overwhelmed them: they broke and ran in panic towards the stream, their fear fed by the knowledge that Thomas, Lord Monson, was notoriously averse to taking Roundhead prisoners. Black

11

Thomas had private scores to settle—a dead brother and a burnt home among them—and this was his day for the reckoning.

Clouds of insects rose from the water as the fugitives splashed through it in the thirty-yard gap between the hawthorn and blackberry tangles; the smoke from their burning wagons thinned, to reveal their abandoned cannon on each side of the rout.

The Royalist infantry surged after them, Monson on his great black horse now leading them. But as he reached the Swine Brook one of his men overtook him—

This was the moment of victory, and also the moment of the act which was to immortalise that victory—and Black Thomas with it—when greater triumphs and commanders would long be forgotten.

The soldier tore off his helmet and filled it with the dirty, reddened water. Then he climbed back up the bank and offered it to the Royalist general.

There was a growl of approval from the footmen as Black Thomas lifted up the dripping helmet high for all to see, a growl rising to a great cheer as he lowered it to his lips, the water cascading on either side down his gilded black half-armour.

Black Thomas had promised.

Black Thomas had fulfilled his promise.

"A Monson! A Monson!"

"God and the King!"

The Royalist infantry shook their pikes and waved their swords in triumph; and the watching crowds on the hillside above, who had been waiting for this above all things, took up the applause.

Henry Digby, observing the spectacle from his post beside an old willow ten yards upstream, grunted his disgust. One well-aimed musket ball would have cut Lord Thomas Monson down to size at this moment, and would have gone some way towards avenging the Swine Brook Field slaughter of the righteous. But he had no musket and today there had been no musket ball with Black Thomas's name on it. That day would come, but it was not yet come.

The dead man beside him raised himself on an elbow.

"He's not actually drinking the stuff, is he?" asked the dead man.

A dying man who had been dabbing his toes in the water nearby laughed. "I wouldn't put it past him. Just like the real thing—and I'll bet they're all damn thirsty by now." He pointed to Digby's plastic container. "It's not poisonous by any happy chance, is it? But that would be just too much to hope for, I suppose."

"The dye?" Digby shook his head, frowning at the implications of the suggestion. "Of course not. It's strictly non-toxic. But I hope to heaven he doesn't drink it. The stream's full of cow-dung."

"Yrch!" The dead man stared at the stream, wrinkling his nose.

"But *they* drank it. And *he* drank it, that's for sure," said the dying man. "And it was probably full of pig-shit then. And it didn't do him any harm."

"I expect they had stronger stomachs than we've got. Probably had all sorts of natural immunities," said the dead man.

"I doubt that," said Digby. "They were rotten with dysentery at the Standingham Hall siege a week later."

"Both sides were rotten with it," countered the dying man. "I was arguing with a chap from Boxall's Regiment last night in the pub. He said the cavalry was queen of the battlefield, when it came to a killing match. But I reckon squitters was queen. More of the poor bastards crapped themselves to death than ever killed each other, for a fact. I had a bad dose of enteritis last summer, and it bloody near killed me, I tell you. And I was full of pills and antibiotics." He nodded wisely. "I should think the safest ingredient in this water back then was probably the blood, and Monson just struck lucky."

As if he had overheard their conversation, the Royalist commander came riding along the bank towards them while his troops surged across the stream in pursuit of the broken Roundheads.

He waved at Digby. "Keep pouring it in, Henry," he shouted. "We want to make sure it goes all the way down to the road bridge—that's where the crowds will be."

Digby waved back and slopped more dye into the stream. It hadn't occurred to the silly man that it was pointless to waste the dye when everyone was churning up the water, but now most of them were across and he wasn't going to argue the toss. It was enough that he understood better than anyone that his role today, though unglamorous, was probably the most important one of all: just as Black Thomas's unhygienic act had fixed Swine Brook Field firmly in the history books, so that it was remembered by people who'd never heard of such crowning mercies as Naseby and Marston Moor, so today's red stream was what would catch the public eye and the public imagination. The afternoon before, when the other officers had been checking out the battle scenario, he had superintended a dress rehearsal of this bit of it for a BBC TV News crew. By this evening with any luck it would be seen in colour by millions, and from those millions there would be some hundreds of would-be recruits. From them the Mustering Committee would be able to raise half a dozen new regiments—good quality regiments of those who knew what they were fighting about, and loved what they knew.

"How long do we have to lie here?" The dying man consulted a wristwatch. "I'm getting damn thirsty—it comes of watching Black Thomas do his thing."

Good quality regiments were composed of better material than the dying man, thought Digby disapprovingly. Wristwatches were strictly forbidden in battle, together with all other anachronisms except spectacles, and even those had to be National Health steel-framed.

He added more dye to the stream. "5.30 for us." The man hadn't even read his scenario properly. "We have to perform for the crowd first."

He pointed towards the ridge, which was already black with spectators who had been released from the retaining ropes by the crowd marshals.

"Don't worry, Phil," said the dead man. "Any minute now we're due for succour from the Angels of Mercy and consolations from the Men of God."

"You can keep the Men of God—you're dead," said the dying man. "Me, I'll settle for an Angel of Mercy to ease my passing. A little bit of succour is just what I need at the moment." He peered around uneasily. "You haven't seen the Lord General anywhere, have you?"

"He's in the next gap," said Digby. "Why d'you want to know?"

"Because he's probably keeping his beady eye on me, that's why. I got chewed up for putting my hand up an Angel's skirt at Overton Moor."

"By the Angel?" asked the dead man innocently.

"Are you kidding? It was my own private Angel. But the Lord General doesn't think a god-fearing man ought to fancy the flesh ih his last agonies—he's a stickler for bloody accuracy. . . . There are times when I think I ought to have been a cavalier. They expect that sort of thing, lucky bastards."

Digby was slightly shocked by the dying man's profanity. It was true that Jim Ratcliffe was meticulous in his requirements. But it was also true that it was becoming a point of honour in the Parliamentary Army that there should be no swearing on the field or off it. He had noticed the previous evening that even after the beer had flowed freely and the politics had become vehement there had been very little swearing among the men of his own regiment.

"Are you sure you shouldn't change sides?" He tried to sound casual.

"Change sides?" The dying man repeated the words incredulously. "Christ, man—my old dad was a miner. I've voted Labour all my life, and I'm not going to change now. . . . Bloody cavaliers, you won't catch me among them."

"Phil talks like a Malignant," explained the dead man loyally, "but his heart's in the right place."

"Too true," agreed the dying man. "Just happens Dave and I don't happen to be a couple of your Eastern Association men. We're low-grade cannon-fodder—what Noll Cromwell called 'old decayed serving-men and tapsters'. We run away when things get too hot, but we bloody well come back again. And we died out there too—" he pointed towards the water-meadow "—before there ever were any Ironsides in their pretty uniforms. This is 1643, remember, not '44 or '45."

He could be right at that, thought Digby penitently. But more than that, there ought to be a use for such cheerful rogues because even in defeat there was a marked reluctance among members of both armies to behave shamefully. The dying man

15

and his friend might become the nucleus of a special group prepared to disgrace themselves—a company of cowards. He might usefully raise the idea with Jim Ratcliffe before the next Mustering Committee meeting. Although he was a successful stockbroker, Jim's enthusiasms for the realism and the Round-head cause were unbounded.

As he emptied the last of the dye from the canister and reached for a fresh one a shadow fell across his hand.

"Keep it up, Henry—keep it up." Bob Davenport's broad American voice followed the shadow. "It's going down great at the bridge, the people there are loving it. If we could bottle it I swear we could sell it for souvenirs.... Casualties ready to perform?"

"Any real casualties?" Digby's private nightmare came to the surface.

"Just the usual cuts and bruises ... plus one minor concussion. No fractures—nothing serious," the American reassured him. "The boys are getting pretty good at looking after themselves."

"Have you seen the Lord General?" asked the dying man.

"Not since he was hit. He's just round the next bush." Davenport looked over his shoulder. "Well, here they come. Do your stuff now."

Digby screwed the dripper-top into the new canister of dye and fitted it into the recess he had scooped out in the bank between the roots of the willow. When he had checked that the red stain was spreading satisfactorily he camouflaged the plastic with the grass he had cut in readiness and climbed back up the bank to where Davenport stood beside the bodies. As the first of the spectators drew near he dropped on his knees beside the dying man, his hands clasped in prayer.

"Courage, good friends," said Davenport in a loud voice. "We must needs look upon this dread day as the hand of the Lord raised mightily against us poor sinners, for it was only He that made us fly from the ungodly hosts."

"Amen to that," said Digby. "For those that He loveth He first chastiseth, even as the mighty Samson was brought low before the Philistines."

"Ye shall be cast down in this wicked world that ye be raised up in the world everlasting," agreed Davenport. "And doubt not

16

that on the dreadful day of judgment the Lord shall know His own."

"He that loseth his life in Thy service shall save it," said Digby.

"Look! He's all covered in blood, mum," said a shrill treble voice in the crowd.

"Sssh!"

"Tomato sauce, more likely," said another voice irreverently.

There was a titter of laughter, which the dying man cut off with a realistic groan. "Lord, Lord—Thy will be done," he croaked.

"Amen," intoned Davenport.

The bushes on the far side of the stream parted and the first of the Puritan Angels of Mercy appeared exactly on cue, a fine buxom girl bursting out of her tight black dress in unPuritan style.

"Water, water," croaked the dying man.

Raising her skirts with one hand and grasping her leather water-bottle firmly in the other the Angel stepped bravely into the water.

"Thou comest as an angel of mercy, sister," said Davenport. "This poor fellow hath need of thee."

The Angel knelt beside the dying man and tenderly lifted his head as she tilted the bottle to his lips.

The crowd murmured appreciatively, cameras clicked, Digby smelt beer and the dying man winked solemnly at him.

Davenport launched himself into his standard five-minute sermon on the wickedness of the Royalists, the diabolical nature of their recent victory, its temporary nature and the inevitable outcome of their obstinate adherence to Popery, prelacy, superstition, heresy, profaneness and other abominations contrary to sound doctrine, godliness and the will of Parliament.

It was good stirring, authentic-sounding stuff and the American put it over with hellfire sincerity, thought Digby. Indeed, it knocked spots off all the modern political harangues he had heard, from National Front meetings to International Marxist rallies, at which each side had bayed for the other's blood, but in dull twentieth-century language lacking the marvellous Old Testament vocabulary which had come naturally to seventeenth-century speakers.

Now the climax was coming—

"The Swine Brook runneth red this day with the blood of the servants of the Lord, shed by those men of Belial whose cause is the horridest arbitrariness that was ever exercised in this world." Davenport pointed towards the stream. "It crieth out for vengeance, and be assured that the vengeance of the Lord of Hosts shall be terrible to behold—"

Digby rose unobtrusively from his knees (those who were not listening open-mouthed to the American were staring pop-eyed down the Angel's cleavage) and made his way back to the stream's edge to check the spread of the dye.

It was still dripping out nicely from the container, and also spreading—

Digby looked down, suddenly perplexed. Where the stream had been stained rusty-brown downstream from the container, now it was also already coloured a vile unnatural pink *upstream*.

He stared to his left, into the dark tunnel of overhanging bushes. Some unauthorised joker was at work up there, spiking the water with a chemical of his own—possibly a toxic one. And that must be stopped quickly.

The look on his face as he turned back towards the crowd was caught by the dying man.

"What's up, Henry?" he said, reviving himself miraculously.

"Somebody's playing silly buggers," hissed Digby angrily.

"Well, you can't go now—the Preacher's just getting to his blood-and-confusion bit. He'll need you for that."

"This won't wait." Digby pushed into the crowd.

The Preacher paused in mid-flow. "Where—" he caught himself just in time. "Where goest thou, brother?" he called out.

Digby raised his hand vaguely. "Upon the Lord's business, brother, upon the Lord's business."

He made his way through the crowd and out round the straggle of blackberry bushes and young hawthorns to the first gap in the thicket, where Jim Ratcliffe was stationed, carrying with him a gang of small boys who were concerned to discover what the Lord's business entailed. But the gap was empty; without the distraction of the Preacher's performance Jim had obviously spotted the tell-tale stain ahead of him.

Somewhat reassured he continued upstream. The next opening

in the undergrowth was nearly a hundred yards on, by a gated farm bridge. That was the most likely place for—

"Mister! Mister!"

The treble yell came from behind him. One of the small boys waved frantically at him, and then pointed at Jim's empty gap.

" 'E's in the water, mister!" yelled the boy.

Digby pounded back the way he had come. Inside the gap, between the high tangles of thorn and bramble, there was a yard of ground beyond which the stream widened into a dark little pool.

" 'E's in the water," the voice repeated, from behind him now.

Two slightly larger boys stood on the bank of the stream looking down. One of them squatted down abruptly to get a better view of what lay out of sight.

"Well, I still think 'e's shamming," said the boy who had remained standing. "It's what they do, like on the telly."

Digby noticed a bright splash of red dye on the crushed grass beside the boy's left foot.

"Get out of the way," he commanded.

As the boys parted he saw that the pool was bright red.

He took two steps forward and looked down.

One thing Jim Ratcliffe certainly wasn't doing was shamming.

PART ONE:

How to be a good loser

I

CROMWELLIAN
GOLD HOARD
WORTH 'MORE
THAN £2M'

By a Staff Reporter

A subtle skein of historical mystery, interwoven with the red threads of piracy, civil war and sudden death, surrounds the discovery yesterday of a great treasure of gold, thought to be worth more than £2 million, at Standingham Castle in Wiltshire.

The discoverer—and the probable owner—of this vast fortune is Mr Charles Ratcliffe, 26, who inherited the castle recently on the death of his uncle, Mr Edgar Ratcliffe, 70, after a long illness.

The gold, nearly a ton of it in crudely-cast ingots, is now under guard awaiting the coroner's inquest which must by law decide its ownership.

Meanwhile, Mr Charles Ratcliffe, who is a Roundhead 'officer' in the Double R Society, which re-enacts English Civil War battles and sieges in costume, has revealed how his special knowledge of the period helped him to discover what so many others, Oliver Cromwell among them, have sought down the centuries.

Yet the story that he has finally unravelled begins, it now seems likely, not at Standingham Castle at all, but far out in the Atlantic Ocean in the year 1630, with the disappearance of the Spanish treasure ship *Our Lady of the Immaculate Concepcion*..

Legend has it that this ship fell prey to one of the last of the Devon sea dogs in the Drake image, Captain Edward Parrott,. of Hartland, whose own ship, the *Elizabeth of Bideford*, was lost that same summer on the North Devon rocks.

It was widely believed in the West Country, however, that Captain Parrott had earlier landed the gold secretly (since

England was nominally at peace with Spain at the time), and then had put to sea again.

No confirmation of this rumour emerged until August, 1643, when during the Civil War a party of Parliamentary horsemen from North Devon led by Colonel Nathaniel Parrott, the Captain's son, took refuge in Standingham Castle to escape capture by the Royalists.

Colonel Parrott and his men reinforced the defenders of the castle, which had been re-fortified by its owner, Sir Edmund Steyning, himself a fanatical supporter of the Parliamentary cause.

They brought it no luck, however. For after a Roundhead relief force had been defeated at the battle of Swine Brook Field, twelve miles away, the castle was stormed by the Royalists and the majority of its defenders massacred.

Both Colonel Parrott and Sir Edmund were among the dead, but it is known that the Royalist commander, Lord Monson, instituted a thorough—but fruitless—search of the castle directly afterwards. The historical assumption (though one not widely maintained until now) is that both the search, and indeed Lord Monson's energetic prosecution of the siege, had been inspired by some knowledge of a treasure brought to the castle by the Roundhead horsemen.

The North Devon legend of Spanish gold now became firmly rooted in rural Wiltshire, strengthened by a second search, reputedly by Oliver Cromwell himself, in 1653. Since then there have been at least four other major treasure-hunting operations, the last in 1928 by the late Mr Edgar Ratcliffe's father.

This long record of failure, which led most historians to discount the whole story, has now been ended by Mr Charles Ratcliffe's brilliant historical detective investigation.

Standing beneath the crenellated outer ramparts yesterday, Mr Ratcliffe, a youthful and colourful figure, said: "I have never believed the experts who said either that there never was any gold, or that Cromwell must have found it in 1653. As a boy I listened to all the old stories, and I believe that local traditions are worth far more than the half-baked facts in the history books."

Mr Ratcliffe, who is a postgraduate sociology student and runs a workers' paper in his spare time, said that he had not searched haphazardly for the gold.

"First I studied all the known facts and compared them with the local tales," he said. "Then I simply put myself into Colonel Nathaniel Parrott's shoes.

"I took my final conclusion to a distinguished historian of the period, and he agreed with me. But I shall tell the full story of that at the coroner's inquest to be held shortly."

And he added intriguingly: "I can say that once I had worked out what really happened I didn't have to search for the gold. I went straight to it."

The only shadow on Mr Ratcliffe's good fortune is the recent death of his cousin, James Ratcliffe, in circumstances peculiarly relevant to—and strangely connected with—the Standingham treasure.

For Mr James Ratcliffe was killed earlier this year during the re-enactment by the Double R Society (of which he was also a member) of that same battle of Swine Brook Field which preceded the storming of Standingham Castle.

The suspicious circumstances of his death are still being investigated by the Mid-Wessex Police Force, following the adjournment of the inquest in June.

The police have stressed that Mr Charles Ratcliffe, who was also present on the fatal mock-battlefield, is not involved in their inquiries.

Our legal correspondent writes: It will now be for an inquest jury convened by the local coroner to decide on the ownership of the Standingham gold. Broadly speaking, buried treasure comes under two categories: that which was deliberately abandoned with no intention of recovery (i.e. burial goods, like that found in the fabulous Sutton Hoo ship cenotaph), and that which was temporarily hidden by an owner intending to recover it (like the Romano-British coin and plate hoards) or otherwise lost accidentally. The latter category provides the classic examples of 'treasure trove' in which, in default of finding a rightful owner, the established principle of English law is that the Crown is entitled to the treasure but grants 'full market value' to the finder. This custom, designed to encourage finders to declare their discoveries, has aroused controversy in recent cases where

25

there has been a marked discrepancy between what the Treasury and the British Museum consider 'full market value' and what dealers on the open market are prepared to offer, since the finder has no redress in law.

In the case of the Standingham gold, therefore, the sum which Mr Ratcliffe will receive depends not so much on the value of the gold, which is easily established, as on his ability to establish original ownership to the satisfaction of the coroner's jury.

Audley glanced from the newspaper cutting to his wristwatch. Although they had been cruising along for nearly ten minutes they had somehow contrived to stay quite close to the airport: somewhere just ahead of them a Jumbo was straining to get airborne, engines at full thrust. Like his own worst suspicions.

Naturally they would have known, because they knew him, that he would arrive back from Washington tired and dishevelled and desperate to get back to the loving quiet of his home and family. More, they would have known that he had confidently expected to do just that, because that had been the deal: two weeks of tranquillity at home in deepest Sussex to complete his report (which could be done in less than one) in exchange for a barely endurable month of American high summer among old friends who could no longer afford to trust him as they had once done.

And most of all, because of that, they would know that he would be mutinous to the limits of loyalty about taking any new assignment before the present one was discharged.

"Very interesting." He handed back the cutting to Stocker politely.

All of which meant they were very sure of themselves, that had to be the first conclusion.

"Did you read about it in the States?" Stocker inquired with equal politeness.

"There was a story in the *Washington Post*. I didn't read the British papers in the embassy, they'd only have depressed me."

Stocker delved into his brief-case. "There's another cutting here."

"I don't want to read another cutting. I want to go home."

26.

Audley kept his hands obstinately in his lap. He noticed as he looked down at them to make sure they were obeying orders that his thumbs were tucked into his fists. According to Faith that was a sure sign that he was miserable, uncertain and vulnerable, and consequently in need of special care and protection. And although he mistrusted his wife's instant psychology as much as he enjoyed her interpretation of the duties it imposed on her it was an interesting fact that one couldn't punch anyone on the nose with thumbs in that position.

"In due course," said Stocker.

Audley re-arranged his thumbs. Not that punching Stocker would do any good whatsoever; besides, Stocker was quite capable of punching back.

"I've a lot of work to do," he said.

"I know. Your report on the current state of the CIA." Stocker nodded. "Sir Frederick told me."

"Did he also tell you it was for the Joint Chiefs?"

Stocker smiled. "Yes, he told me that too, David."

The christian name was an olive branch.

"Well, Brigadier—" Audley trampled the olives—"it isn't going to get done by remote control. I intend to write it now, while it's fresh in my mind. Could be it's not without importance."

"I'm sure it is. But this is more important." Stocker lifted the second cutting. "In fact if your time in Washington hadn't run out today we would have brought you back today anyway —no matter what."

"We?"

"Sir Frederick and I." Stocker paused. "And others."

"Others?"

Any chance of a reply to that question was blotted out by the roar of another big jet. This time the noise was almost unbearable, with the brute force of the sound vibrating the car as it slowed down at the entrance to a lay-by on its nearside. There was a police car—a large, vividly-striped Jaguar—parked in the entrance so that there was only just sufficient room for them to squeeze by. The uniformed man at the wheel raised his gloved hand to Stocker's driver, beckoning him on.

It wasn't a custom-built lay-by, Audley realised. Once upon a time, before the runways had swallowed the fields, this had been the line of the main road lurching in a drunken meander between the quiet hedgerows, Chesterton's rolling English road to the life. But when the new highway builders had amputated this unnecessary loop they hadn't bothered to grub up the tarmac, and now the unrestrained hedges had sprouted into trees which screened it from the passing traffic. But for the jets, it would have been an admirable place for love in the back seat.

But there was no love in this back seat, nor would there be any waiting for him in the back seat of the car parked in the shade of a gnarled crab-apple tree, an anonymous new wedge-shaped Leyland 2200 of the sort he and Faith had contemplated buying in the autumn, in patriotic replacement for his rusting old 1800. In a more peaceful, more honourable world he would be returning to her now.

He waited until the jet thunder had become a distant rumble.

"Others?"

"The Joint Chiefs... among others."

"Uh-huh? You mean Sir Frederick and you and the Joint Chiefs... and others... all cried my name with one voice in their hour of need?"

"Something like that. Something very like that." Stocker was so sure of himself that he was prepared to be magnanimous. Audley recognised the tone. Magnanimity was the civilised victor's final body-blow to the defeated.

"I'll bet."

"You should be flattered, David. This is an awkward one, but you have the right equipment for it."

Audley strained to make out the features of the man in the back of the 2200. "I have the right equipment for rape, but I've no intention of letting anyone make a rapist of me, Brigadier."

"That wasn't quite what we had in mind for you." Stocker was almost genial now. "It's your brain we need, not any other part of you. You won't even have to do much leg-work—I've detached Paul Mitchell and Frances Fitzgibbon to do all that, directly under your orders. And you can have anything else you want within reason, short of the Brigade of Guards." He paused. "If you like you can choose your field co-ordinator too."

Now that *was* flattering, thought Audley. To be given two

bright field operatives who had worked with him before was commonsense. But to be allowed to choose a co-ordinator was patronage on a grand scale.

Unfortunately it was also rather frightening.

"We'll give you Colonel Butler, if you like." Stocker actually smiled as he baited the hook with the best co-ordinator in the department. "He's free at the moment."

Audley was saved from not knowing how to react to that by the opening of the 2200's rear door. The mountain was coming to Mahomet.

"It's entirely up to you, anyway," said Stocker mildly, offering the second cutting a second time. "And naturally we're not going to insist on anything. But . . . well, you read this first, David, before you make up your mind."

They weren't going to insist. Audley watched the 2200 as though hypnotised. Of course they weren't going to insist; with his own money and what he could earn—Tom Gracey had as good as promised a fellowship for the asking—he could flounce off in a huff any day of the week. The pressures were much more subtle than that, though.

The occupant of the 2200 stepped out of the shadow on to the sunlit tarmac.

Of course they weren't going to insist. They didn't have to.

He took the cutting—

A TON OF GOLD
FOR RED CHARLIE

Half a lifetime's professional interest in newspapers identified the typography instantly: this was the popular version of the dignified story he had read earlier.

Dressed in a flowered shirt and with his long hair curling trendily round his collar, a 26-year-old revolutionary told last night of his amazing discovery of Cromwell's Gold—a whole ton of it.

But Charlie Ratcliffe, who inherited near-derelict Standing-ham Castle in Wiltshire only six weeks ago, is not yet willing to reveal how he found the treasure which is likely to make him one of the richest men in Britain.

29

Audley looked up as Stocker opened the car door for the man from the 2200.

"Thank you, Brigadier. No—it's all right. I'll sit here." The Minister drew open the extra seat from its fastening on the partition which separated them from the driver. "There's plenty of room, I shall be perfectly comfortable ... Did everything go satisfactorily?"

"Yes, sir. We were in and out in five minutes."

"Good." The Minister turned to Audley. "I must apologise for the unorthodox approach, Dr Audley. At least you were spared the usual inconveniences. And it was necessary, you understand."

"Of course, Minister." At least the man didn't try to sugar the pill with a diplomatic smile, thought Audley, which saved him from the pettiness of not smiling back. But then this one was the best of the bunch, and more than that a good one by any standards; he wouldn't smile in this sort of situation unless he encountered something worth smiling about. "Or let's say I'm beginning to understand."

The Minister stared at him for a moment, as though he had expected a different reply. Then he nodded. "But you were reading one of the cuttings. I think you'd better finish it before we go any further."

Audley stared back into the cool, appraising eyes behind the thick spectacles before lowering his own to the fragment of newsprint. There were times when it wasn't disgraceful to be out-stared, even diminished. In that better—and non-existent—world which he had been mourning a minute or two back this man might have been the leader of his party, rather than a senior member of an embattled flank of it. Half his mind struggled with the printed words and the meanings beneath them—

... *treasure trove inquest shortly to be held.*

And in the meantime an inquest of another kind—of suspected murder—stands adjourned. Its subject is James Ratcliffe, Charlie's cousin ...

—while the other half grappled with the Minister's presence and the meaning beneath that.

Politics. They were the nightmare grinning on every intelligence chief's pillow; the wild card in the marked pack, the extra dimension in a universe which already had too many dimensions.

In his time he had watched the Middle East and the Kremlin as he was watching Washington now, and their politics were to him never more than academic matters to be assessed only in terms of his country's profit or loss.

But British politics were different. And so were British politicians, even this man for whom he was already half-inclined to break the golden rule of non-involvement.

... however. But country memories are long, and for the price of a pint in the oak-beamed public bar of the Steyning Arms the locals will still tell you the tale of Cromwell's Gold and the bloody siege of Standingham Castle on the hill above—the gold for which so many treasure hunters have searched in vain ...

He needed time to think. Time to figure the forces required to bring the Minister to a lay-by behind some bushes at the end of a runway.

But there was no time. He re-read the last three paragraphs as an act of self-discipline before looking up.

The same stare was waiting for him. One reason the Minister was here was to see in the flesh the man who had been selected for a particular job. There was no substitute for that.

"I've heard quite a lot about you, Dr Audley," said the Minister.

"None of it true, I hope," said Audley.

"Exaggerated, perhaps. Or it may be that you've had more than your share of luck over the years."

"I wouldn't deny it. But then ... wasn't luck the chief qualification Napoleon looked for in his marshals?"

"Yes, it was." The Minister nodded. "But I've always preferred Wellington to Napoleon, myself."

Audley smiled. "As a general, I hope. I seem to remember that he was a deplorable politician."

"True." The smile wasn't returned. "And the moral of that—?"

Audley shrugged. "Good generals usually make indifferent politicians. One should stick to one's profession after the age of forty—I think that I should be just as ... unlucky ... if I became involved in politics at my age, don't you think?"

The Minister regarded him thoughtfully. "Yes, very probably. In fact neither of us should seek to meddle in the other's—ah—

sphere of activity. If we both agree on the broad principles there's a lot that should be taken on trust, wouldn't you say?"

The oath of allegiance was being put to him more quickly than he had expected, thought Audley. But at least it was phrased in the best feudal spirit, with the acceptance that loyalty was a two-way obligation.

"For example—" the Minister continued smoothly "—whatever political mistakes the Duke made he did lay down one guiding principle for times of crisis, a rule to which I wholeheartedly subscribe: 'The King's government must be carried on'. I intend to see that it is carried on, and that is why I'm here now."

Audley tried another smile.

"I've said something that amuses you?" The Minister frowned.

"No, Minister. I was smiling at myself for jumping to the wrong conclusion for your being here."

"Indeed? Which was—"

"That otherwise I might have gone off to sulk in my tent. I didn't want to go to Washington in the first place—not simply because I don't like to spy on my friends, but because I don't like being buggered about. Because I know why I was sent, in fact."

Stocker gave a warning cough. "David—"

"No, Brigadier. If the Minister has heard quite a lot about me he may as well hear this too. I'm a hard-liner in East-West relations, Minister. I dislike the Russians, and I hate Communists. And with the Helsinki nonsense coming up my face didn't fit at all—I'd become an ancestral voice prophesying war. Or if not war then treachery. So I was banished to the New World with the promise of a fortnight's extra holiday after that, and then a choice of research projects on NATO security. Which promise is about to be broken as thoroughly as any of the undertakings the Soviet government may have appeared to give at Helsinki. And Sir Frederick Clinton knows that *that* just might have been enough to break the camel's back."

"You're beginning to sound suspiciously like a prima donna, David," said Stocker.

"Beginning? Brigadier, I *am* a prima donna. If you insist on giving me damned difficult arias—like this one—" Audley waved

32

the newspaper cutting "—I've no choice in the matter. So if you want someone else to sing this, you get whoever you can. But if you want me to sing it, then you damn well have to put up with me, temperament and all." He turned back to the Minister. "So?"

The Minister smiled. "So you'll sing for us?"

"Of course. The Queen's government must be carried on, one way or another. If you're prepared to take me on trust, I'm prepared to take you, Minister. Sir Frederick gave you good advice."

"That you would trust me face-to-face? Obviously he knows you very well."

"Too damn well for my own good. And I know him too."

"He also says that you're good at finding things—that you once recovered a lost treasure for him."

"I've found a number of things for him. And people. But in this case the treasure appears to have been already found. So what exactly do you want me to find?"

"What makes you think we want you to find anything?"

"Well, you surely don't want me to solve a murder for you. Because solving murders isn't my forte. Murder is for policemen —just as politics is for politicians."

Again the Minister smiled, though more coldly this time. "*Touché*, Dr Audley—I'll try to remember that. But you've read the two cuttings: what do you make of them?"

"Textually, you mean? You want a comparison between the two?"

"That would be interesting—for a start."

Audley looked down at the cutting in his hand. Cromwell's Gold—and now Charlie Ratcliffe's gold—was an incomparable 'silly season' story for any newspaper by any standards. It was every reader's Walter Mitty dream come true: a ton of gold uncomplicated by taxes and death duties. Besides such a fortune even the biggest football pools win looked like a lucky afternoon at the bingo hall; but more than that it was a quick fortune won not by luck, but by the sweat of the finder's intelligence, and therefore deserved as no chance fortune could ever be. Only sour grapes would disapprove of Charlie's riches.

Except for one dark suspicion.

33

"All right... Two cuttings, two papers... One a heavy-weight Sunday, the other a popular Monday." He raised the second cutting. "But the difference goes deeper than that."

"How—deeper?"

"Ratcliffe gave the story to the Sunday. But he didn't give a thing to the daily—there isn't a single first-person quote from him, not a real one. It's all second-hand, or out of their cuttings morgue."

"Inverted revolutionary snobbery, perhaps?"

"Perhaps. But also a mistake."

"Why a mistake?"

"Because it never pays to be unfair to the press when you've got a good story. This Ratcliffe—he's not quite as clever as he thinks he is, if that's what he did."

"I'm still not quite with you, Audley."

"Well, it's like this, Minister. He gave the Sunday a splendid story about the discovery of a great treasure, and that's what their story is about. But he gave the daily paper nothing, so they had to dig up the story for themselves—and they dug up a new story. But it's not a treasure story, it's a murder story." He looked towards Stocker. "What about the rest of the daily press? Did they write about treasure—or murder?"

The Brigadier's expression soured, as though the thought of the British press as a whole was distasteful to him and the only good newspaper was a dead one. Then he nodded.

"Meaning... murder?" Audley smiled. Obviously it wasn't quite the moment to admit that some of his best friends were journalists. "Of course they did. That's where the best story is. But if he'd saved a bit for them, or if he'd been fair all round, they might have felt a tiny bit inhibited about putting his skeletons on display so prominently. But he didn't—so they weren't. Of course, as a revolutionary he might have lost either way, but this way he made it a certainty."

He passed the cutting to the Minister. "Read it for yourself. It's not really about gold, it's about murder. They say that he killed the pair of them, first the son and then the father."

"The old man died of cirrhosis," said Stocker.

"A mere detail. He simply anticipated his murder—and that

was why Cousin James had to go first. But Charlie wanted the estate, and Charlie got it, that's what it amounts to."

"The estate?" Stocker growled derisively. "The estate is little more than the land on which Standingham Castle stands. And that—"

"Is near-derelict?" Audley grinned, warming to the task of imagining the extent of Charlie Ratcliffe's villainies. "And no doubt the old man was up to his neck in debt—don't bother to tell me. It's all there between the lines."

"It is?" The Minister looked down at the cutting, then back at Audley. "I must say I don't see it."

"You don't see it, Minister, because you don't need to see it—you already know it." Audley paused. "The man who wrote that—the reporter, or the re-write man or the sub-editor, or whoever—I hope they pay him what he's worth. There's not a word in it any lawyer could quarrel with. But what it amounts to is that Charlie found the gold, or at least he established to his own satisfaction where it was. Only he didn't want any arguments about ownership—or problems with death duties, either. And if there was doubt about the ownership, then if the father died before the son he might have to face double death duties—which is why the son had to be killed off before cirrhosis got the father. So he killed the son, waited for nature to take its course with the father, and then came up with the goodies. How's that for size?"

"Very neat." The Minister stared at Audley thoughtfully.

"And substantially correct?"

The Minister nodded slowly. "Substantially . . . yes, it very probably is. I don't dispute that." He lifted the cutting. "But there's nothing here that says as much. In fact they go out of their way to say that he didn't do it."

"Oh no, they don't." Audley shook his head. "They most carefully don't say that. What they say—or what they very clearly imply—is that he *couldn't* have done it."

"Very well—couldn't. In this context it amounts to the same thing."

"Not at all. It amounts to the opposite, Minister."

The Minister frowned. "Are you suggesting that 'couldn't' means 'could'?"

35

"No. I'm saying that 'couldn't' means *did*." Audley sat back. "Not in law, of course. Otherwise the editor would be in trouble now. But we're not a nation of lawyers anyway, Minister. We're a nation of detective story readers."

"So?"

"So we know a perfect crime when we see one—means, motive, but no opportunity. The locked room, the flawless alibi, the unshakeable eye-witness. And Charlie Ratcliffe has seven thousand eye-witnesses to testify that he didn't do it, has he not?"

The Minister nodded again, clearly puzzled. "Yes."

"Right. But everyone knows exactly what Hercule Poirot would say to that: 'Here is a man with seven thousand witnesses to his innocence, so my little grey cells tell me that he is the guilty one, *mes enfants*. Seven thousand witnesses must be wrong.' "

Audley was suddenly aware that he was trying to out-shout a jumbo jet which had stolen up on him and now seemed to be passing ten feet above his head. He noticed also that Stocker was smiling.

The Minister waited until the jet thunder had faded. "So what do your little grey cells tell you?"

It was time to consult his thumbs again, thought Audley. Stocker's smile had faded with the jet engines, but the memory of it still reverberated. "That I'm in the process of being conned."

"You . . . are being conned?" The Minister cocked his head on one side. "I'm afraid I don't understand, Dr Audley."

"Murder is for policemen, Minister—I've already said so. If you want me to . . . pin the rap on Charlie Ratcliffe I'm afraid you're going to be disappointed. I won't do it."

"Won't?" The Minister's voice was silky.

"Can't."

"You think he's innocent, then?"

"On the contrary. You've already told me he's guilty. I wouldn't dream of disbelieving you, Minister."

"And the seven thousand witnesses?"

Audley shook his head. "I don't mean he did it himself—as I'm sure you didn't either. But for one per cent of £2½ million I could put out a contract on anyone you care to name—or let's say two per cent, inflation being what it is . . . No, I'm sure

36

he's guilty. But I'm also sure that I'm not the man to prove it."

"Why not?"

"I've told you. First, it's not my skill. Finding enough proof to convince twelve good men and true isn't something I've ever had to do, I wouldn't know where to start, never mind finish.

"And second, it's a police job. It *is* their skill—they know how to do it, and they're damn good at it, too. If it can be done, they'll do it—and if they can't do it then I can't do it." He stared hard at the Minister. "And since you're here now I must assume that they can't."

The Minister relaxed, with just the ghost of a smile edging his mouth. "A fair assumption. But you haven't taken your logic quite far enough." The smile grew. "And that is your skill, I gather."

It was an open invitation to go straight to the heart of the matter, thought Audley. But for some reason the Minister was unwilling to spell it out, but wanted Audley himself to deduce it.

He stared out of the car window at the crab-apple tree in the hedgerow. There was a crab like that in the spinney behind his own kitchen garden wall at home, and like this one it was laden with fruit. The late frost and the bullfinches had played havoc with his carefully tended Blenheims and Cox's Orange Pippins, but the devil himself looked after the crab-apples. And if what the Minister said was true then it looked as if the devil had kept a friendly eye on Charlie Ratcliffe too.

So they were morally certain that Charlie Ratcliffe was the killer, or at least the killer's paymaster, but they couldn't prove it. But that had happened before and would happen again: there were some you won and some you lost, and there was no use weeping about it. Those were the ones you notched up to experience, hoping that the Lord of the Old Testament would keep His promise about repayment in His own time.

But Ministers of the Crown had no time to worry about such things in any case. Murderers caught and murderers free could only be statistics to them. All murderers were equal before the law.

Even revolutionary murderers.

Audley looked back at the Minister as innocently as he could.

"Tell me about Charlie Ratcliffe, Minister. I'm afraid I'm not very well up in revolution at the moment."

Stocker fished a yellow folder out of his brief-case. "Charlie Ratcliffe, David," he said.

Audley accepted the folder. It was crisp and new, like the typescript within it.

Charles Neville Steyning-Ratcliffe.

Interesting, that. Despite battle and murder, and Puritan revolutions and Royalist restoration, and Protestant revolution and Hanoverian succession, and industrial revolution and democratic succession, and the rise and fall of the British Empire, and two world wars and the rise and fall of the Labour Party and Trades Union succession ... despite all that there was still a Steyning in possession of Standingham Castle after over three centuries of accelerating social change.

They must be a shrewd, tough line, the Steynings.

The Steyning-Ratcliffes.

Charlie Ratcliffe.

He felt the smooth, thick paper under his fingers. That was interesting too—if anything even more interesting. Not Department paper and not a departmental typewriter. Not a photocopy from the Special Records or a typist's copy of a print-out from the Central Computer. But, for a bet, if he now called for a photocopy on a print-out from anywhere else, then this would be what he would get.

Well, they had been careless—

Born April 23, 1949—

A mere baby, relatively speaking.

—careless. Which was all the more reason why he must not be careless in his turn and ask them the direct question that was on the tip of his tongue: what had there been in the original file on Charles Neville Steyning-Ratcliffe that wasn't fit for David Audley's eyes?

Much better to hold on to that question. So long as it remained unanswered there would be an area of uncertainty. But there were ways and means of dealing with that, and as long as it remained officially unasked he had a nice little excuse with which to account for future failure.

Educated at—

He read the typed pages through carefully. Until the last one they contained nothing of unique, or even very special, interest; Charlie Ratcliffe was no different from his fellow activists among the privileged youth of the West, from the Berlin Wall to the Golden Gate, the product and victim of his age.

Born a century earlier he might have carried the flag or the Gospel into darkest Africa. Born fifty years later—or twenty-five years after that—he might just have managed to get his name on the village war memorial, with the lost generations of First World War subalterns and Second World War bomber crews.

But *Born April 23, 1949* he had become the founder and editor of *The Red Rat*, which appeared to advocate an odd mixture of perfect peace and bloody revolution, in which all men not hanging from lamp-posts were brothers.

"Well..." he closed the folder and met the Minister's stare again "...I would have thought you'd have done better to enlist a good team of sharp lawyers rather than me, Minister."

"Why lawyers?"

"You don't want young Charlie to get his hands on his ton of gold. And the easiest way to do that would be to prove it isn't his."

The Minister nodded. "And how would we do that, Dr Audley?"

Audley shrugged. "I'm not a lawyer. But..."

"But?"

"Well, I would think you could make a damn good case that it belongs to the Crown, for a start."

"How do you make that out?"

Audley thought for a moment, imposing the facts on the first cutting's interpretation of the treasure laws. "Okay. Charlie found it, and he found it on his own land—correct?"

"Correct."

"So if it had been lost then he gets the full market value—right?"

"Yes."

"Uh-huh. But it certainly wasn't lost—as if anyone could lose a ton of gold on dry land. It was hidden by—" Audley stopped abruptly.

"By Colonel Nathaniel Parrott," said Stocker.

Audley stared from one to the other of them. It just couldn't be as easy as this, with Stocker and the Minister listening politely and answering politely, and helping him out every time he stumbled. Because if there was one thing the Minister and the Department had at their beck and call it was a complement of sharp Government lawyers.

"Go on, Dr Audley," said the Minister.

Audley shook his head. "There's no point. If you could take it away from Ratcliffe legally then you wouldn't be here now. Which means that somehow he's got you by the short hairs."

The two men exchanged looks. Then the Minister nodded. "Yes ... well, you're substantially correct on both counts, I must admit. We would prefer not to see a fortune pass into Charlie Ratcliffe's hands, for reasons which don't concern you directly ... And we naturally did look very closely into the legal-possibilities. In fact it was the first thing we considered."

And that figured, thought Audley with a twinge of personal bitterness. When it came to separating people from their money by fair means or foul, Her Majesty's Civil Service had nothing to learn from the Great Train Robbers.

"We even contemplated encouraging the Spanish Government to raise the issue of original ownership." The Minister's nose wrinkled with instinctive distaste.

"You mean—Parrott's ownership? Back in the seventeenth century?"

"That's right." The distaste was masked now. "But there are certain—ah—legal difficulties in that area."

Not to mention political ones, thought Audley. To sup at that Spanish table any British politician would require a very long spoon, and a social democrat like this man would never be able to find a spoon long enough for safety.

"In any case there seems to be little doubt that Parrott was the owner, in fact and in law, by inheritance from his father," the Minister continued. "And that he hid it, intending to recover it later. That presumption is overwhelming."

"It could have been the other fellow who hid it—Steyning."

"It makes no difference. Parrott was the owner. And the moment he was dead it belonged to his heir."

His heir. That was the point, of course; all that flummery

40

from 'our legal correspondent' about treasure troves and fine points of English law paled into nothing if there was an heir.

Because then a much older and stronger law could be invoked: that it was someone's *property*, protected even in this semi-socialist society by the most sacred laws. Only in Charlie Ratcliffe's own revolutionary Utopia, where all property was theft, could there be any argument about that. Which was an irony because—

"His heirs," said the Minister. "And their heirs, Dr Audley."

Audley had reached the same point of repetition as he spoke, but he still stared across the car incredulously. After three hundred years—after three hundred years, then this was a coincidence which overshadowed that irony as a skyscraper did a mudhut.

"Minister—are you telling me that Charlie Ratcliffe is Nathaniel Parrott's heir?"

"I am indeed."

"As well as the Steyning heir?"

"Is that so incredible to you?"

"It's one hell of a coincidence."

The Minister shook his head. "Not really. The Parrotts and the Steynings were related and they had a common heir who married a Ratcliffe, that's all. Unfortunately for us there isn't a shadow of doubt about the descent either; because although the Ratcliffes have managed to lose practically every acre they inherited, with the sole exception of the land on which Standingham Castle stands, they've never failed to produce a male heir, right down to Charles Neville, who is literally the last of the line. With no pretenders and no rival claimants."

No pretenders and no claimants—and no arguments, thought Audley. Charlie Ratcliffe could hardly be better placed if he had struck oil, not gold: he himself, unaided, had found his own property on his own land.

"The last of the Ratcliffes," repeated the Minister, "and now the richest. And consequently the most dangerous." He lifted his hand to adjust his horn-rimmed spectacles on his nose. "And there is apparently absolutely nothing we can do about it. As things stand the coroner's inquest will be a mere formality, so it seems. And that's just two weeks from today."

41

Audley looked very carefully from one serious face to the other. If what the Minister had said was true, literally true, he knew exactly what the Minister meant.

Only in England . . . in Britain . . . here was a Minister of the Crown, holding one of the most powerful posts in the Government, and a very senior Civil Servant, one of the most senior officers of the security service, explaining to him the niceties of a three-hundred-year-old inheritance and their inability to control its fate.

There is absolutely nothing we can do about it and we're running out of time.

It could only happen in Britain. Or maybe in the United States, for all the scandals of recent years (perhaps even because of them!). And, to be absolutely fair, perhaps still in one or two of the other Western democracies. . . .

Only in the West, then—the West which Charlie and his kind hated and despised—only there would Charlie and his inheritance present any problem whatsoever. Elsewhere another minister would only have to nod, and another civil servant would take the nod and pass it down the line to someone whose job it was to translate ministerial nods into executive actions for the Good of the State.

· But not this Minister, not this Civil Servant. Nor this State, thank God!

And the proof of that, if any proof beyond his own judgement was needed, was that they would never have come to him to get their problem solved. He was even less skilled at committing murders than he was at solving them.

So what the devil did they want, then?

"Dr Audley." The Minister's voice was sharp suddenly.

"Minister?" Audley realised he had been looking clear through the Minister.

"If you're thinking what you may be thinking, then don't. There's to be no killing."

"Sir—" Stocker bristled defensively.

"It's all right, Brigadier." Stocker's reaction defused Audley's anger before it had had time to spark. "You do yourself an injustice as well as us, Minister. So perhaps we'd better get back to your problem ... and I would have thought the law was still your best bet there. Better than me, anyway."

The Minister sat in silence for a moment, as though slightly confused by the reactions he had stirred. "The law?"

"The law's delay, more accurately. There has to be a fuzzy edge to it somewhere—enough to hold things up, anyway. If you want to stop Ratcliffe getting his hands on ready cash. ... Is that the object of the operation?"

"It is, yes."

"And do I get to know why?"

The Minister shook his head slowly. "You don't need to know that, Dr Audley. Let's just say Ratcliffe can cause all kinds of trouble with it on a scale we can't handle at this moment."

"Then I would have thought someone would have already supplied him with the necessary funds."

"But everyone would have known where they came from then. And that would have compromised him totally." The head went on shaking slowly. "The whole trouble with this money is that it's ... shall we say, respectable?"

Point taken. In revolutionary circles Russian gold and Chinese gold—even at a pinch Libyan gold—was tainted. But Cromwell's gold had been purified by three hundred years in the ground.

"I see. ..." Audley pursed his lips. "Well, in that case I'd let the Spaniards contest it. You don't need to give it to them—you can argue against them publicly. But you can use them to delay the pay-out."

"Of course we can. But you're forgetting your basic economics; we can delay the pay-out in a hundred and one ways, nothing easier. What we can't affect is the credit. And at this moment Charlie's credit is as solid as a rock in the City. In fact he's already negotiating a big loan at a very reasonable rate of interest."

"That's where we need you, for a start," said Stocker. "We can hit his interest rate even if we can't do anything else. Through you."

"Through me? How?"

The Minister smiled. "In certain restricted circles you have a reputation, Dr Audley."

"Restricted—?" Audley stared at Stocker, aghast.

"Very restricted, naturally," continued the Minister soothingly. "We wouldn't be shouting your name from the rooftops. It would be more in the nature of . . . dropping the word in the right place—that we aren't satisfied with the situation as it is . . . and that we are doing something about it."

"Dropping my name, you mean."

"Only in the first instance. And only at the very top, of course . . . where you have a reputation, as I've already said."

"A reputation for what?" Audley was again appalled and flattered at the same time, as well as being intensely curious. To have a fame that could go before one like the rumble of thunder before the storm was gratifying, even if the sound could only be heard by a few; but to risk losing the element of surprise was a very high price to pay for that gratification.

"For what . . ." The Minister looked to Stocker for aid.

"You make things happen," said Stocker brutally.

"And that is exactly what we want, Dr Audley." The Minister adjusted his spectacles again. "In the matter of Charlie Ratcliffe's gold, we want something to happen. And we want it very urgently."

II

AUDLEY DROVE WESTWARDS at his own speed, which was slow, and by his own route, which was by every small country road he could follow without too much difficulty. If he was late they would just have to wait for him.

As he drove he reviewed his predicament, and decided he didn't much care for it. He had a high regard for the efficiency of the police, but if Charlie Ratcliffe had bought himself a pro from London, or even from abroad, then they had never had a proper chance. And on a cold trail he himself stood no chance at all.

A cold trail which had suddenly become important. Well, at least he could understand the urgency of it: once that inquest jury had pronounced its verdict there was nothing anyone could do to stop Charlie Ratcliffe doing whatever it was they feared he would do. And maybe the Minister himself was his next target.

But that wasn't the real maggot in the apple, just a small bruise on the outer skin of it. The maggot was politics.

The Department *never* involved itself in internal politics, and no matter how much the Establishment feared Ratcliffe's ability to make a nuisance of himself with a ton of gold in his war chest, that still wasn't the Department's business—it was just the Establishment's bad luck. So someone very heavy must have leaned very hard on the Department—especially after what had happened with Nixon and the CIA.

Which could mean one of two things.

Either—*Yes, this is an interesting assignment. So we'll bring our best man back from Washington ... David Audley. Brilliant mind, remarkable record, blah, blah, blah. ...*

Or—*Yes, this is a bastard job—if it goes wrong there'll be hell to pay, and the odds are it will go wrong. So who's expendable in the awkward squad at the moment—*

There was a cowman in the road ahead, bright in his orange-

45

banded safety jacket, motioning him to stop and give way for a milking herd on their way to the byre. He had noted the *Cattle Crossing* sign fifty yards back, and the tenth of his brain which read the signs had already lifted his foot off the accelerator.

If that was the case—

The first of a stately procession of beautiful fawn-coloured Jerseys nosed her way out of the gate on the cowman's left.

If that was the case it would be immensely satisfying to give the Minister what he wanted. But it would be much more prudent to aim at an attainable target.

Respectable failure?

No, that would be beneath his honour. He had promised the Minister, and that promise was binding. But he had not promised the Minister he would risk his neck and his career—as he would have done if the enemy had been a foreign one and not a dirty little jackal who cracked the bones of politicians' indiscretions to get at the scandalous marrow within.

Not failure, then. But he wouldn't aim at a total victory; he would fight a limited war strictly within the Geneva Convention, dropping no bombs beyond the Yalu and keeping his gloves on all the time. The Minister himself had spelt out the rules after all, so that was fair enough.

The leading Jersey nodded at him in agreement across the bonnet. That was decided then. For once he would behave himself, and, if he resolved that from the outset, he ought to be able to organise the mission without any scandalous incidents.

All he had to do was to operate in a regulation manner, using as many operatives and as much equipment as they would let him have. These could be deployed in complicated operations, while he himself was engaged in exhaustive researches into—into what?

The Jerseys were pouring out now, stepping daintily with their forefeet, but lurching boney hindquarters and distended milk-bags behind them as though their rear halves had been added on from some different and much more ungainly animal.

Into the seventeenth century, of course! Into the Civil War, and the Gold of Standingham Castle—and even into the Double R Society itself He ought to be able to lose himself safely in all of those without offending anybody very much. Meanwhile others could research into Charlie Ratcliffe and *The Red Rat*.

He closed his eyes and tried to remember what the *Rat* looked like. He had only seen the thing once, together with a report of an investigation into the charge that the underground and semi-underground press was being funded by external subversive organisations.

Which, apparently, it wasn't. ... And all he could really remember was the origin of its title, which had derived not so much from Charlie's own name as from an insult hurled at him during some political rally—

You bloody little Commie rat!

Which Charlie, in the best political tradition, had seized on and gloried in—*If I'm a rat, then the plague I carry is death to the oppressors of the workers!*

Good rousing stuff, that. Much better than the smudgy, crudely-printed character-assassination sheet packed with half-truths, innuendoes and near-libels which had taken its name from that violent occasion.

Audley opened his eyes and smiled at a doe-eyed heifer which had thrust her dripping black nose at him through the window of the car. The rich sweet smell of cow was infinitely preferable to the sour smell of hate and envy that rose from *The Red Rat's* pages.

All the same, *The Red Rat* had had a clean bill of health. For all that it occasionally came up with an uncomfortably genuine morsel of scandal—which it usually ruined with crass exaggeration—there had been no hint of foreign manipulation, KGB or other. The only string to it was the shoestring on which it ran: it had almost certainly avoided the legal consequences of its most outrageous accusations because it wasn't worth taking to court, not because of the victims' generosity.

Now it would have to tread more carefully. But now it could also afford to tread more heavily.

He drove on steadily, stopping first to purchase a bottle of beer and a pie, and then to turn two pound notes into small change.

The Jerseys had relaxed the last of his Atlantic tensions, the

47

Jerseys and the quiet of the countryside, the green and yellow countryside of the last days of harvest time.

There hadn't been so much stubble-burning this year, he noted approvingly. But what was saddening was the epidemic spread of Dutch elm disease which was browning the leaves everywhere with a false autumn. It looked as though the day of the elm was over in southern England, his own elms among them.

He realised he was seeing all around him what he wanted to see, not what should be uppermost in his mind. The countryman was seeing the fields and the trees, just as the property developer would see choice building land, and the psephologist would pass from one parliamentary division to the next, remembering each one's electoral swing.

What he should be seeing now was not the peaceful countryside of the 1970s, but the war-torn land of the 1640s, the divided England of the last great English Civil War.

Except that was easier said than done, because for all his degree in history there wasn't a great deal he could recall about the seventeenth century—

King versus Parliament.

Cavaliers versus Roundheads.

Dashing Prince Rupert versus dour Oliver Cromwell.

Cavaliers—wrong, but romantic.

Roundheads—right, but repulsive.

And, of course, the Roundheads had won, and dear old Sir Jacob Astley, surrendering the last Royalist army, had summed up this and all other wars—*You have now done your work and may go play; unless you fall out amongst yourselves.* . . .

Which the victorious Roundheads had promptly done. Because now, in place of the King and his cavaliers, they had Cromwell and the terrible New Model Army which had won the war—the unbeatable Ironsides who knew what they were fighting for (more or less), and loved what they knew.

It was coming back, thought Audley. Some of it, anyway.

And then Cromwell had ruled England with his New Model sword, and a great many people had felt the edge of it—the Scots and the Irish and the new young King Charles II . . . and the

Dutch and the Spaniards, and even the Algerine pirates, by God!

And the English themselves most of all, and they hadn't liked that very much—

In the name of Lucifer, Amen; Noll Cromwell, Lord Chief Governor of Ireland, Grand Plotter and Contriver of all Mischiefs in England, Lord of Misrule, Knight of the Order of Regicides, Thieftenant-General of the Rebels, Duke of Devilishness, Ensign of Evil, being most wickedly disposed of mind—

—they hadn't liked it at all, having a man who made the trains run on time, and solved the parking problem, and evened the balance of payments by throwing a sword on to the scales.

Yes, it was coming back, but he needed much more precise information than this before he could decide what to do.

He assembled his small change in neat piles and dialled the London number of the ancient banking house of Fattorini.

"David Audley for Matthew Fattorini, please."

"Will you hold the line please, Mr Audley." Polite voice, polite pause for checking Matthew's personal list. "I'm putting you through now, *Dr* Audley."

A shorter pause—"Hello, David! I thought you were in Washington."

"You know too much, Matthew. I was, but now I'm not... And I need to pick your brains."

"Pick away, dear man—brains, pockets, it's all the same— empty."

Since Matthew Fattorini was certainly one of the shrewdest men in London, and would be one of the richest there before he retired, that was a mild departure from the truth, thought Audley.

"Gold, Matthew."

"Uh-huh. Buying or selling?"

"Neither."

"Pity. Lovely stuff, gold. Price is just about to go down, too."

"I want information, Matthew."

"Don't we all, dear man! But if you want to know whether the Portuguese are going to sell some more of their reserves—and they've got at least 800 tons still—or how much the Russians are going to sell for that US grain, you've come to the wrong man—sorry."

"Not that sort of information. Historical information."

Silence. Audley fed the coin box again.

"What sort of history, David?"

"Sixteenth, seventeenth century."

Another moment of silence. "Wouldn't be Cromwell's gold by any chance, would it, David?"

Audley grinned into the mouthpiece. "I told you, you know too much, Matthew."

"Read the papers, that's all. Lots of interesting things in the papers—you should know, you spend most of your time keeping the best stories out of 'em. But still lots of interesting things. Some of 'em very nearly true, too."

"Like a ton of gold? Can that be on the level, Matthew?"

"Why not, David? Ton of gold weighs the same as a ton of wheat. It's just worth more—and easier to move, that's all."

"Did they ship that sort of cargo from America?"

"In the seventeenth century? Dear man, that was the main cargo from the Spanish American colonies for years—gold and silver, plus gems and spices. I know for a fact that California was producing up to eighty tons a year in the 1850s, and Australia even more. If you think of all the gold-producing areas in the Americas—well, Francis Drake picked up tons of the stuff, gold and silver, in that one raid of his in the 1570s. And that must have been all from the current year's ore, they wouldn't have left the previous year's production just lying around, would they now?"

"But in one shipment, Matthew?"

"You mean all their eggs in one basket? Yes, I see. . . ."

"And with pirates and bad weather—"

"Ah—now you're being deceived by your own historical propaganda. The English—and the French and the Dutch too—always dreamed of Spanish treasure ships, but they very rarely captured one. They travelled in convoy, for a start. And there were very few men of Drake's calibre . . . which was of course why the Spaniards made such a fuss about him. Besides, this shipment of yours was much later—in the 1620s or 30s, if I remember right, wasn't it? That is the one we're talking about, I presume?"

50

The mixture of disinterested interest and casual helpfulness was almost perfectly compounded, thought Audley.

"You wouldn't have a personal interest in Charlie Ratcliffe's credit, would you, Matthew?"

"Hah! Now who knows too much for his own good, eh?" Matthew chuckled briefly. "But as it happens—no. I'm not a crude money-lender. And if I was ... there are some people I wouldn't lend money to."

"But there are people who might?"

"If they thought the profit and the risk matched up—I know of one such." There was an edge to Matthew's tone. "Though now you're showing such a laudable interest in Spanish-American economic history, am I entitled to hope that he's going to be in trouble?"

"You're not entitled to hope for anything, Matthew."

"Pity. But what you really need is an expert historian, my friend."

"I know. I suppose you don't happen to have one in your counting-house, do you?"

"Not bloody likely. But I can give you a name." Matthew chuckled again. "You won't like it though, I tell you."

"Why not?"

"Why not? Hah—well you remember that long streak of wind-and-piss on our staircase at Cambridge—the one who got a First despite everything his tutor could do? The one who read *The Times* aloud at breakfast?"

"Nayler?"

"Professor Stephen Nayler to you, you hireling. He's transmogrified himself into a Fellow of St Martin's, and he's also by way of being a television pundit on matters historical for the BBC. But I expect you've seen him on the box, haven't you? Or do you just watch the rugger and *Tom and Jerry*?"

"What's Nayler got to do with Charlie Ratcliffe's gold, Matthew?"

"Why—everything, dear man. The blighter's going to do a programme of some sort on it. A sort of on-the-spot re-enactment, complete with young Charlie dressed up as his revolting ancestor.... So if you go crawling cap in hand to the great man himself he'll surely help you."

"I should very much doubt it. We never got on with each other."

"Got on? Dear man, he hated your guts—you were the ghastly rugger-playing hearty who nearly pipped him for the senior scholarship. And that's precisely why he'll help you, if you abase yourself suitably. Where's your psychology?" Matthew Fattorini clucked to himself. "No, he won't be your problem.... It's young Charlie you want to watch out for."

"Indeed?" If Matthew was fishing, this was one time he'd find nothing on the hook.

"Indeed and indeed." Fattorini gave a grunt. "Oh, yes—I know what you're thinking: you play with the big rough boys, and he's just a juvenile revolutionary. But I mean it all the same, David."

"You know him?"

"Never met him in my life. But I know he's a man with a lot of gold."

"Gold—meaning power?"

"Not just power. Gold changes people, believe me."

"You should know, Matthew."

"I do." Fattorini's voice was serious. "But my gold is all on paper. Ratcliffe's is the real thing, and it's all his. And what's even more to the point is he's handled it—a lot of it. They say you're never the same after that, it turns little pussy-cats into tigers. Remember Bogart in 'Sierra Madre'? Don't you forget that, David...."

Audley picked up the remains of his money and walked back to collect the beer and the pie, his reward for being right about Matthew Fattorini's usefulness.

He sat on the grass, swigged the beer, munched the pie and thought about how much Matthew must dislike the anonymous source of Charlie's present credit. That in itself was interesting.

But Nayler was something different. All he could remember was a spotty face, uncombed hair and a long, lanky body. Plus, of course, the voice which had driven Matthew and himself from the breakfast table all those years ago. But if he'd got that senior scholarship he could hardly be stupid, anyway.

He swallowed the last fragment of pie, washing it down with

the last draught of beer, and sighed deeply. It had been a bonus that Matthew had known as much as he did, confirming the Brigadier's information about the fund-raising. And Matthew had even produced the right reaction at his interest in the subject. But in the meantime, here and now and in the sacred name of duty, he was going to have to undertake some cap-in-hand crawling.

He retraced his steps unwillingly to the phone box, piled up his coins again, and obtained Nayler's college number from directory inquiries.

There was always hope that the man was out. Or even that he wasn't up at all, since term had nowhere near started, and every self-respecting don would be away from college until it did. Or even that he was happily and fruitfully married, and was taking his wife and his seven ugly and precocious daughters to Bournemouth for a prolonged summer holiday. Then he could honourably get someone else to do this job.

But he knew even before the Porter's Lodge answered that it wouldn't be so. All the laws of chance decreed that anything anyone didn't want to happen as much as that *had* to happen, no matter what the mathematical odds against.

"What name shall I give, sir?" inquired the Porter politely.

"Audley. David Audley." Audley closed his eyes. "We were ... up ... together many years ago, you might remind him."

And there wasn't the slightest possibility that Nayler wouldn't help him. Plus not the smallest fraction of that slightest possibility that he wouldn't settle a few old scores in doing so.

"Hullo?" The voice set Audley's teeth on edge. "Hullo there?"

"Professor Nayler?" Audley opened his eyes to glare at the dying elms. "This is David Audley. Do you remember me?"

"But of course! How are you, my dear fellow? Flourishing, I hope."

The machine asked for more money.

"Well enough." Audley swallowed.

"Jolly good." The words were qualified with an audible sniff. "What is it that you're doing now—teaching is it?" Nayler managed to make teaching sound like sewing mailbags.

"No." That was all he could manage. But he had to do better than that, for the Minister's sake if not for his own.

"No? But you did publish a little book not so long ago, didn't you? I seem to recall seeing it mentioned somewhere."

The scale of the insult had a steadying effect. It was on a par with reading *The Times* aloud at breakfast.

"Yes. But I work for the Treasury now." That was safe. But more to the point, it was also sufficiently impressive.

"The Treasury?" Nayler sounded disappointed. "Jolly good. . . . So what can I do for you, then?"

"We're working on the Standingham Castle gold hoard—you may have read about it in the press?"

"The Standingham Castle hoard?" Nayler was elaborately casual. If Matthew was right he must have all the facts to hand by now, but he wasn't going to admit prior knowledge of the question.

Audley felt better now, even a little ashamed that he had ever let his temper rise; in such circumstances as these flattery did not belittle the flatterer, only the flattered.

"We're looking for an expert to confirm some of the historical facts. Naturally, your name was the first one to come up, Professor."

Nayler bowed to him over the phone. "What is it you want to know?"

"Just the broad details. Did the Spaniards really lose a major shipment of gold at that time?"

"Yes, they did. There's a newsletter from the Fuggers' Antwerp agent reporting it overdue."

"All that gold in one ship?"

"Yes . . . well, that was due to a series of unfortunate accidents. The treasure fleet put into Havana *en route* from the mainland ports—Nombre de Dios and Porto Bello and so on. But two of them had been damaged in a storm, and they transhipped their gold into the *Concepcion* and the *San Salvador*. And then, during the second storm in the Atlantic, when the fleet was scattered, the *San Salvador* sprang a bad leak and they transhipped again when the weather moderated. So the *Concepcion* was carrying a quite exceptional cargo when the third storm broke."

"And then they were scattered again?"

"That's correct. But the *San Salvador* made port and the

Concepcion didn't—that was how the first news of the loss reached Europe."

"I see. Whereas in fact old man Parrott scooped it up for himself?"

"That was the legend in North Devon, certainly. It was never substantiated, of course."

"You mean, they took a treasure ship with a ton of gold—and nobody blabbed?"

"Ah—no, Audley. It wasn't quite like that. The story was that Edward Parrott landed the gold secretly at Shipload Bay, because England was at peace with Spain and what he'd done was the blackest piracy and couldn't possibly be publicly admitted. And then he stood out to sea again and made for Bideford—the *Elizabeth of Bideford* was his ship. But then the storm caught him—"

"Another storm?"

"They called that year 'the Year of Storms', Audley. The fourth one that summer took six ships between Padstow and Hartland Point—including the *Elizabeth of Bideford* on the rocks of Morwenstow. Only three of her crew made the shore and lived."

"Including Edward Parrott, I take it?"

"Including Edward Parrott. And none of them talked."

"Then how did the legend start?"

"I said three got ashore and lived. There was a fourth who came ashore farther down the coast, a very young boy. The local story was that he babbled of a great treasure of Spanish gold before he died."

"Hmm. . . . Not only the local story but the old, old story. No wonder no one believed it later on—'the dying survivor babbling of treasure' would have been the kiss of death to it."

"But in this instance it was the truth, Audley."

It looked as though Professor Nayler belonged to the wise-after-the-event brigade.

"It certainly looks that way, I agree."

"I should think so. The idea that this young man—what's his name . . . Ratcliffe—could rob Fort Knox does seem a somewhat quaint conceit, if I may say so. But then I suppose you Treasury people have to leave no stone unturned, eh?"

Audley wondered idly for a moment how his opposite number

in the KGB would have conducted this inquiry, then thrust the thought out of his mind. That way lay sinful and very dangerous heresies.

"We're rather more interested in establishing why the—ah—young man was so sure the gold existed. After all, the experts said it didn't."

"Oh no, not *all* the experts, Audley. No indeed!" Modest pause for the shaking of distinguished head. "I've long had my suspicions about that little episode."

"You thought the gold did exist?"

"I thought there was a strong possibility." Nayler was hedging slightly now. "Of course there was no direct evidence, of course. As things stood it was—ah—a mere footnote. Or not even that, really."

Message received: if Nayler had really believed as much, which was bloody doubtful, he hadn't been willing to commit himself in print as saying so. But no matter—

"No direct evidence? Meaning there was indirect evidence?"

"Circumstantial evidence Or shall we say inferential evidence?"

We could say what we liked as long as we said something useful, thought Audley tightly. "Apart from the timing of the disappearance of the *Concepcion* and the wreck of the *Elizabeth*?"

"Oh yes, indeed. I shall be saying as much on the television shortly, on their 'Testimony of the Spade' programme—BBC 2, of course."

Of course. No vulgar commercials there—except for Professor Nayler.

"Indeed? Well, you wouldn't care to give me a brief preview? I—and the Treasury—would be in your debt then, Professor. For our ears only, as it were?" Uriah Heep couldn't do better than that, by God!

"I don't see why not. It's really quite simple when you know how to interpret the facts. . . . You see, Audley, the gold went to ground in North Devon after it was landed. Edward Parrott was a prudent man, he knew exactly what would happen if word of it reached the Government. He . . . he knew the score, you might say—if you will forgive the colloquialism."

Pompous bastard!

"You mean—he didn't want to hang in chains with the other pirates in execution dock?"

"Hang in chains?"

"You said it was the blackest piracy."

"And so it was, Audley, and so it was. But I mean the *political* score. You mustn't think of the Parrotts as mere nobodies; they were squires and gentlemen. Edward Parrott sat for Hartland in the first three of Charles I's parliaments—he owned the seat. And his son Nathaniel sat in the other two, the Short Parliament and the Long Parliament. So they were very well aware of the political situation."

Audley cudgelled his memory viciously. He knew now exactly the game Nayler was playing—and winning, petty though it was: the price of information was that he must crawl for it, admitting his ignorance.

On your knees then, Audley—for God, Queen and Country!

"What was the political situation?"

"Tck, tck, tck!" Nayler tutted contentedly down the line at him. "You have forgotten a lot, haven't you, my dear fellow! All those tutorials, all that sherry old Highsmith poured down you—has it all gone for nothing?"

God bless my soul! thought Audley in genuine surprise, remembering for the first time how Nayler had envied his happy and boozy friendship with old Dr Highsmith, which had made their early evening tutorials as much social occasions as academic ones. Had that really been niggling the silly man for a quarter of a century?

But the sudden recollection of those evenings was like a benison—those summer evenings, long and cool, and winter ones dark and cosy, with the mist rising off the river.... And the quick irony of Nayler's sarcasm now was that it unlocked his memory as nothing else could possibly have done: old Highsmith had been a born teacher saddled with an arrogant young ex-soldier who fancied himself as a budding medievalist and maintained that nothing of very great interest had happened after the year 1485—

The tide of memory surged back: Charles I had angrily dissolved his Third Parliament one March day in 1629—which Firth had called "the most gloomy, sad and miserable day for

57

England in five hundred years"—and hadn't called another for eleven fateful years—

And it had been whisky, not sherry.

Audley nodded to the shade of Dr Highsmith through the dirty window of the phone box.

"Yes, I'm afraid you're right, Professor. It's all gone now, all quite gone," he admitted abjectly.

The shade grinned and nodded back at him approvingly. The old man had always held that what one knew about oneself was what mattered, not what other people thought they knew.

Nayler sniffed contemptuously."The Eleven Years' Tyranny, Audley. The King tried to govern without Parliament. So he had to have money—this was the time of Ship Money and monopolies and the revived Forest Laws—surely you remember *that*?"

Humbly now—"Yes, I do now you mention it."

"I should think so too! And there was Edward Parrott—or *Sir* Edward Parrott he had to become compulsorily because he owned estate worth more than £40 per annum, and pay through the nose for it; that was another of the King's tax-raising dodges —there he was, sitting on the greatest single treasure to reach this country since Drake sailed into Plymouth fifty years before ... and there was nothing to equal it until Anson took the Manilla galleon a century later ... there he was, sitting on a king's ransom. Or in that political situation it was more like a kingdom's ransom. Certainly it would never have been sent back to Spain—never."

A kingdom's ransom. Well, maybe it was still that—in the wrong hands at the wrong moment in time ...

"And he was against the king, of course."

"Edward Parrott?" Nayler made a judicious sound. "Say rather, Edward Parrott was for Edward Parrott. He belonged to an older era—he could remember Drake and the others, he'd sailed with them as a young lad. And by the 1630s he was an old man too—that last shipwreck ruined his health. It was his son, Nathaniel—*your* Parrott, Audley—he was the one who was against the King. A left-wing back-bencher in Parliament in 1640, he was—one of the Vane-St. John faction."

"So why did he wait so long to lay hands on the gold?"

"Because he didn't know where it was, that's why. Not until the very end, in 1643, when his father was dying."

"How do you know?"

"For certain, we don't know. But by '43 he was an up-and-coming Parliamentary officer, one of Cromwell's trusted lieutenants, we do know that. And we also know that he left his command in the Midlands right in the middle of the campaigning season, when things weren't going too well for Parliament, to be at his father's deathbed. Through Royalist country, too, that meant."

"And that wasn't filial piety?"

"Filial stuff and nonsense! There was no love between them."

"Only gold?"

"Nothing else makes sense. The old man died on August 1, according to the Parish burial register. Ten days later Nathaniel was at Standingham Castle."

"And just what is the significance of that, Professor?"

"Time and place, man—time and place."

"The Steynings were related to the Parrotts, I gather."

"More than that. Nathaniel Parrott's heir was his daughter, his only child. And she was married to Steyning's only surviving son. The other two Steyning sons had already been killed in the war. So Edmund Steyning and Nathaniel Parrott had the same granddaughter—their joint heiress."

"Steyning was a strong Parliament man, obviously."

"Fanatical. Parrott and Steyning were two of a kind, even though Steyning was past his soldiering days. Both fanatical Parliament men—and fanatical Puritans too. Blood, politics and religion, Audley: you can't bind two men more closely than with those three."

Despite his dislike of Nayler Audley found himself nodding agreement to that. Family and politics and religion . . . dead children and a live grandchild . . . those were the solid bricks of the Steyning-Parrott alliance. The Civil War had only bound them tighter together, becoming a make-or-break cause for both families.

And the gold . . . normally the possession of gold divided men more than it united them, but in these peculiar circumstances it would have been the best cement of all—a loan on behalf of

59

their joint grandchild's future, an investment in the service of everything that they believed in.

"So, when you think about it intelligently, Audley, Standingham Castle was the one place Parrott could really feel safe in between North Devon and London."

Audley frowned. "You mean—he went there deliberately? The newspaper report said he was chased there by the Royalists."

Nayler gave a derisive snort. "My dear Audley—you don't really believe what the newspapers say, do you? Besides, he may simply have been chased where he intended to go."

"Even though it was being besieged?"

"The siege was a rather intermittent affair, or it had been up to then, certainly. And Standingham was a great stronghold too; Monson was considerably reinforced that last time, of course."

And maybe the incentive was greater, thought Audley grimly. With a ton of gold as the prize Black Thomas would probably have chanced his arm on the gates of Hell.

"Hmm . . . You said 'time' as well as place, Professor."

"I did indeed—don't be dense, my dear fellow. Time and place are what makes the thing certain in my mind. There was absolutely no other reason why Parrott should ride out of his way to Standingham—it wasn't as though the news of his father's death was of the least importance to anyone. He should have gone straight back to his regiment, where he was urgently needed. That's Point One.

"And Point Two is that he took far too long to get there in any case. That is, if he'd still been travelling the way he'd come. Which of course he wasn't, because now he had a ton of gold to transport. And that would mean wagons or pack horses, probably pack horses—or pack ponies, seeing that he was coming from the West Country. But for much of the route he'd be passing through Royalist-held territory, so that would mean using back-roads and circling the main towns and villages. Quite a deal of night-marching too, I shouldn't wonder . . . all of which would play the very devil with the men and the animals."

True enough, Audley conceded grudgingly. The man might be a bastard, and for sure he was being wise after the event, but he'd done his work properly all the same.

"I see. He had to have somewhere to rest up *en route*."

"At last you're beginning to see the light! Somewhere safe, with someone he could trust. Preferably about halfway to London. Standingham Castle and Sir Edmund Steyning." Nayler paused. "All inference, of course—all hypothesis. But when you throw a ton of gold into the scales you'll see that I'm right. . . . And if you're looking for more detail, I suggest you switch on your little television the Sunday after next and it'll all be there."

Indeed it would. And Charlie Ratcliffe's claim to fortune would be established to the satisfaction of tens of millions, too; established so that even those who loathed everything which he stood for would concede his right to his loot.

So the gold was real.

And the emergency was real.

The phone pipped for more money and he automatically fed the last of his change into it.

"Are you phoning from a call box?" Nayler managed to make the simple question sound contemptuous.

"Uh-huh. . . . One more thing, Professor: where do the Ratcliffes come into the story?"

"The Ratcliffes? Oh, they simply had the good fortune to marry the granddaughter—the Steyning-Parrott heiress. She was the only survivor of the whole affair, you know . . . and later on she became Cromwell's ward. It's interesting that he never married her off to anyone—interesting and possibly significant, because he was one of the first to look for the gold. . . . But then after the restoration of the Monarchy in 1660 she prudently secured her estates by marrying the first impoverished Royalist who came her way. A sharp fellow by the name of Charles Ratcliffe, oddly enough."

The original Charlie Ratcliffe.

"Even without the gold it was a good match for him," continued Nayler. "His family had lost everything in the war, confiscated or sold—I don't know which, and she brought him about five thousand acres in exchange for his name. It was a good English compromise, even if he was a bit of a bounder."

Pirates, religious and political fanatics—and now bounders. If Charlie was a throwback to the seventeenth century he had

61

everything going for him, no doubt about that, from the Parrott-Steyning-Ratcliffe connection.

But time was running out—

"You don't happen to know how the gold was found, do you, Professor?"

Nayler chuckled malevolently. "Yes I do—as it happens. But that's classified, I'm afraid, Audley. You'll have to wait your turn for that like the rest. It's a little surprise we've got up our sleeves, don't you know."

Bastard, bastard, bastard.

"But I'll tell you this, Audley: they were clever, Parrott and Steyning were. Both devious and ruthless men, no question about that. Just you wait for my little television programme, eh? Clever and devious and ruthless—and Parrott was the more ruthless of the two."

The pips sounded, and an obscene insult formed on Audley's tongue.

But then Dr Highsmith shook his head: revenge was a dish which should always be served cold.

"Thank you, Professor. You've been extremely—"

The phone cut him off. Extremely, unpleasantly, humiliatingly helpful. Nothing was going to shake the historical existence of that gold. The first cutting had been accurate enough. It remained to be seen whether he could improve on the second one.

III

The signpost was just where the Brigadier had said it would be, exactly at the crest of the ridge. But then the Brigadier was always exact.

Audley parked his new 2200 carefully on the verge and studied the sign without enthusiasm. After his initial resistance he had felt the old inevitable curiosity stirring, not for the job itself, but for the ultimate *why* hidden somewhere at the heart of it. But now the reaction to the curiosity was setting in: such curiosity was well enough for Rikki-tikki the young mongoose, but for a respectable middle-aged husband and father it was a poor substitute for the soft breasts and soft cheeks of home after a long journey from foreign parts.

The sign was small and newly painted, or even brand new, and it bore the legend *To the Monument* in capital letters, and *Swine Brook Field 1643* in lower case beneath them.

He climbed stiffly out of the car and surveyed the landscape. The crest of the ridge was quite sharp, almost a miniature hog's back compared with the undulations to the east and west of it.

But Swine *Brook* had to be the key, and in the valley to the west a straggle of willows and thick bushes marked the line of a stream. On his right the pastureland ran down towards the stream, flattening for the last two hundred yards into a rich water-meadow.

Swine Brook Field: the field where they once let the pigs loose.

He followed the signpost's finger down a rutted track along the line of the hog's back between overgrown hedges of bramble and hawthorn. If this had been the battle-front of one of the 1643 armies it would have been a strong position, no doubt about that with the hedge to hide the musketeers and the reverse slope to the east to snug down the cavalry out of sight.

Except that he didn't know which side had fought where at Swine Brook Field yet, only that it had been the King's Cavaliers who had won the day.

Cavalier—wrong, but romantic; Roundhead—right, but repulsive.

Which .side would Sir David Audley have been? Would he have followed his head or his heart? Or his religion? Or his father? Or his county? Or the source of his income?

But there was another thing for sure: of all wars, civil wars were the cruellest, 1640s and 1970s no different. Because the winning and the losing was rarely the end of them, as old Sir Jacob had seen—

Paul Mitchell was leaning on a farm gate set back in the thickness of the hedge, waiting for him with well-simulated patience.

No mistaking Paul. The first time Audley had seen him, across a table strewn with maps and documents in the Military Studies Institute, he'd been hidden under a near-revolutionary shock of mousey hair, and the last time the shock had been tamed to an army trim, blond-rinsed. Now the mouse-colour was back and the length too, with a van Dyke beard and moustache, cavalier-style and flecked with ginger. But no disguise, natural grown or artificial, could hide the predatory Paul underneath; at least, not from the eyes of the man who had recruited him to the Queen's service.

At the time, almost at the first glance, it had seemed the clever thing to attempt it; and every aptitude test and training report since then had confirmed his intuition. If there was any logic and justice to promotion, Paul would be running a section in five years' time, and a department five years after that, and the whole bloody show five years after *that*.

And in the meantime, what could be more sensible than to let him win his spurs under the control of the man who had identified his natural talents at a glance?

God help us all, thought Audley. *Paul is a fine feather in my cap—and how glad I am that I won't be wearing that cap in fifteen years' time!*

"Hullo, David. You're looking bronzed and fit."

For a bet, Mitchell knew where he'd been these last weeks.

"Bronzed and fit, my eye! I'm tired and bad-tempered, and you had better believe that.... Good afternoon, Paul. You look like a sociology lecturer at a radical polytechnic. Does this gate open, or do I have to climb over it?"

"It doesn't open."

"But you have to watch out for your trousers—there's a strand of barbed wire on the top, just this side. I've already torn my jeans on the damn thing," said Frances Fitzgibbon as she came into view at Mitchell's shoulder. "And I think I've spiked my bottom, too."

Audley stared at her against his will. The thought of Frances Fitzgibbon's little bottom was arresting, as was the thought and sight of all her other components, miniature though they were. It wasn't that she was in the least beautiful, or even that she was pretty except in a pert, early-flowering, childish way. But at first sight she was the sensual essence of every man's imagined indiscretion with the girl glimpsed across the shop counter.

"Good afternoon, Mrs Fitzgibbon—Frances," said Audley carefully.

It was always the same: after that first sight the truth about Frances Fitzgibbon dowsed desire like a bucket of ice-water. Despite appearances—which so totally belied reality that she was worth a fortune to the department as she stood, torn jeans and all—Frances was a kindly and serious-minded young woman trapped in the wrong body, who deserved a better fate than having to work with Paul Mitchell... and maybe with David Audley too.

"How are Faith and little Cathy?" asked Frances.

"They were fine when I last saw them some weeks ago."

The brown eyes became sympathetic. "Like that, is it? They double-crossed you again? Poor David—I'm sorry."

"And I'm sorry about the—barbed wire."

Mitchell grinned. "I offered to render first aid, but she wasn't having any."

The eyes flashed. "I should hope not!"

Mitchell too, thought Audley. But that was the predictable male response, a sort of protective lust, and at least they were of an age. Two more babies.

"Never mind, Frances dear," Mitchell went on unrepentantly, "you have an honourable injury On Her Majesty's Service to console you—

Then will she strip her ... jeans and show her scars
And say, 'These wounds I had on Swine Brook Field'

—and David has us to console him."

Babies. Or if not babies then mere children, they had given him to do this job. Clever children, but children all the same. And now they were making him feel older than he really was, and not a little jealous too.

"Some consolation!" murmured Frances.

Audley cleared his throat. He had to stop this sparring and start asserting his authority.

"Very well, then..." He pointed to the plain stone cross which rose from the gass a dozen yards down the hillside. "I take it that is the monument, and Swine Brook Field is beyond it."

"That's right," said Mitchell. "And the stream down there is the Swine Brook, no less."

Audley was unhappily aware that he had observed the obvious, and that Mitchell had capped him deliberately by adding the equally obvious.

"So what happened?"

"What happened..." Mitchell paused momentarily. "Well, we're standing just about midway along the spectator line. They filled in right along the ridge—" he spread his arms out on each side "—about a quarter of a mile to the left and right of us here. And there were ropes strung along to keep them from spreading too far down the hill and getting mixed up in the battle. So—"

"I meant, what happened in 1643?" said Audley waspishly. It was just possible that Mitchell hadn't considered it necessary to take his researches that far back, and nothing would put him down more surely than having to admit a little healthy ignorance.

"In 1643?"

"In the battle. Swine Brook Field, 1643," said Audley with exaggerated patience. "I like to start at the beginning."

"Okay." Mitchell shrugged. "We're on the attack line—they came over the hill from behind us—"

"Who is they?"

Mitchell looked at him uncertainly. "You don't know anything about the battle?"

"If I did I wouldn't be asking. Who came over the hill?"

"The Royalists." Mitchell's voice was just a shade sharper. "The Roundhead relief convoy was travelling up the valley, on the old road to Standingham alongside the stream, more or less."

"A convoy?"

"Wagons and carts, that's right. They call it a battle, but the truth is it was more like an ambush—or an overgrown skirmish that worked like an ambush. The Royalists weren't really lying in wait for them, they were simply trying to stop them getting to Standingham and this was where they collided. It just happened to work out badly for the Roundheads and perfectly for the Royalists, that's all."

"What was in the wagons?"

"General supplies, but mostly cannonballs and gunpowder, apparently....There was this man Monson—Lord Thomas Monson, or 'Black Thomas' as they called him—who was besieging Standingham Hall. It wasn't a big affair: Monson had about 700 men and there were maybe 250 inside the perimeter at Standingham—maybe less. In fact, it was more like a local feud, because the Monsons of Ingham Hall and the Steynings of Standingham Castle were neighbours. Only they just happened to hate each other's guts."

"Because Monson was a Royalist and Steyning was a Roundhead?"

"That was the way it was. But that wasn't the only reason why they hated each other. There was also bad blood between them over a lawsuit of years before, when they'd both laid claim to the same piece of land somewhere, or something. And the King's court ruled in Monson's favour—he had more influence with the King, so the story goes. It was a typical feud situation—like a range war in the Wild West."

Audley nodded. "I see. So when the Civil War broke out Monson naturally sided with the King."

"Exactly. And Steyning declared for Parliament."

"So when Monson laid siege to Standingham Hall, then Steyning sent to Parliament for help. And they sent him these supplies?"

"That's right. And when Monson heard about it he appealed to the King, and the King lent him two regiments of cavalry, and he rode back hell for leather to head off the supply column. Also, at the same time, he ordered up 300 of his best men from the siege lines to block the old road at the top of this valley." Mitchell pointed upstream. "He probably planned to rendezvous here before the Roundhead convoy arrived. But they arrived ahead of schedule and ran into the road-block first, and they were just about to deploy against it when Black Thomas reached the ridge here with the cavalry."

"I see. And being a good cavalier he charged straight in and beat them?" Audley stared down the hillside. The question was almost unnecessary; if the country had been anything like this in 1643 then the unfortunate Parliamentarians wouldn't have stood a chance, caught deploying in the open by the Royalist horsemen on the ridge above them. Charging at the gallop was the one thing the cavaliers did well from the start of the war, he remembered. The problem was to stop them from charging too far, right through the enemy and off the battlefield altogether. But here on Swine Brook Field, the Swine Brook itself would have prevented them from doing that. Plus, no doubt, the prospect of plundering the wagons.

"Yes, that's just about it," agreed Mitchell. "Most of the convoy escort ran away, but the Royalists butchered a couple of hundred on the banks of the stream. It was all over in a quarter of an hour."

"It all sounds rather dull," said Audley.

"It sounds rather nasty to me," said Frances.

"The gentry killing the peasantry, you mean?" Mitchell raised an eyebrow. Then he grinned at Audley. "She's a proper little Roundhead at heart, you know. A Puritan maid despite appearances."

There was more truth in that than Mitchell intended, thought Audley.

"I simply don't find killing attractive," said Frances coolly. "Or military history interesting."

That was one deliberately in Mitchell's eye, for that had been his chosen career before Audley had tempted him into one even more suitable for his talents, as Frances well knew.

"Well, as a battle so-called it was rather dull," Mitchell nodded at Audley, wisely ignoring her challenge. "But it did pro-

duce one celebrated anecdote that lost nothing in the telling. A
real bloodthirsty story—literally bloodthirsty."

"Litefally?"

"Literally, it's the exact word for once. You see, Black
Thomas was so desperate to get here before the Roundheads
did that he wouldn't let his men halt. Kept them going non-
stop after they'd run out of water, and it was a hot August day
—hot and humid, because it had rained during the night before.
So by the time they reached this ridge they were pretty damn
thirsty, and they'd been grumbling about it.

"So when he finally got them here he pointed down to the
Swine Brook—which was beyond the enemy, of course—and told
them there was plenty of water there, and they could drink to
their heart's content when they'd reached it. All they had to
do was to remove the base, vulgar fellows who were in their
way.

"At least, that's the story according to Royalist propaganda
as told by *Mercurius Aulicus* in Oxford afterwards. But the
Roundheads had a different version—according to *Mercurius
Britanicus* in London. He claimed that since Black Thomas had
sold his soul to the devil, water couldn't quench his thirst, only
blood. And when he reached the stream it was running red with
the blood of the slain, so he ordered a trooper to bring him a
helmet-full, which he promptly drank, thus proving he was in
league with Beelzebub."

"Yrch!" exclaimed Frances. "You are disgusting, Paul."

"Not me, Frances dear. This is straight *Mercurius Britanicus.*"

"And what really happened?" asked Audley.

"A bit of both, I'd guess. They would have been thirsty right
enough. And he could well have said 'There's water down there',
or some such thing."

"And did the stream run with blood?"

"That's the story. There were a lot of men killed along it, so
there's no reason why it shouldn't have. It wouldn't be the first
time it's supposed to have happened either—didn't the River
Cock run red at Towton in the Wars of the Roses?"

"But would they have drunk from it then?" asked Frances.

"You bet they would. Thirsty men have drunk a lot worse
than that—and been grateful for it." Mitchell nodded towards

Audley. "David'll quote you *Gunga Din* in support of that, if you like—how does it go?

> *It was crawlin' and it stunk,*
> *But of all the drinks I've drunk*
> *I'm gratefullest to one from Gunga Din.*

That right, David?"

Word perfect, thought Audley suspiciously. Paul Mitchell had done his homework on Swine Brook Field; or it might be that with his military history background, and his eerie faculty for total recall of every fact he had ever encountered, no homework had been needed; but by the same token he wouldn't have forgotten Audley's own weakness for quotations, particularly from Shakespeare and Kipling, and that he was now deliberately and maliciously exploiting it.

"Absolutely correct." In other circumstances he might have capped Mitchell with another quotation. But with Mitchell it might be as well to resist such temptations. The young man's knowledge was once more going to be as useful as his brains, and he could see now why the Brigadier had supplied him. But it was going to take some getting used to, the handling for the first time of a subordinate who could equal him at his own game, and had no scruples about trying to do so.

"That's very apposite, Paul. And most interesting." He smiled patronisingly. "So the Royalists won the battle of Swine Brook Field. Now then—"

"But there's more to it than that," cut in Mitchell quickly. "You see, if it hadn't been for that—the bloodthirsty Monson story—it's a hundred to one we wouldn't be here now. Because the Double R people—the Royalist and Roundhead Society—arranged to have the stream run red again for their mock battle. And in the end it was that which gave the game away. The murder, that is—"

"No, Paul." Audley held up his hand. "I want to get that first hand." He looked at his watch. "We're due to meet the police at the scene of the crime in ten minutes from now. I need to hear their side first before your interpretation of it."

That was the truth, or at least the truth only slightly bent to bring it home to Mitchell that it was David Audley, not Paul Mitchell, who was running the operation.

"What I want now, before we meet them, is a rundown on this Double R Society. Not the mock-battle, just the Society," Audley said innocently, still pretending to concentrate on Mitchell.

Mitchell's face fell. "Oh—well, you'll have to ask Frances about them, they're her pigeons."

"I see. . . . Well, Frances?" He turned towards her.

With Frances there were no special reservations to be made. But there was, he was instantly reminded, one disconcerting tendency to be mastered. Being all of eight inches taller than she was, he was forced to look down on her, and in looking down he found it extremely difficult to stop at her face. Indeed, no matter that the faded denim shirt was chastely buttoned to the neck—by some unjust alchemy that seemed to emphasise what it was intended to conceal—he found himself now looking directly at her chest.

Damnation!

He tried again. One quick look at her face—

"The Double R Society?"

And then away from her altogether. Anywhere.

"In one word . . ." If she had observed the first glance she gave no sign of it. Probably she was used to men with eyes like organ-stops, poor girl. "In a word—weird."

"Weird . . . meaning?"

She shook her head. "It's not easy to explain. There are a number of these Civil War groups . . . the Sealed Knot was the first one. Then there's the King's Army and the Roundhead Association, who operate together. They all do pretty much the same thing—mock-battles for charity mostly. Charity and the fun of it, that's how it seemed to me at first . . ."

"On the actual battlefields always?"

"For choice. They will put on a show anywhere, of course. But they prefer authentic locations. They like to get as close to the real thing as possible."

Weird. He had to make allowance for her prejudice against military history—and against war itself. Weird or not, these Civil War buffs would start out with two strikes against them so far as Frances Fitzgibbon was concerned.

71

"And they do it for the fun of it, obviously. Dressing up and all that?"

"That's what I thought at first." Frances frowned. "But there's more to it than that...I don't know about the other groups, but with the Double R Society it's rather more complicated. They stage the battles for charity like the others, with thousands of people watching. And the battles are combined with seventeenth-century fairs and plays and concerts—also like the others. But they don't actually do all this for the spectators and the audiences—if nobody turned up they'd do it just the same. They do it for *themselves*, if you see what I mean. It's not a game or a hobby, it's almost an obsession. And in a strange way it's even more than that...not just obsession. There's almost an element of *possession*."

"You mean—they don't just play at being Royalists and Roundheads? They *are* Royalists and Roundheads?"

"I think that's what I mean..." She nodded doubtfully. "But I still don't really understand what makes them tick."

"There's a lot of *esprit de corps* in the different regiments, that's for sure," agreed Mitchell. "They have their own badges and they're proud of them."

"Oh, no—it's more than that, Paul. The other Civil War groups have that too."

"I don't just mean that." Mitchell caught Audley's eye. "They're also extremely knowledgeable. And they won't let you join just to have a punch-up in costume; you have to know your history pretty damn well first."

"You're both in the process of joining, I gather?" Audley looked from one to the other.

"That's right—in fact we've both just joined. Young Frances there is a brand new Angel of Mercy for God and Parliament—" Mitchell pointed and then tapped his own chest "—and I'm one of King Charles's laughing cavaliers."

"A Malignant," murmured Frances.

"A Malignant. And a profane and licentious limb of Satan— that is, if I can find a horse in time for Saturday." Mitchell smiled boyishly at Audley. "That was the chief reason they let me in so quickly. There's a waiting list for the pikemen and musketeers, so they vet them much more carefully. But they're dead short of people willing to supply their own horses. Once I showed my heart was in the right place *and* I had a horse, I was in." The smile broadened to a wicked cavalier grin. "Whereas they're always on the look-out for good-looking Angels of Mercy, I suspect. . . . Though I must say, Frances, you're going to have quite a problem looking like a modest Puritan maiden. You haven't got the figure for the job."

"Fiddlesticks!" Frances turned towards Audley. "But Paul's right about having to have one's heart in the right place. You can't join the Roundhead Wing or the Royalist Wing unless you believe in the appropriate politics."

Audley nodded. "Naturally. I'd expect the Royalists to believe in the monarchy, and the Roundheads to believe in Parliament."

Frances shook her head. "It goes much further than that. They asked me which party I'd voted for in the last General Election."

"They?"

"There's a membership committee which meets once a month to interview applicants. We were lucky to get a hearing so quickly—it's quite a complicated procedure, really."

"You can say that again," agreed Mitchell. "They've even got a form to fill in—with spaces on it for religion and politics, and God knows what else."

"So what did you tell them?"

Mitchell laughed. "I told 'em what I thought they wanted to hear: that I was a good Tory and a practising member of the Church of England. And that I thought socialism was as bad as communism—they liked that almost as much as when I said I had my own horse."

Audley looked at Frances.

And at Frances's bosom.

Damnation again!

"I had a different committee," said Frances. "And I told them I was a paid-up member of the Labour Party. Which happens to be true."

"I asked my lot what they would have done if I said I was a Marxist-Trotskyite," said Mitchell.

"And?" Audley felt the sun hot on his face.

73

"There was one chap with a sense of humour. He fell around as though I was pulling his leg—as though the idea of anyone being a Trotskyite was a joke. But the other one next to him took it seriously, like I'd said something dirty. And he said that Anabaptists and Fifth Monarchy men and Levellers all went into the Parliamentary Wing."

So that was the way of it, thought Audley. Or it looked very much as though it *could* be the way of it. And if it was—

"I think your policemen have arrived." Frances pointed down the hillside towards the Swine Brook.

"I left my field-glasses on the monument," said Mitchell. "One look through them and we can be sure."

Audley followed him down to the stone cross, his mind too full of possibilities to take anything else in.

If that was the way of it . . .

Mitchell adjusted the field-glasses. "That's Superintendent Weston. . . . And the sergeant."

Audley found himself looking at the inscription chiselled into the granite:

SWINE BROOK FIELD

1643

*We are both upon the stage and must act
the parts that are assigned us in this
tragedy; let us do it in a way of honour.*

And so they must. Except if that was the way of it, then it was unlikely that there would be much room for honour.

IV

"WESTON'S A SHARP fellow, don't be deceived by appearances," warned Mitchell. "He goes by the book—they all do, of course—but he's got quite a reputation, according to Cox."

So Mitchell had consulted their own Special Branch superintendent, thought Audley. A very thorough young man, Mitchell ... in his place he would have done exactly the same, because Cox's memory was encyclopaedic. But it was still another score to Mitchell that he had known exactly who to go to for first-hand information.

He stared at the memorial. It not only looked new, it was new: he could see the fragments of fresh mortar trampled into the grass around it.

He pointed. "How long has this been here? Not long?"

"A month. Wherever they do a re-enactment the Double R people always set aside some of their profits for a memorial if there isn't one already there. It's part of their public relations," said Mitchell. "Are we going to see Weston and the sergeant now?"

A thorough young man. . . . He took in the inscription again. It summed up very well the sad plight of the moderate man pushed at last by the extremists to take his stand, and discovering then that he had delayed too long and that the only chance left to him was to join one hated side or the other.

Like—who was it? The man had also had a memorial dedicated to him, on a battlefield of this same Civil War where he had fallen, he remembered having seen it years before.

"Are we going to see Weston?" Mitchell repeated.

Who was it? It suddenly became important to Audley to dredge the name out of his memory, as though it was the key to other forgotten things. Mitchell wouldn't have forgotten, damn him.

Not John Hampden. He had a memorial somewhere—at

Charlgrove, where Prince Rupert and the Royalists had killed him. But Hampden had been a Parliamentarian. This man had been a Royalist ... and a poet—

Falkland!

Little Falkland, with his ugly face and his shrill voice; but everyone had loved him for his kindness and his generosity and his learning. . . . And when the last hope of a negotiated peace had vanished and he had understood at last that whoever won, the moderates on each side had lost, he had saddled up and joined the King's cavalry and had calmly and deliberately ridden to certain death.

Suicide while the balance of the mind was undisturbed.

But not a mistake that David Audley would make.

"This quotation—" he looked at Mitchell "—who's it from? Falkland?"

"No." Mitchell eyed him curiously. "Why d'you ask?"

"Because I want to know. Not Falkland?"

"No." Mitchell stared at the memorial. "It could have been at that, I suppose. . . . But actually it was William Waller, the Parliamentary general. He was writing to old Sir Ralph Hopton before they fought each other at Landsdown—they'd been comrades years before in the German wars—"

"I remember." Audley nodded. Surprisingly he did remember, too: Hopton had written first, hoping to win over his old friend, or at least to win time. And Waller had rejected his overture, but in the noblest terms—

With what a hatred I detest this war without an enemy ...

He felt his confidence begin to flow again, diffusing inside him like the warmth of a hot drink on a freezing day. Mitchell was a very thorough young man, as he had proved again this minute. But that was a virtue to be used, not to be feared.

"Right. I shall now see Superintendent Weston and the sergeant." He didn't want either of them with him down there beside the Swine Brook: each would put him off his stroke, though in very different ways. But in any case they would be better employed elsewhere. "By myself."

They looked at him questioningly, and that was good.

"When does the—the Double R Society fight its next battle?"

"Easingbridge, the day after tomorrow—Saturday," said

Mitchell promptly. "They're putting on a performance at the annual fête and flower show. Do you want us to be there?"

"Can you get a horse in time?"

Mitchell shrugged. "If you pushed me—I guess so."

"I'm pushing." Audley turned to Frances. "And you must be there too."

"No problem." She nodded readily. "All I need is a costume."

"Good. . . . Now, in the meantime, Frances, I want you to research the Roundhead—ah—"

"Wing." Mitchell supplied the word.

"The Roundhead Wing. And particularly how Mr Charlie Ratcliffe fits into it. But don't be too obvious with the questions." He swung back to Mitchell. "And you, Paul—"

"Let me guess. Would a ton of gold be close?"

"Close enough. What d'you know about it?"

"Only what's been in the papers. The Brigadier told me to lay off it until you gave the word, just to check out Swine Brook Field." The corner of Mitchell's mouth lifted. "But I can add two and two as well as the next man."

"And what do you get?"

"Giving Charlie Ratcliffe a fortune is like handing a stick of gelignite to a juvenile delinquent: he's going to want to play with it one way or another, and either way something's going to get damaged."

"A whole box of gelignite, more likë," said Frances.

So they'd done their homework, and something more. But with two like this that was to be expected.

"You want me to go down to Standingham?" asked Mitchell.

Audley shook his head. Sending someone as keen as Mitchell to Standingham was just asking for something violent to happen, and that would never do.

"Not yet. It's research for you, my lad. I want to know all there is to know about that gold of Ratcliffe's—chemical analysis, and so on. And I want to know more about the history, too. The experts all said there wasn't any gold; I want to know why he thought differently."

Mitchell perked up at that. "You think somebody sparked him off?"

"At the moment I don't think anything, except my feet ache."

Audley turned towards Frances, steadying his eyes on her face with a conscious effort. He must think of her as someone's daughter. "I want you to concentrate on the Double R Society, Frances, remember. It's only information I want, nothing else."

He watched them climb the gate and disappear down the track between the hedgerows.

He had laid that last bit on rather too thick, the bit about information. There wasn't anything she could get other than that, and the frown she had given him back said as much. He must try to sound more like his usual belligerent self next time.

He began to descend the hillside.

At one time or another he had walked across quite a few battlefields, he reflected, and many of them had featured ridges not unlike this one: Vimy and Waterloo, Cemetery Ridge at Gettysburg and Senlac Ridge at Hastings, Hameau Ridge on the Somme where he had first got to know the real Paul Mitchell. . . . One of his ancestors had even died on a ridge at Salamanca, riding at General Le Marchant's side.

Of course this ridge was small beer compared with those, but it now shared with them the lack of any distinguishing mark which singled it out as a place where men had once buckled down to the serious business of killing each other. Just as the more recent marks of the Double R Society's mock-battle had faded, so there were no residual emanations of King Charles I and his Parliament, the Lord's Anointed and the Lord's Elected Representatives.

Or, presumably, of what had also been staged here on behalf of Mr Charlie Ratcliffe.

He could see Superintendent Weston waiting for him.

If Cox had said Weston was a sharp fellow then he was a sharp fellow; because Cox himself, for all that he looked like a retired PT instructor, had a mind like a cut-throat razor.

So it would be better to make a friend of Weston than to try and bullshit him with the letter of introduction he carried in his pocket.

* * *

"Superintendent Weston?"

Tinker, tailor, soldier, sailor . . . retired PT instructor . . . none of those, certainly. Say, a middle-aged country doctor with the authority of half a lifetime of births and deaths behind him.

"Dr Audley." The Superintendent advanced towards him, but the sergeant stayed back like an obedient gun-dog waiting for his signal.

Confidence tempered by caution.

"I'm sorry to have kept you waiting, Superintendent."

"That's all right, sir. It's quite nice to have an excuse to get away from my desk for an hour or two."

Caution plus neutrality. But no overt hostility, and in Weston's place Audley knew that he would be hopping mad behind an identical façade.

"Your Chief Constable will have told you why I'm here." Audley paused significantly. "It's on the instructions of the Home Secretary."

Weston nodded slowly. "In connection with the Ratcliffe investigation." He matched Audley's pause, second for second. "And you want my sergeant."

And that, of course, was adding injury to insult: bad enough for some anonymous Home Office official to descend on a hard-working police force empowered to ask questions without the obligation of answering any in the midst of a stalled murder case, implying dissatisfaction in high places; but to detach a useful officer from the duty rota when the force was already over-stretched—all forces were over-stretched—that had to be beyond the bloody limit.

Yet Weston still appeared cool enough and that was no good at all for the sort of answers that were needed. Somehow he had to be made to drop his defences. But pulling rank wouldn't achieve that any more than a straight appeal for help, which would only be despised.

He realised suddenly that he was staring fixedly at Weston, and that Weston was returning the stare with interest. In another moment they would be in a staring match.

"I gather he was your man on the spot." He shifted the stare to the sergeant. "In fact, very much on the spot."

He took in the younger man in detail for the first time.

Younger was right; over the years he had grown accustomed to the truth of the cliché that police constables grew younger and younger as one advanced into senility. But now the sergeants were growing younger too: if Weston passed as a middle-aged country doctor, Sergeant Digby could have been a first-year medical student, no longer wholly innocent but as yet unmarked by his profession.

Another baby to make him feel old and jealous.

And another *clever* baby, if what the Brigadier had said was to be believed.

"You'll have read his statement, then. And the others." Weston's voice cut through his line of thought.

"His statement?" Audley frowned stupidly. Maybe they weren't babies after all—a month of humid Washington and a few hours' flying, and he couldn't keep his mind on the job for five consecutive minutes. Maybe they weren't babies at all—maybe he must just be getting too old.

Weston heaved a carefully-controlled breath. "Transcripts of all the statements taken in the course of the investigation so far have been sent to the Home Secretary." He paused, watching Audley impassively. "I assume you've studied them, sir."

Statements.

Of course there had been statements. Dozens of statements, hundreds of statements. Names and occupations and places and times and facts. Statements to be checked and cross-checked and double-checked. Statements to be read and re-read and sieved and strained and refined.

That was what a murder investigation was: not a brilliant *tour de force* by a Sherlock Holmes, but an organised routine carried out by dozens of men and women working sixteen hours a day.

Of course there would be statements. In fact, with the Ratcliffe investigation the way it was that was all there would be at this moment. Just statements.

And nine times out of ten the police could be pretty sure that somewhere in that mass of paper was the name they wanted, and that if it was there they would get to it in the end. Not by luck —the whole system was built to eliminate luck as far as possible, because luck had to be arbitrarily good or bad in equal proportions—but by the cold mathematics of routine multiplied by team work multiplied by sixteen hours a day.

Only this had to be the tenth time; the time when there was no name and all the multiplication was ruined by a final zero factor. And if Superintendent Weston was half as good a policeman as Cox believed him to be, then he would know it. The trick was to make him admit it. . . .

Why not the truth? thought Audley suddenly.

He smiled at Weston. "No. I haven't read any statements."

"No . . . sir?" Weston's impassivity was a work of high art.

"Not one single word." The truth was supposed to set men free, perhaps it might set them both free now. "Just two newspaper reports."

Weston continued to stare at him expressionlessly, reserving his right to burst into laughter or tears.

"Four hours ago . . ." Audley consulted his watch casually ". . . actually rather less than four hours ago . . . I'd never even heard of either the Ratcliffe family or Swine Brook Field. As a matter of fact I was on a jet from New York four hours ago—minding my own business."

At last the hint of an emotion showed on Weston's face: one corner of his mouth twitched.

"But now you have to mind ours for us?"

"It does rather look that way." Audley nodded slowly, then converted the nod into a negative shake. "But I wouldn't have read the statements anyway."

"No?" The twitch became the beginning of—it might be a snarl or it might be a smile.

"No." The implications of that he had to let Weston work out for himself: it had to be either an insult or a vote of confidence, according to whether Cox's assessment was wrong or right.

A smile.

"Quite right too. Take you a week to read—and then you'd only be where we are."

Cox had been right.

"Which is nowhere?"

"Which is nowhere." The smile completed its journey and

then vanished. "And you work for the Home Office, Dr Audley —is that right?"

Polite disbelief. *Am I right?* meaning *I am wrong, aren't I?* Cox had understated the reality.

"Does that matter, Superintendent?"

"Not to me, sir. To my sergeant it might, I'm thinking."

Audley flicked a glance at the sergeant, to find that he too was being carefully scrutinised. He wondered whether the sergeant was thinking *he's old for this job*, just as he'd been thinking a few moments before how very young the sergeant was. But then the sergeant could hardly know what the job was, of course.

And that was one aspect of the truth which must be ducked. "I'll try not to keep him too long."

"No skin off my nose. He isn't really one of mine, not yet."

"Not . . . one of yours?"

"He's been attached to me for this case."

Audley frowned. "You mean he's not CID?"

"He has been. And he will be again before I'm very much older. But at this moment he's uniform branch."

They were up to the second of the two things he needed from the Superintendent before he had asked the first vital question. But Weston had already half answered that with his suspicion that Audley wasn't just a Home Office busybody: clearly he'd already smelt a rat in the Ratcliffe case.

"Tell me about him, Superintendent."

"Sergeant Digby?" Weston's face hardened. "He's a good copper. With the makings of a very good one."

"He looks very young . . . to be a sergeant."

"You think so?" Weston managed to look amused without softening his expression. "This time next year he'll be an inspector."

Well, well! thought Audley. But then—why not? The police fought an unending war against crime, and in war the company commanders were often no older than Sergeant Digby. No doubt there'd been plenty of fresh-faced young captains-of-horse in Cromwell's panzers, the New Model Army.

"Indeed?" And, come to that, it didn't take much imagination to turn Paul Mitchell into a hard-faced young colonel, not yet out of his twenties. Ruthlessness had never been the prerogative of old age, after all.

"Scholarship boy, Henry Digby was—Fenton Grammar School, before it went comprehensive." Pride and regret were evenly distributed in Weston's voice. "And they went for flyers then, too. Eleven 'O' levels he had, and three 'A' levels—good ones, too. Could have gone to university for the asking, and his mother wanted him to. A teacher, that's what she had in mind for him.".

"But he wanted to be a policeman?" Familiar pattern, even if the ambition was eccentric: all those examination honours were no good if mother couldn't pass her psychology test. Likely she'd have stood a better chance of making a teacher of him if she'd insisted on helmet and handcuffs.

Weston nodded. "Three commendations in his first two years. One year as a detective constable, and I marked him for accelerated promotion myself. . . . We sent him to Bramshill."

"Bramshill?"

"Police College. One of the top three of his year."

"But then you put him back into uniform?"

"That's the rule. Uniform sergeant for one year. Then automatic promotion to inspector—and I'll have him as one of mine if it's the last thing I do. He's the sort we need, a born thief-taker if ever I saw one . . . bright, but not flashy. That's the way they made 'em at Fenton Grammar when old Jukes was headmaster. So you be careful of him . . . sir." The hard look was granite now. "I want him back when you've finished with him, too."

"I wasn't thinking of kidnapping him, Superintendent."

"No?" Granite veined with calculation. "Just so he doesn't acquire a taste for Special Branch work, that's all."

"Recruiting for the Special Branch isn't one of my duties, that I promise you." Audley returned the look. "But you think this is shaping into a Special Branch case?"

"I didn't say that."

"You didn't, no." Not much, by God. That was further confirmation of the as yet unasked question. But they'd come back to that when the time was right. "So . . . bright, but not flashy. A good copper. A real thief-taker."

"Aye." Weston was no slouch himself: he was tensed up for the next question already.

83

"And yet he's a member of this ... this Double R Society."
One controlled nod. "That's correct, sir."

"And the Roundhead Wing of it, presumably, yes?" That was mere deduction: the one thing the Brigadier had said about Digby was that he'd been down by the stream throughout the battle, a mere stone's throw from the scene of the killing.

Another nod. So Sergeant Digby was a Roundhead.

"Who are perhaps a little weird?"

"Some of them are. And some of the Royalists too," Weston admitted. "But not Sergeant Digby."

"It doesn't surprise you that he's a member?"

"There are plenty of perfectly respectable citizens on both sides." Weston was doing his best to sound matter-of-fact rather than defensive. "Amateur historians and teachers and such like— a few retired army officers too.... And the prospective Labour candidate for this area is a Roundhead officer, actually."

Audley shook his head, smiling. "You haven't answered my question—actually."

Weston shrugged. "We encourage our men to have their own hobbies. Sergeant Digby attended one of these mock-battles when he was a uniform constable."

"On duty, you mean?"

"That's right. We always have three or four men at these things, for crowd control and such like—they can draw as big a crowd as a second division football match, these mock-battles. We've had up to ten thousand people for a big one. So the Society asks us for men, and pays for them ... and we throw in half a dozen special constables for free."

"I see. And he attended one and then became interested?" Audley nodded. One of those eleven 'O' levels had to be History, and maybe one of the 'A' levels too. And for a bet, the history of the sixteenth and seventeenth centuries was still more popular among schoolmasters than that of the nineteenth and twentieth centuries now, just as it had been in his own schooldays. So that figured well enough.

But it damn well wasn't the only thing that figured—and that figured even better, Audley thought triumphantly as he stared at Weston.

We encourage our men to have their hobbies.

I'll bet we do!

"Have you ever been to one of these battles, Superintendent?" Try as he would, he couldn't make the question sound innocent.

"I have, yes." And try as he would, Weston had the same trouble with his reply. "Have you, sir?"

"No. Not my . . . scene, as they say." And not Superintendent Weston's scene either, for a hundred-to-one bet. "But I'm learning fast—about the police as well as the Civil War."

For a moment they stared at each other. Then, as abruptly as it had disappeared a few minutes before, the smile came back to Weston's mouth. But this time the humour spread, crinkling up the whole face.

Finally Weston grinned broadly. "All right, Dr Audley—I give you best there. He did get interested, I told you no lie. It was partly because he is interested in history, too."

"But you were interested too, eh?"

Weston beamed. "It's a pleasure to do with business with you, Dr Audley."

"Even your own business?"

"Better you than some fool who thinks he knows all the answers."

"Quite so. Whereas I don't even know all the questions yet. . . . So he came to you and asked permission to join?"

"Not to me. This was while he was still in uniform as a constable."

"Of course. I was forgetting. He went to his uniform superintendent." Audley nodded.

"That's right. But he was due for a CID transfer in a few months' time, and his super knew I had my eye on the Double R people."

"Uh-huh. . . . So you gave him your blessing—you even encouraged him." The pleasure, thought Audley, was mutual: this must be a good force, in which the men in charge of the different branches were on the same side, unlike some of those in his own service.

"One volunteer's worth a dozen pressed men. And young Digby was made to measure for what I wanted."

"Which was?"

Weston thought for a moment, staring up sightlessly towards

the ridge. The hottest part of the afternoon was almost spent, but with no breath of wind the skyline still shimmered with heat. There wasn't a sign of life or movement anywhere. In an hour or two, with the first cool of evening, it would be different; but now the landscape seemed exhausted, almost stupefied.

It was hard to imagine that the hillside, this same hillside, had once boiled with murderous activity—that Black Thomas's cavalry had swept down it, desperate with thirst.

Audley licked his lips. On second thoughts that thirst wasn't so unimaginable. And he'd already decided that one place was as good as another when it came to killing, hadn't he?

Weston turned back to him. "How much d'you know about these Double R people?"

"Not a lot yet." Audley returned the look candidly. "But I think at the moment I'd rather like to avoid jumping to conclusions. Which is pretty much the answer to my question, I suspect: you didn't just want an inside man—a spy. Would that be about the size of things?"

"That's very good, Dr Audley. You're absolutely right. Crime's one thing and prejudice is another, and the copper who mixes them up only makes trouble for himself. My business is crime."

"You had a prejudice against them?"

"Not to start with. It was more like curiosity."

"Professional curiosity?"

"Indirectly, I read about one of these battles they staged, when there were a dozen people carted off to hospital. And it occurred to me if that had been a football match I'd have thought 'Aye aye—the local yobbos are getting out of hand'. So I went to have a look at one of their shows for myself, unofficially."

"And—?"

"Well, they differ, of course. The Sealed Knot—pretty respectable . . . the King's Army—lots of beer and good fellowship. Both keen on their history. Discipline not bad really. Safety regulations . . . well, improving, let's say."

"Safety regulations? So there's an element of danger—but if they cart people off to hospital obviously there is. Silly question."

"Not so silly. Before I read that newspaper report I'd assumed their battles were glorified pageants—cream puffs at five yards sort of thing. And after I'd seen one...well, I must say I was surprised by what I saw.

"I suppose the size of the battle plays a part in it. Sometimes there are only three or four dozen putting on a parade and a bit of old-fashioned drill at a fête—'Shoulder Your Pikes' and 'Advance Your Pikes', that sort of thing. But the first big fight I saw the Double R people stage, down in the west of the county it was...there were six or seven hundred of them, and it wasn't cream-puffs at five yards at all—it was pretty brutal. They really went at each other."

"Undisciplined, you mean?"

"No, they were disciplined all right. Just like the others. They keep together in their regiments, as they call them. And they charge each other in their regiments too, I can tell you."

"Like a rugger scrum?" Audley tried without success to envisage a rugger scrum in seventeenth-century battledress, with three hundred a side. "But they're carrying pikes, aren't they...?"

"And swords. And there are musketeers." Weston nodded.

"They charge each other with pikes...Christ! I can see that would be dangerous. It's a wonder there aren't more hurt!"

"Yes...but at the last moment they port their pikes—hold them up diagonally across their bodies—and then smack into each other."

Weston slapped his open hands together graphically. "And then they push like buggery until one side gives up. Or their officers break it off." Weston stopped suddenly. "But you say you don't want to hear this sort of detail yet?"

"Oh, I don't mind the technicalities." Audley glanced at Weston, unwilling to probe too obviously. What he wanted must be given freely or not at all, that was the essence of it. "But what I still don't quite understand is why all this interested you.... That is, after you'd seen it.... I mean, so they were playing soldiers—maybe a little roughly. But that's all it amounts to: playing soldiers. The Americans have been playing their Civil War for years. And now they're busy playing the War of Independence. If you don't force people to wear uniforms they'll put them on of their own accord. At least, some people will. And so long as it's historical—so long as it isn't

87

para-military.... You're not suggesting the Double R Society is para-military in seventeenth-century drag, are you?"

Weston stared at him in silence for a moment. "No, not exactly para-military."

"What then?"

Again Weston said nothing for a few seconds. Then he shook his head doubtfully. "If I tell you I'll be helping you to jump to conclusions, that's for sure."

Audley shook his head. "I'm rather afraid I've already been helped to this one, so the damage is already done. But I'd be interested to find out whether it's the same one—and I'll make allowances for your prejudices, Superintendent." He smiled the sting out of the words. "So you went on the look-out for—ah —yobbos having a licensed punch-up. And you found ... something more interesting, maybe?"

Weston pursed his lips. "To be honest, Dr Audley, I'm not at all sure what I found—not yet, anyway." He paused, as though unwilling to commit himself. "Just let's say as a policeman I'm prejudiced against ... politics."

So there it was, thought Audley: the confirmation of what Paul Mitchell and Frances Fitzgibbon had encountered, passed on with all the caution and non-partisanship of the man in the middle, the good copper. There was an irony there which neither of the extremes could stomach, and against which they therefore blinkered themselves: to the far left Weston was a Fascist pig marked for the lamp-post, and to the far right a potential tool to be flattered and used; whereas in reality Weston's breed regarded both sides with equal contempt as it protected each from the excesses of the other.

"Just so," he agreed sympathetically. "Not para-military so much as para-political. And what was it brought you to that conclusion?"

"They sang the wrong tune."

"I beg your pardon?" Audley frowned. "They sang—?"

"The wrong tune, aye." Weston gave him a grim little smile. "Funny thing was, I almost missed it. Because, you see, I didn't really go on the look-out for yobbos. Or shall we say—I didn't expect to see any of my yobbos, not at that sort of gathering. Not quite their style, if you see what I mean."

83

True. Yobbos might, or might not, know a great deal about football, but it was unlikely that any of them would be able to satisfy the Double R Society's membership committees.

"Of course. I was forgetting—it was the casualties you were interested in. You wanted to see how they'd got themselves organised."

"That's right. And after I'd seen them fight their battle I was in two minds about packing it in and going home. I'd seen what I came to see. But then I thought..." he shrugged "...I was there, so I might as well see the whole thing out. See how they behaved off the battlefield when they'd had a few beers, talk to them and see what made them tick, and so on."

Thoroughness. The mark of the good copper.

"So I waited." Weston continued simply. "And as they marched off the field I heard them singing. One lot of Cavaliers were singing a dirty song, and some of the Roundheads were singing hymns. But then there was this regiment at the rear, pikemen, all in red coats and steel helmets. Charlie Ratcliffe's regiment, it was."

"Yes?"

"They were singing *The Red Flag*, Dr Audley."

V

THE POLICE HOUSE at Standingham was a solid, red-brick dwelling, with a well-regimented garden which looked as though it was inspected twice a week by a superior officer who regarded weeds as law-breakers.

After dropping Digby outside it, Audley took the car forward a couple of hundred yards to the forecourt of the Steyning Arms, where it mingled unobtrusively with those of the pub's early evening drinkers.

He would dearly have liked a pint now himself, but that would have to wait. It was bad enough to allow the mere indulgence of his curiosity to rule his judgement, though if pressed he could argue that now, if ever, was the time to look the place over, before Ratcliffe could possibly be aware of his presence; but whatever the argument, it would be pointless to expose his presence to the public gaze without good cause.

And there was the rub, though: there was really no point in coming to Standingham now, if ever, and he was only doing it because Nayler's smug references to his "little television programme" had galled him—the idea of Stephen Nayler squatting on any secret that interested David Audley was like an itch on the sole of his foot; he couldn't go on until he'd taken off his shoe and scratched it properly.

The sudden movement of the white picket gate of the Police House, for which he'd kept one eye cocked on the rural scene reflected in the car mirror, caught him by surprise. Sergeant Digby had transacted his business with remarkable despatch.

But then the Sergeant Digbys of this world would transact all their business smartly in their accelerated progress to the top, he decided, watching the young man's light infantry advance. The Good Fairy at the Digby christening had endowed that infant with every virtue necessary for success in the police service, except perhaps an extra portion of imagination. And even that, when one thought about it, might have proved more of a hindrance than a help in his superiors' eyes, if it had been granted.

"You've been quick," said Audley encouragingly.

"Had a bit of luck," said Digby breathlessly, jerking his head back towards the Police House as he spoke. "PC Cotton—I worked with him before he was posted here, when I was a DC, so I didn't have to mess around explaining things. And he knows this patch like the back of his hand."

"Including the castle?"

"You bet. Only two men there now. Caretaker-handyman—name of Simmonds—for the inside, and old Burton the gardener for the outside. Caretaker'll be there now, but Burton'll most likely be in there—" Digby nodded towards the Steyning Arms.

"Charlie Ratcliffe not in residence, then?"

Digby shook his head. "Doesn't fancy the place at all, apparently. He didn't even stay there when he was treasure-hunting—stayed at the pub most of the time. At least, stayed until the last two or three days before he found the gold—then he must have camped on the site, Cotton reckons." Digby paused. "All by himself."

"By himself?"

"That's right. When his uncle was alive there was a house-keeper and a trained nurse as well as the handyman and the gardener. After the old man died he paid the two women off and kept the men on. But when he came down to look for the gold he packed them off on holiday—told them to keep away until he sent for them. Which was about three weeks, Cotton says."

"So he found the gold single-handed, you mean?"

"He hired a tractor with a front scoop from a local farmer, but otherwise he was alone right up until the morning he announced he'd found the gold."

"A tractor?" Audley frowned. "It wasn't in the house, then?"

Digby looked at him in surprise. "Oh, no. It was in the kitchen garden, over by one of the gun-bastions along the north rampart—right out in the open, so Cotton says. He was one of the first outsiders to see it."

"What happened, exactly?"

"That morning? Well, Ratcliffe had it all organised, that's for sure. The first thing Cotton knew about it was when Ratcliffe phoned him up, about ten o'clock. Cool as a cucumber, Cotton says. He simply said he'd found his family treasure, and would Cotton kindly telephone the local coroner because it was his job to take it in charge now, for the time being anyway. And he'd better phone his divisional HQ as well, because once the coroner had taken it then there'd be a security angle."

"And what did—ah—Cotton say to that?"

"He asked what the treasure consisted of. And Ratcliffe said it was gold, about a ton of it, give or take a hundredweight or two."

"He said that?"

Digby nodded, deadpan. "Cotton reckons he'd dug it up bit by bit over those three days, and then worked out exactly what he intended to do. Because by the time he got there on his bicycle there were a dozen of Ratcliffe's long-haired friends standing guard over it—he'd seen some of them drive through the village that morning, before the phone call. And he had others patrolling the grounds to keep people out as well, and they weren't there the previous day. Or not in the village, anyway."

"His long-haired friends?" Audley considered the possibilities. "Meaning Ratcliffe's regiment of the Roundhead Wing, I take it?"

Digby shrugged. "I don't know. But ... probably."

"So he kept everyone out of the castle grounds, did he?"

"Not everyone. He let in the people he wanted—he'd phoned a Sunday newspaper, and the others caught on double-quick. Cotton says it was a nightmare, the next week or two, with journalists and sightseers. But when they found they couldn't get into the grounds unless they went in through the front gate they cleared off—the sightseers did, anyway."

Audley stared at the dashboard. Cool as a cucumber and bloody well organised, Charlie Ratcliffe had been, sitting day after day on a steadily increasing pile of gold ingots—and night after night, alone in the midst of his ancestral loot.

The gold of the Indies. King Philip's gold. Captain Sir Edward Parrott's gold. Colonel Nathaniel Parrott's gold. And then nobody's gold for over three hundred years.

And now Charlie Ratcliffe's gold by every law and every

custom that made any sense. It was hard not to be on Charlie's side, even with the as yet unproved—and probably unprovable—suspicion that he had played most foully for it. Because there was a much older and crueller law which applied to gold, a law which transcended every other one: those who had the guts to find it and the wit to keep it were its natural owners. Once it would have held force of arms as well as wit, now it took law as well. But unless Charlie Ratcliffe could be proved a murderer public opinion would be on his side, no matter what his politics.

"But now there are only two of them looking after the place?"

"So Cotton says." Digby nodded. "It was a nine-days' wonder —and apparently there's nothing much to see now but one damn great hole in the kitchen garden, like a bomb hit it. You won't have any trouble finding it, he says." He glanced shrewdly at Audley. "If you still want to."

There was nothing here for him—for either of them—thought Audley. But Digby didn't know about the secret Nayler had dangled in front of him over the telephone, which was a private matter, having nothing to do with gold or politics or murder.

"I still want to—yes."

Self-indulgence.

"All right." Digby was deadpan again. "Cotton will go along to the house and talk to the handyman, and I'll go to the pub and talk to the gardener. That should give you a clear run for an hour or so."

The young sergeant had come to the same conclusion, that Swine Brook, not Standingham, was their only hope; and that this side-trip was either pointless or the product of some information which Audley was keeping to himself. If it had been Paul Mitchell sitting beside him there would have been signs of rebellion, or snide comments at the least; but Digby, mercifully, was better disciplined.

"How do I get into the castle grounds from here?"

"Ah—now I've got you something that may help there." Digby produced a tattered booklet from his coat pocket. "I borrowed this from Cotton. There isn't any modern guide-book to the castle, because it's never been open to the public. But there was this old Methodist minister who wrote a history of the place back in Victorian times, and there's a map in the back which shows

93

the layout . . . it's a bit out of date, but the castle part hasn't changed—the village has expanded to the south, that's all, Cotton says—"

He opened the booklet carefully and spread out a dog-eared and yellowing map on his lap. "We're just about *here*—on the fold—on the north edge of the village by that dotted line. . . ."

Audley studied the map. The village in the old queen's day had been huddled around the river crossing, with the castle on the hillside above—

"What's this other castle?" He pointed to the map.

"That's nothing. Or there's nothing there, anyway—that's the old castle site, it says," said Digby dismissively. "It'll all be in the book—this is our castle *here*, and you can get to the line of the old ramparts up that track beyond the pub *there*—" he pointed ahead across the car bonnet "—just by that bus stop. If you follow the ramparts round you'll come to the kitchen garden on the north side, but you'll be out of sight of the castle all the way."

It was on the tip of Audley's tongue to suggest that he could read a map as well as the sergeant, if not better, having been reading maps since before the sergeant was out of his nappies. But there had been nothing in the sergeant's voice except helpfulness, any more than there was nothing now but politeness in the way he offered the old guide-book once he had folded the map back into it. So perhaps young police sergeants naturally took senior Home Office officials to be doddering incompetents when it came to practical matters.

"Thank you, Sergeant," he said with equal politeness. "I'm sure I shall manage very well now."

· Digby regarded him doubtfully for a moment. "Well, it's half-past now. Cotton can ring the caretaker, that'll pin him down. And then I'll deal with the gardener in the pub."

"If he's there."

"If he's not, then he's on his way. Half an hour every night without fail, Cotton says, and I can make him stay longer. Will an hour be enough for you?"

Five minutes.

Audley looked down at the venerable guide-book which,

94

according to Digby, would answer all his questions about Standingham Castle.

The History of the Village and Castles of Standingham. By The Reverend Horatio Musgrave, BA, Resident Minister of the Methodist Congregations of Standingham, Worpsgrave and Long Denton.

On the next page the Reverend Musgrave himself frowned up at him out of a luxuriant frame of hair and side-whiskers and beard, the very pattern of the late Victorian clergyman.

'The felicitous tranquillity of Standingham in our own peaceful and enlightened times conceals a sad history of fratricidal warfare and intermittent pestilence which cannot but provoke the reflection that the blessings of education and scientific progress, sustained and advanced as they have been by the proper study of the Gospel of Our Lord Jesus Christ, have conferred on the British Nation signal benefits which are nevertheless insufficiently understood by the generality of the population.'

Evidently the Reverend Musgrave was determined to use his history to point a moral, if not to adorn a tale, in the best Victorian tradition. Which, in the circumstances of less peaceful and felicitous times, his latest reader might be allowed to skip—

'That same happy juxtaposition of highways and waterways in the midst of an industrious and prosperous agricultural community which has lately resulted in the extension of the Great Western Railway's passenger and goods services to the district served to identify the earliest settlement at the con-fluence of the rivers Irthey and Barwell as a place of some importance—'

More paragraphs to skim across. Anglo-Saxon ploughman, marauding Danes, iron-fisted Normans with the tax-man's Domesday Book in their baggage, adulterine castles going up like mushrooms when the kings were weak—and coming down smartly when they were strong... the Black Death wiping out the original settlement beside the Barwell, and the new settlement

95

beside the Irthey being burnt during a peasant rising...
well, no one could say that the Reverend Musgrave was really
exaggerating the horrors of everyday life in rural Standingham
in the good old days—

'It was in the early fifteenth century that Sir Edward de
Stayninge was granted the right to crenellate his manor on the
ridge above the Barwell, on the site of the earthworks of the
earlier castles; of which there yet remains not one stone upon
another to testify the feudal pride before which the might of
France crumbled at Crécy and Agincourt. For having espoused
the cause of the wicked Richard Crookback, slayer of the
innocent Princes in the Tower—'

Well, that figured. Because if there was one thing for which
the lords of the manor and the villagers of Standingham alike
could be relied on, it was to back losers. If there was a lost cause
to hand, or a disaster of any sort going, then Standingham was
first in the wrong queue; it was only to be expected in due course
that Sir Piers de Stayning, having lost the 'e' off his name, should
also ride to Bosworth Field in 1485 with the wrong army and lose
the rest of it.

A cycle bell roused him from the contemplation of late medi-
eval lawlessness to catch twentieth-century law in all its majesty:
whether it was because of the price of petrol or from a wise
return to old-fashioned police methods, PC Cotton's superiors
had provided him with a bicycle rather than a car. And for a bet,
the sight of a large, properly-helmeted policeman on a tall
bicycle moving steadily and silently round his patch under his
own power did more to deter the local lads from petty crime
than an anonymous car driver in a bus conductor's flat cap.

Just a couple more minutes of the Reverend Musgrave, then—
and he could finish the sad history on foot anyway...

'It was not until the second decade of the sixteenth century
that a collateral descendent, Sir William Steyning, having
secured the reversion of his uncle's estates, commenced the
construction of the great house on the Irthey Ridge, across
the pleasant open valley of the Willow Stream. Using stone

from the castle ruins, he raised a residence in the Tudor manner which, though still taking the style "castle", was yet an edifice at once more commodious and more comfortable than the frowning fortresses of earlier times, testifying both to the greater confidence of the gentry in their security of tenure and to the power of the monarch to impose his will on their feudal ambitions. It was to be a tragic irony of history that this gracious home, with its noble aspect and high-mullioned windows, was to feature in the most famous and melancholy chapter in our brief chronicle of former days.'

Audley shook his head at the text. It was maybe tragic, but hardly ironic that Standingham had received a bloody nose during the Civil War; the village was simply running true to form. Even the fact that it had been staunchly Parliamentarian, following its lord of the manor as so many places had done, and yet had still managed to ruin itself although Parliment had won the war, was a predictable occurrence. He could only hope that in reviving the family fortunes Charlie Ratcliffe had also re-animated the slumbering fiend who turned every Standingham event into a misfortune.

The track beside the bus stop sported a mouldering notice-board bearing the legend NO THROUGH ROAD, but, if the Reverend Musgrave's map could be relied on, it led nevertheless straight up the ridge to the old sallyport beside one of the bastions along the south rampart.

'Had the Lord of the Manor of Standingham been young and vigorous when King and Parliament parted from one another on the great issue of England's liberties in the year 1641, then he would have assuredly have followed his inclination toward the banner of one or other of the belligerent parties—'

Very true. The Reverend Musgrave could no more resist stating the obvious than he could pass up the chance of using a ringing adverb or adjective.

'And, conversely, had he been old and unversed in the arts

97

of war he would doubtless have stood aloof from the fratricidal strife which then ensued—'

True again. So presumably the lord of the manor, Sir Edmund Steyning, had been neither young and vigorous nor old and unversed in the arts of war—

'But it chanced that Sir Edmund Steyning was neither.'

Bingo!

'In Edmund Steyning, it might be said, piety and enthusiasm for the Protestant cause combined with a fiery and martial spirit which no physical handicap could altogether extinguish. From his earliest manhood he had followed the drum, first under the veteran Dutch commanders in their long war against Catholic Spain and then under the greatest captain of the age, the veritable "Lion of the North", King Gustavus Adolphus of Sweden, in his homeric struggle against the Imperial tyranny of the Holy Roman Empire on behalf of German Protestantism.'

There was no doubt where the Reverend Musgrave's sympathies lay. No doubt he had also thundered from his pulpit against Catholic emancipation in his own time, so he certainly wouldn't miss a chance of recalling the armed Catholic might of the Counter-Reformation—

'It was on the glorious field of Breitenfeld, when his hero and mentor smote the Catholic power, that the accident befell which ended Sir Edmund's active career. For, while attending to his duties with the Swedish field artillery which was a novel feature of Gustavus's army, he was desperately wounded by the premature explosion of a quantity of gunpowder. Although attended by the king's own surgeon, his life was despaired of for many weeks; and even when that indomitable spirit and iron will which sustained him throughout his life had triumphed over his injuries, it was in a body so shattered by war that no thought of further service could be entertained.'

The track levelled between two low brick walls. Peering over the parapet of one, Audley realised he had reached the line of the Great Western Railway's extension which had once been attracted by the Reverend Musgrave's 'happy juxtaposition of communications'. He was glad that the old Methodist minister was no longer alive to see the change which another century's educational and scientific blessings had wrought on the railway: its tracks had long since been torn up and young trees were already pushing their way up through the granite chippings. So far as Standingham was concerned, the railway age was as much part of bygone history as Sir Edward de Stayninge's crenellated manor.

'It was to his patrimony at Standingham that the crippled hero returned, from a Europe now wracked by the worst excesses of the Thirty Years' War, which had reached its apogee in an unparalleled outburst of ferocity, unsurpassed since the fall of the Roman Empire, with the last vain and discredited attempts of the Papalists to impose uniformity on the unconquerable Protestants of the North.'

Hadn't it been six of one and half a dozen of the other? Or was it that Musgrave had had to contend with a Newman-trained Catholic priest in his combined parishes? No matter—

'Yet even here, amongst the lush water-meadows of the Irthey and the Barwell, the stormclouds of war were gathering. Debarred by his physical infirmities from taking part in the events which preceded the English Civil War, Sir Edmund was yet not unaware of their genesis, which were borne upon him not only because of his staunch Protestant sympathies, but also because of the excesses of his Catholic neighbour, Lord Monson, ever a favourite with the Queen and her priests.'

Enter the Demon King himself, good old Black Tom!
And here was another sign, a printed poster pasted on to hardboard: PRIVATE. TRESPASSERS WILL BE PROSECUTED. To which, in an egalitarian spirit which Charlie Ratcliffe ought to

have approved, someone had added BALLS with a red felt-tipped pen.

'It seems likely, indeed, that Monson's enmity and depredations, threatened in times of uneasy peace, had already animated Sir Edmund to plan that unique and formidable line of circumvallation which, even after the ruinous passage of two and a half centuries, yet remains for the discerning student of fortification to marvel upon; and which, with the aid of his willing and sturdy tenantry, he was to encompass so speedily when the war commenced.'

Audley looked around him. The Irthey ridge, which he had been steadily climbing, was now so heavily wooded that he had passed into the line of old Edmund's circumvallation almost without noticing it. But here, where the track passed through what had seemed like a natural cutting in the hillside, he had actually come upon what the Reverend Musgrave required discerning students of fortification to marvel upon.

Directly ahead of him was a pair of ancient wrought-iron gates festooned with rusty barbed wire and heavily padlocked. But the track had curved first round an isolated mound crowned now with trees, the roots of which straggled between the remnants of what looked like stonework. Except for the narrow beaten path up to the gates there seemed no rhyme or reason in the construction, though.

'One cannot but reflect with satisfaction on the surprise with which Monson and his be-ribboned cavaliers, flushed with their early successes, gazed upon the cunning defences with which Sir Edmund had girdled his property in their absence, and upon which they were to dash themselves in vain for two long years—'

Audley looked round again, and then retraced his steps to the point where the path had begun to sink into the cutting.

Cunning defences? If they were, then they were as confusing as the Iron Age earthworks at the entrance of Maiden Castle, two thousand years older than Roundheads and Cavaliers, and their cannon—

Cannon?

He swung on his heel. Of course!—This had been the age of cannon, and he had been thinking foolishly of castles and towers!

That sudden steeper rise in the hillside wasn't hillside at all, but the earth shifted from the ditch ahead. A—what was the name?—a *glacis*, that was it.

And the mound in front was a ruined horn-work, with ravelins on each side of it, behind the counterscarp, and with the flanking bastions of the main ramparts ahead of him. He was in the middle of a classic seventeenth-century defence line, far in advance of anything the amateur soldiers of the English Civil War normally built, much more in the style of Vauban and the great French military engineers.

But, of course, Steyning hadn't been an amateur soldier at all, but a veteran of a dozen battles and sieges from the North Sea to the Baltic, who had learnt his trade from the great Gustavus Adolphus himself. There had been scores of others like him in both armies—men like Hopton and Waller, and the Scotsman Leslie—who had taken the same tuition, but they had all been fighting in the field, whereas Steyning had been caged by his injuries in his own great house in the middle of Royalist territory—caged with his Protestant zeal and his military know-how—

And, by God, he'd been an artillery expert too, if the Reverend Musgrave could be relied on! So he'd done the only thing left within his power to do: he'd turned his home into a strongpoint, overlooked by his enemies until too late, so that no one had had the knowledge or the resources to dislodge him. Or the incentive either ... until Colonel Nathaniel Parrott had descended on him with a ton of gold in his saddle-bags.

And then—

'Indeed, Standingham Castle might well have endured all the shocks of war until Cromwell and Fairfax had crowned the Parliamentary cause with the laurels of victory, but for the malevolence of fortune which, by a singular coincidence, visited upon Sir Edmund a second and final disaster.'

* * *

Audley glanced at his watch. The details of the second disaster would have to wait. A railing thickly encrusted with barbed wire now surmounted the rampart, but the beaten path he'd been following seemed to indicate that there was a way in to his right, among the trees.

He followed the path through a thicket of holly bushes until the way was blocked by a moss-covered tree-trunk. Where the tree had fallen there was a gap in the overhanging roof of leaves and also in the rampart above him: the fallen tree had grown on the very lip of the old parapet, and in falling had dislodged a five-yard stretch of it into the ditch below. Although the break had been long since plugged with a tangle of barbed wire, the abrupt end of the path and the regular footholds printed up the side of the bank of earth clearly marked the barrier as being weaker than it looked from below. But then the usual run of trespassers probably didn't wear good suits, thought Audley as he clambered up; this was the second time today that he'd had to negotiate barbed wire, even though the field gate on the ridge above the Swine Brook—and Frances Fitzgibbon's spiked backside—seemed like distant memories.

When he reached the wire, however, he saw at once that its strength was an illusion, for the whole concertina was held in place by an unbarbed loop hung loosely over the twisted end of a broken railing: surmounting the cunning defences of Standingham Castle wasn't going to be such a problem after all, thank heavens!

He lifted the loop and stepped gingerly over the remains of the old railing. But then, as he was in the act of refixing the loop, he felt a sharp tug at his trousers, behind and right down by his heel.

Holding the loop in one hand and cursing under his breath at his clumsiness, he reached down to free the snagged material, only to encounter something warm and wet and soft.

There was something licking his hand.

Audley looked down into the eyes of a beautiful, half-grown red setter.

The red setter grinned at him, gave an excited but perfectly friendly little yelp, and made as though to grab his trousers again: the discerning student of seventeenth-century fortification was being invited to play a game with an idiot dog.

Correction: an idiot bitch. A beautiful, half-grown, well-groomed, amiable and totally inconvenient idiot bitch of a red setter.

Audley's brain accepted the information. That the bitch was friendly was no surprise to him, because he was accustomed to animals liking him, even though he had no special affection to return. He had grown up in a household where there were only two kinds of animals: the ones which were eaten and the ones which worked for their living, guarding, mousing, pulling or carrying. He had never quite understood, when he became old enough to want to analyse their reactions, why they rewarded this unsentimental attitude with trust and affection, but he had had to accept the fact of it, that animals liked him. Maybe they just liked being treated like animals.

But it wasn't the setter's behaviour that mattered, it was the combination of her presence and her appearance. She wasn't just anyone's dog running loose in search of canine adventure: that shining coat had been brushed not long ago, and the little brass plate on the real leather collar shone pale with recent polishing.

This wasn't anyone's dog, it was *someone's* dog. And the someone must be close at hand—and on the wrong side of the wire.

He dropped the loop into place and turned his full attention to the setter.

"Here, girl," he commanded conversationally, extending the licked hand for further examination. "Have a good smell, eh?"

The bitch strained forward towards the hand, first sniffing and then slobbering over each finger in turn, tail beating with excitement. When he was confident that she was sure of him Audley bent over her, slid his sticky hand over her head and eased the collar sideways so that he could read the name on the brass plate.

Burton, Castle Lodge, Standingham.

"There's a girl—there's a beautiful girl." He stroked the sleek head. "Aren't you a beautiful girl then?"

The bitch nodded at him, steadied and soothed by the sound

and the touch. If only she could speak now she would have answered all his questions; instead she offered a dusty paw.

Audley shook the paw. "Pleased to meet you."

But where's your master, beautiful girl? Is this the way he comes down from the Lodge to take his evening pint? Is he close by now, beautiful girl?

The bitch cocked her head on one side, looked straight at him, and then looked directly over his shoulder.

Audley straightened up slowly to give himself time to gather all his wits together, and then turned to look along her line of sight.

"Good evening," he said.

The setter's master was a tall, thin man with an all-weather face and an upstanding brush of grey hair less well-groomed than his dog's coat.

" 'Evening."

A quiet-spoken man too, though his voice seemed to release the setter from Audley's spell: she leapt up the side of the gap and came to heel obediently at the sound of it.

"You've got a good bitch there," said Audley.

"Aye." Absently, without taking his eyes off Audley, the man —Mr Burton, I presume—reached down to touch her head, and she quivered with pleasure at the touch.

"Maybe a little too friendly with strangers, though," said Audley, smiling.

The grey brush shook disagreement. "Not usually. If you were a bad 'un she'd set her teeth to you, likely."

Well, that was a compliment. And if Burton trusted his dog's instinct perhaps David Audley should trust his own also—and play to win when there was nothing left to lose. He was the wrong side of the wire after all, clear beyond the notice to trespassers.

He cocked his head on one side as the dog had done. "Oh aye? Then I take it she's left her mark on Master Ratcliffe already then?"

For a long moment Burton considered him. Then one corner of his mouth lifted. "Would have done if I'd let her," he admitted.

Audley nodded, first at the man and then at the dog. He'd

made the gesture and it hadn't been rejected. But the next move wasn't his.

Another moment passed. "You wouldn't be from a newspaper, I don't think?" It was more a reflection spoken aloud than a question. Or if a question, thought Audley, remembering his old Latin master, it was a *num* question, with the answer *no* built into it.

"No, I'm not from a newspaper. But I want to see what they weren't allowed to see all the same."

For a second or two after he had spoken Audley was afraid he had gone too far too fast. But instinct was still in charge, and instinct was all on the side of frankness now.

The man took a step forward and offered his hand. "Well then ... you'd better come up out of there then, hadn't you?" he said simply.

Help evidently didn't include conversation; Burton simply led the way along the path on the rampart, zigzagging between the trees in silence while the setter bitch rushed ahead in an attempt to discover the longest distance between two points. On their right the ditch was so choked with undergrowth that the counter-scarp and glacis slope were almost invisible; on the left Audley caught occasional glimpses through the trees of the house itself, all windows and chimneys. On this south side it was quite close to the defences, he remembered from the Reverend Musgrave's map.

He could have found his way to the kitchen garden just as well on his own, and Sergeant Digby would be worried sick at Burton's failure to arrive on schedule, so this turn of events would have little profit to it if he couldn't persuade the man to talk. But however eloquent his agreement with his bitch—that Charlie Ratcliffe was a bad 'un—he didn't look like a talkative man.

Audley quickened his pace. "You know Master Charlie well, do you?"

For a dozen paces Burton gave no sign of having even heard the question. Then, without pausing, he spoke over his shoulder.

"Not really—since he was a nipper."

Audley waited for elaboration, but none came. With a man

105

like this, a man of few words, every word had to work an eight-hour day.

"He came here when he was young?"

"Aye."

"And not since—up until now?"

"Aye." Pause. "But he's not changed, though."

That confirmed the record. Charlie hadn't really got on with either his cousin or his uncle, whose political and social persuasions were very different from his. He was the *faute de mieux* inheritor of an impoverished estate for which he had shown no love and in which he had shown no interest until very recently.

"What was he like—as a boy?"

Burton took another dozen paces and then halted. Half turning he waited for Audley to come alongside him. They stared at one another in silence.

"What you after, mister?" The question was as direct as the stare.

"Information."

"To cause trouble?"

No lies, thought Audley. Burton would smell a lie as quickly as his bitch smelt a rabbit.

"No."

Burton stiffened. "No?"

"The trouble has already been caused. And I didn't cause it. What I cause isn't called trouble."

There was a rustle of leaves and the bitch appeared, summoned by the tension between them. She came to heel again precisely as she had done at their first meeting, and Burton reached down in exactly the same way to touch her head. It was as though there was a current passing between them.

Audley reached forward, offering his right hand to the bitch again.

Lick or bite?

He felt the warm, wet tongue on his fingers.

"What was he like when he was a boy?" he repeated the question.

Burton nodded slowly. "Same as now. A chancer."

A chancer?

What was a chancer? Something more—or less—than an opportunist. A taker of risks, a twister—

"He never cared for nobody born, nor nothing made, nor nothing growed." Burton paused. "He never did, and he never will. Not till he's six foot under."

The bitch shivered at the pronouncement of this anathema and Burton swung back on to the path, releasing her and striding away. All the words he had to give on Charlie Ratcliffe had been said.

The trees ended abruptly on the ruin of a corner bastion and the rampart curved away along the crest of the ridge above open country. Audley realised that they had been following the contour line all the way round the spur of land on which the house had been built—having seen it he could no longer think of it as a castle, despite its name. And here, on the northern and more open side—this must be the Reverend Musgrave's 'pleasant open valley'—only the chimneys were visible.

And sure enough, there across the valley on the lower ridge above the Barwell beyond it, were the earth walls of the old castle, four or five hundred yards away. Obviously it had been built above the original village which the Black Death had wiped out; and built long before the days of gunpowder and cannon which made it a death-trap under any guns planted on this higher ridge. No wonder the Cavaliers had found this a hard Roundhead nut to crack! For, with the lie of the land to his advantage, old Sir Edmund had raised his glacis and rampart simply by moving the earth from the great ditch between them, leaving the ridge to do the rest of the work of shielding his manor.

Burton had stopped and was pointing along the rampart.

Audley took the guide-book from his pocket and opened the map. The walled kitchen garden was sited half way along the southern defence line, tucked behind 'The Great Bastion'. Within it, right next to the bastion itself, was a small cross marked 'The Memorial' . . . well, here at least the Double R Society wouldn't have to expend any of its funds on a pious monument to the real thing.

He turned back to the text—

'... a second and final disaster. For, having given shelter to a
party of Roundheads led by his kinsman Colonel Nathaniel
Parrott, a trusted lieutenant of Oliver Cromwell, Sir Edmund
was more fiercely assaulted by the Royalists than ever before.
By this time, however, he was reduced to casting his own
ammunition with lead from the castle roof and making his own
gunpowder with materials prudently laid in store; and it was
while attending to the latter that he was killed in the explosion
of a magazine behind the north wall.'

Oh, careless Sir Edmund! Once might be called bad luck, but
twice—well, that lesson ought to have been better learnt ...

'History does not relate whether this misfortune was due to
inadvertence or to a stray shot from the enemy, for there was
none left to tell the tale; all that is certain is that he and his
principal officers perished instantly in the ensuing disaster in
circumstances and upon the very spot that are recalled by a
monument raised by his posterity, Mr Algernon Ratcliffe JP,
esteemed father of the present Lord of the Manor, upon the
two hundredth anniversary of its tragic occurrence:

'Stranger! Now gaze on gallant Steyning's urn,
Who ne'er upon the foe his noble back did turn,
But, Earth to Heaven, was untimely sent
By fierce explosion. Mark the dire event!
Once close besieged, now by dread Death set free,
Lord, from Life's Battle take my Soul to Thee!

'Now, once again, we may observe the role of the hero in the
divine plan, which the death of the noble General Gordon at
Khartum in recent times must surely remind the reader. For,
deprived of Sir Edmund's guiding hand and implacable resolve,
the defences on that instant crumbled. The great cannon being
dismounted (which it had been his constant charge to play
upon the foe), the enemy burst in upon the defenders at that
point, scattering all before them. Colonel Parrott, the sole

survivor of the explosion, took to horse and essayed to escape (and who shall cry "faint heart" or "treachery" in such an extremity?), only to perish in the carnage which ensued.'

The gold, thought Audley suddenly. Why was there no mention of the gold?
Burton waved at him again.
"Just coming."

'For sure it was that, as the holding of Standingham had been a great feat of arms, so was its overthrow the more terrible. In a letter to King Charles (who had furnished him with a body of soldiers, together with siege armament), Lord Monson wrote: "In the extirpation of this nest of viperous rebels above 200 persons were slain, and an hundred taken prisoner, mostly of the baser sort: together with a great store of plate and all manner of household stuff, together with gold and silver pieces, being the fortune of the late owner, to the value of 3,500 *l*., other than that taken by our soldiers, they being in the heat of battle." Here it was that dark deeds were committed, it being rumoured that Colonel Parrott had brought with him a great treasure into the castle. But that brave man being beyond the power of his enemies to question, and certain poor prisoners revealing nothing, even upon torture, no part of this was ever discovered (giving rise to the legend which is even yet cherished by local folk); this even though much further damage was wrought to the fabric of the house and surviving buildings, the which was laid at Lord Monson's door, so that when he was shortly afterwards slain by a bullet through the mouth at the battle of Newbury it was said of him that "he sought the gold and drank the blood of the godly in his life, but he found but one ball of lead and drank his own blood in his death".'

Nasty. The sack of Standingham had been nasty—the proportion of killed to captured emphasised that as no mere words could—and the exultation of the godly Reverend Musgrave over Lord Monson's come-uppance was nasty too. But what was certain was that Charlie Ratcliffe hadn't derived much use from the Musgrave *History*, because Musgrave obviously rated the gold no higher than legend and rumour.

Burton was waiting for him beside an enormous cannon, Sir Edmund's original monster now bedded in a carriage of stone and set in the middle of the bastion between two pyramids of equally ancient cannonballs. But Audley had eyes neither for the man nor the gun, only for the kitchen garden behind and beneath them.

Killed in the explosion of a magazine behind the north wall—
But that had been over three hundred years ago, not the day before yesterday!

And yet there, directly below him, was a huge raw crater in the earth, surrounded by all the debris of an explosion: uprooted apple trees, dead in full leaf with the fruit hanging obscenely at unnatural angles, crushed rose bushes in bloom and piles of broken stone half buried in heaps of soil. Even beyond the area of total devastation the garden was scarred by wheel tracks which ran straight across flower beds and neat grass paths as though they hadn't existed. The whole place looked as though a battle had been fought across it, like the gardens of Normandy after D-Day. The fact that it had been a garden in full bloom, full of fruit and flowers, somehow made the scene more horrible; but what made it worse even than that was the feeling that the destruction beyond the crater had not really been mere careless-ness, but a deliberate act, with each tractor journey cutting through a different and hitherto undamaged area.

Burton read the stricken expression on his face. "Makes a man feel sick, don't it?"

Audley nodded. Sick was the right word. If a child had done this the stick would have been needed; in an adult, the psychiatrist.

"Did he hate you, from way back?"

Burton shook his head. "Didn't even remember my name. *Them*, maybe he did . . . maybe he didn't. I can't rightly say."

"But they're dead."

"Aye." Burton surveyed the ruin of his work. "She loved flowers when she was alive, the old lady did. Roses and dahlias and chrysanths, mostly. And daffs in the spring . . . filled the

110

house with 'em. And after she died the old man kept them on. Said they reminded him of her, like." He stopped suddenly, as though he felt he'd spoken too much.

Audley stared down at the pile of stones. He could make out the top of a cross with one arm broken off short, and nearby lay an accusing fragment of inscription:

MARK THE DIRE EVENT!

So that was the way of it: to get at the gold Charlie Ratcliffe had torn up the memorial to his ancestor with no thought of reassembling it afterwards.

But that absence of piety in Charlie Ratcliffe was hardly surprising; what *was* surprising was that he had known exactly where to dig. And, judging by the depth of the crater, where to dig deep indeed.

I put myself into Nathaniel Parrott's shoes.

Hiding a ton of gold ingots presented a great many problems, the more so when it had to be done in the middle of a siege, with the garrison all around. For if Parrott and Steyning had decided that the castle was doomed they could hardly rely on death shutting all the mouths of those who might have an idea of the hiding place.

Although in fact death had done just that very neatly indeed. Too neatly?

And, by God, death had also covered up the hiding place too, for this was the site of the original explosion—the site of the powder magazine.

Audley stared into the crater. *Clever and devious and ruthless,* Nayler had said, and they'd been all of that, Parrott and Steyning —all of that and more.

The powder magazine would have been strictly out of bounds. They had dug their hole in it, and dug far deeper than was necessary.

And then filled it in.

And then made a brand new hole above it—and who would think of looking for a hole in the bottom of another hole?

And they had killed the men who had hidden the treasure at the same time.

111

Audley frowned. The men had included Edmund Steyning himself.

Parrott.

'Colonel Parrott, the sole survivor among the senior officers, took to horse and essayed to escape—'

The murderous bastard!

The murderous double-crossing bastard.

"You got what you came for?" The question was a formality; Burton had been watching him intently.

"Yes."

Like Nathaniel Parrott—like Charlie Ratcliffe: it had maybe taken a murderer to spot a murderer.

"That's good, then," said Burton.

Not really so good, thought Audley. There was nothing more here for him, on the scene of a successful seventeenth-century crime. If there was any chance of catching Charlie Ratcliffe it could only be somewhere back on the site of the twentieth-century crime, beside the Swine Brook.

VI

AUDLEY HATED ENGLISH heatwaves.

He could put up with foreign hot weather, even Washington weather, which was natural and inevitable. But English heat was like a betrayal by an old and dear friend whose greatest virtue had hitherto been a comfortable and reliable moderation.

And worst of all was hot English darkness, which always made him wonder, when he awoke after a few minutes (or was it a few hours?) of sweaty, unrefreshing sleep, whether he was in England at all.

He reached across tentatively under the single sheet to reassure himself. There were only two thighs in the world like that. Once upon a long ago time there had been other thighs, but none of them had had Faith's superb temperature control, cool in summer and warm in winter.

He was at home in his own bed in the midst of a heatwave, with the weathermen's records melting one by one around him—

Not since the summer of 1948 . . .

Not since the summer of 1940 . . .

Hot and dry.

But the summers of the 1640s, especially the summer of '43, had been warm and wet, which spelt poor harvests and bad, unhealthy military campaigns.

No more doubts now. He had been thinking of the summer of '43 when he had finally drifted off. Now he would think of it again for want of anything better to think about.

Anno Domini One Thousand, Six Hundred and Forty-Three.

What had 1643 to do with 1975?

He felt the sweat running down his throat.

Nothing.

But that had been a bad summer for Parliament and the Roundheads, no two ways about that. Maybe not with hind-sight, because even defeat was teaching Master Oliver Cromwell

113

and Sir Thomas Fairfax their new trade the hard way, the way Grant and Sherman had learnt it.

But without hindsight...

Beaten at Charlgrove in June, and that good man John Hampden dying in agony from his wound; beaten at Lansdown the next month by the Cornish infantry, and doubly beaten against the odds at Roundway Down a few days later by the Royalist cavalry.

Bristol, the second city of the Kingdom, stormed by Prince Rupert before July was out, and other towns falling like skittles: Poole and Dorchester, Portland and Weymouth, Bideford and Barnstaple—Henry Digby counting them off on his fingers across the dinner table—Gloucester in danger, Exeter on the verge of surrender, Lincoln and Gainsborough lost.

Trouble in Kent, trouble in London. And a rising even in Cromwell's own East Anglia.

Plague in Waller's army—the warm, wet summer at work.

And John Pym, who held it all together from London, fighting the cancer in his gut that was killing him by inches and which would have him in the ground before the year was out.

Money desperately short, troops deserting for want of it— *Money*. That was what 1643 had in common with 1975.

· In 1643 Pym was already levying taxes such as Charles I had never dreamed of, taxes on everything but the prime necessities of life—and even they would be taxed before the thing was finished. Money not just for weapons and powder and soldiers' pay, but also to buy the Scottish army.

This wasn't Digby, this was his own memory. Digby knew about the battles and how they had been fought, but he didn't know what had brought the armies to the battlefield.

Money.

The Scots, to their credit, would fight the King for the sake of religion. But to their eternal discredit—and their subsequent utter defeat—they would only do it at a price and a profit.

"Darling—are you awake?" Faith turned towards him.

Money.

He knew there had been something bugging him about Swine Brook Field, and that was it. In August, 1643, both armies had been at full stretch, the Royalists to take Gloucester and the Roundheads to relieve it. But they had each detached men they could ill afford to spare to intervene in a piddling little country house siege, little better than a feud between two local magnates who hated each other's guts because of an old lawsuit.

"Darling..."

But if there had been gold at Standingham Castle—if money and promises would make the Scots march it would also make them stay north of the border. Was that what both sides had thought?

"Are you awake, darling?"

And since the King was far shorter of it than Parliament, that made it doubly important for Parliament to stop him getting it, even in the depths of their bad summer.

That was why Swine Brook Field had been fought.

Was that what Charlie Ratcliffe had thought too?

"Sorry, love. Did I wake you up?" He stroked the cool thigh gently.

"You would have woken me up if I'd been to sleep. You've been grunting and mumbling like a mad thing."

Audley felt guilty. She had wanted to talk and he had been too tired. And instead he had merely kept her awake.

"I'm sorry."

She gave a gurgling chuckle. "Oh, I don't mind you grunting and mumbling, darling. It's when you wake up and start thinking that you're really disturbing—you don't make a sound then, and the noise is deafening."

"The noise?"

"You get tensed up when you think. You went absolutely rigid just now—did you have a brilliant idea? I hope you did, anyway. I don't mind being kept awake by brilliant ideas."

"Not exactly brilliant, but an idea." Audley smiled into the darkness: she was as irrepressibly unawed about his job as she had been when she'd first met him. And he was still what he had been to her then—a cross between a high class refuse collector and the municipal pest officer, two unrewarding but necessary posts. Someone had to fill them, and she just happened to fancy the someone who did...

"And top secret, I presume," she murmured.

"Not really. I was just thinking that the sinews of war are made of gold."

"Not very profound."

"But still true."

"Hmm ... if it wasn't just past midnight I might argue that ideas were better than gold."

"Ideas?" Audley squinted at the luminous hands of the bedside clock. It was only just past midnight: no wonder he hadn't woken her up, he hadn't been asleep for more than half an hour. And yet he felt as if he'd slept for hours. "All right, I'll give you gold plus ideas, that ought to be unbeatable."

"And that was why Cromwell was unbeatable? It was his gold you were thinking about, I take it?"

She'd read the same story, only a day late and with more misprints, in the *Guardian*.

"But of course it wasn't his gold, was it?" she continued. "I mean he didn't find it, did he? That Charlie Ratcliffe must be a smart young man."

Bright, but not flashy—no, that was Henry Digby.

"I like your Sergeant Digby," said Faith suddenly, as though she'd been eavesdropping on his stream of consciousness. "I'm half-glad you brought him here to sleep."

"Half-glad?" He wished he could see her face. "What does half-glad mean?"

"It means ... that I enjoyed meeting him. He's intelligent and he has good manners. He's even quite good-looking in a homely sort of way."

"In America 'homely' means 'plain'," said Audley irrelevantly.

"Well, we aren't in America. Nice looking, then, if you want to play with words. You ought to introduce him to Frances, they're both the same sort of person."

"I might just do that some time. And that's the glad half of half-glad, is it?"

"Yes."

"And the unglad half is that he's in my equivocal company?"

She reached for his hand. "You're not equivocal. But he's very young, David."

They were all very young, God help us. Mitchell and Frances and Henry Digby. And Charlie Ratcliffe too.

"It's a young man's game, love. You should be worrying about me."

The cool hand squeezed his hot hand. "I have to think that you can look after yourself, my darling."

Audley stared into the darkness for a moment without answering, holding the cool hand.

"He's a policeman, love. A policeman with three commendations too, and they weren't just for seeing old ladies across busy streets at rush hour either, you can be sure of that."

The hand relaxed. "So he takes his chances?"

"Exactly. He takes his chances. And since this is England and not Ireland, those are pretty damn good chances."

"Well, you just make sure they are, that's all."

"So you be careful of him . . . sir."

First Weston, now Faith.

Weston had said it twice though—

"You've got him for a week, the Chief said. Or ten days at the outside, that'll take in Easingbridge and Standingham. After that we want him back—undamaged."

"Standingham? You mean there's a mock-battle there too?"

Weston registered surprise. "They haven't told you much, have they!"

"I didn't ask for much. I get what I want in my own way and in my own time, Superintendent. Don't you do the same?"

Weston gave a non-committal grunt, then nodded grudgingly without replying. Audley was aware suddenly that he'd lost a part of the treacherous ground on which he'd built a bridge between them; at best it was a ramshackle, temporary affair, and without constant attention it would sink without a trace.

Yet here had to be a reason for this loss.

"So there's to be a mock-battle at Standingham?"

Another nod. "Aye. A full-scale one. The Easingbridge affair's only a one-day stand, but Standingham's a two-day job."

"In honour of Charlie Ratcliffe's treasure trove?"

"I suppose so." Weston shrugged. "There's never been a

re-enactment there before, anyway. The old man wouldn't have one at any price."

A full-scale two-day event. And in the ordinary course of things, a Civil War spectacle could draw a Second Division crowd, up to ten thousand people. But with the publicity Charlie Ratcliffe and the Cromwell's treasure had had ... plus the smell of unsolved murder drifting from Swine Brook Field ... that might lift it into the First Division.

So Weston was apprehensive. Only it couldn't have anything to do with handling a First Division crowd, because when it came to crowd control the British police hadn't anything to learn from anyone. And this was only a crowd of First Division size anyway, not of First Division disposition.

But still apprehensive.

"Will you be there, Superintendent?"

"At Standingham—yes. At Easingbridge—probably."

"On the Ratcliffe case? So you're not giving up?"

"On a murder we never give up. We're running down the Incident Room, it's true. But we're not giving up."

No Statute of Limitations on murder. And as murders went, this was still a young one. But there was something wrong with the way Weston had answered that question, a hint of weariness as well as wariness. Or vice versa.

So it came down to a straight question, delivered with no frills.

"You're not going to solve this murder, are you?"

Not even a question. *If it can be done, they'll do it ...*

"Meaning we're not going to charge anyone?" Weston paused. "No, we're not going to solve this one. Off the record."

"Off the record—understood."

"Thank you. . . . And neither are you, Dr Audley."

And if they can't do it, I can't do it.

"Why not?"

"Because this murderer's long gone." Weston stared directly at him, unblinking. "In my opinion. And also off the record."

Straight from the horse's mouth.

"Professional?"

"Professional." The answer came back so quickly that it

had obviously been ready-wrapped and just waiting for collection.

"In your opinion. Off the record."

"Of course. There's no proof. No evidence." Weston showed his teeth in the travesty of a smile. "Seven thousand witnesses. Nearly five hundred statements. But no evidence."

Brigadier Stocker would have known that perfectly well.

"Not a clever amateur? Or even a lucky one?"

"An amateur." Weston sniffed. "It's just barely conceivable, Dr Audley. Very clever and very lucky and very daring. Or very stupid and very lucky and very daring.... Anything's possible. But not probable."

"Especially as I'm here."

"You improve the odds, for a fact." The teeth showed again. "But you didn't call them."

Audley drew a deep breath. "Thank you for trusting me, Superintendent."

"My duty to." Weston shrugged. "No more questions, then?"

"No more questions. I only had one that was worth a damn, and you've just answered that very fairly."

Weston acknowledged the gratitude with a nod. "So what are you going to do now?"

"I wish I knew." Audley inclined his head towards the young sergeant. "Perhaps he'll have another flash of inspiration—"

They had moved towards Sergeant Digby then.

"Well, just you make sure he is, that's all," said Faith. "You just keep your eye on him. So long as you do that he won't come to any harm."

"Aye. And he won't do anything useful either—" Audley stopped suddenly.

"You've had another bright idea," said Faith accusingly.

"Mmm ..."

"Well, have you?"

He'd have to go through the sergeant's evidence again.

"I don't know ... I was just thinking that someone else might have said much the same thing before the battle of Swine Brook Field a few weeks ago."

119

"And does that qualify as a bright idea?"

Bright idea. In the circumstances that was a joke he couldn't bring himself to laugh at.

"That's right. A little late, but better late than never." He turned back his corner of the sheet and sat up in bed. "And it's telling me to get up and make myself some black coffee."

"But you've only just come to bed."

"But I feel as if I've slept half the night already. And I won't go to sleep for hours now, I'll just keep you awake, love." He leaned over and kissed her accurately on the lips. Cool lips, nice cool soft lips. A sensible man wouldn't get up and make himself coffee. But a sensible man would have explored this bright idea hours earlier, and this must be his penance. "I have to do some noisy thinking."

"Oh, very well—if you must." She yawned. "Just don't wake up Cathy. And don't wake up Sergeant Digby either."

He reached with his toes for his slippers, and with his hand for his dressing gown. Everything was exactly to foot and to hand in the darkness, with no blind groping. And no blind groping in his brain, either: he knew at last what he was doing.

Cathy's bedroom door across the passage was open, as always. In the soft light of the shaded 25-watt bulb outside he could see her lying under the sheet with the abandoned innocence of childhood, long legs and slender arms resting where they had fallen. That was how the dead on the battlefield lay, uncaring and oblivious of prying eyes.

Mustn't think of that now, he shook his head fiercely. Must leave her to her dreams, to pursue his own nightmares.

He stared past the sleeping child into the darkness of the open window beyond her. Somewhere out there lay Charlie Ratcliffe secure in the dreamless sleep of success.

Dreamless until this moment, when a stranger bent his mind towards the tiny flaw in his otherwise perfect crime.

Now was the instant when Charlie ought to stir uneasily for the first time.

VII

Audley drew the crudely cyclostyled pages of the Battle Scenario out of the plastic folder.

7. The battle will commence at 3.15 p.m.

He had left the pages in the wrong order, from the time when he had read them through quickly the first time, just before dinner.

Henry Digby had watched him in silence as he read, without any sign of expectation. And that had annoyed him a little— that loyal assumption that he would get nothing more out of them than Superintendent Weston—and everyone else—had done.

But now, thanks to Faith, things were different.

Now there were four names on his blotter.

Swine Brook Field: Battle Scenario.

Swine Brook Field: Murder Scenario.

—and it had annoyed him because it was correct. If there had been nothing here for Superintendent Weston then there couldn't possibly be anything here for anyone else.

Only now, as he ordered the pages, he realised that he was smiling to himself. For now the game had changed. Or the rules of the game, which had shackled Superintendent Weston, had been abolished—that was the difference.

1. Roundhead Objective: to raise siege of Standingham Castle, or alternatively to deliver supply of artillery shot and to reinforce garrison.

Royalist Objective: to prevent above and to capture supplies for own use.

Of course it wasn't surprising that the Royalists too had been short of powder and shot after the siege of Bristol and with the siege of Gloucester in prospect. And as Digby had explained, they had been fatally short of ammunition at the battle of Newbury next month.

121

Unimportant.

2. *Topography: At the battlefield site the Swine Brook flows between two parallel ridges, with the Old Road to Standingham (ten miles distant) running beside stream, the course of which is marked by clumps of vegetation.*

Audley closed his eyes for an instant, in an effort to recreate not what he had seen a few hours earlier, the ten-week growth which had sprung up since the Murder Squad had painstakingly cut back the bushes in a search for non-existent clues, but the Swine Brook as it had been—

"It wasn't like this, sir."

"No, Sergeant? Then tell me what it was like."

'Clumps' hadn't been altogether accurate. Except for the thirty-yard gap in the centre, where Digby had been stationed under one of the willow trees with his canisters of red dye, the tangle of blackberry and hawthorn bushes had formed an almost continuous and impenetrable hedge on each side of the stream —an overhanging hedge which met and interlocked above the water.

Members of both armies will cross the Swine Brook ONLY between points x and y (see Màp 'A')...

In fact, members of both armies *could* only cross the stream in that gap, between points x and y.

Under Sergeant Digby's eye.

And then, on the far side, the farm track running beside the stream, and beyond it the field of wheat stubble, freshly cut and dotted with bales of straw.

But it hadn't been a stubble field then—

Members crossing the Swine Brook must NOT walk on the growing corn, but will keep STRICTLY to the track, where they will form up in regimental groups...

The Double R Society knew which side its bread was buttered; they were always very careful to keep in with the local farmers.

"... I see, Sergeant. So you were under this tree, pouring in the dye."

"Yes, sir." Digby wasn't overawed, just ten times as cautious as Weston had been. But there was no percentage in rushing him or pushing him, as he had pushed Weston. He had enough time at least to try to win the young man's confidence during the first twenty-four hours.

"A rather dull job."

"Sir?"

"A dull job, pouring dye."

"I was recovering from a sprained ankle, sir."

"Sprained in the line of duty?"

"Yes ... sir."

And now a sprained tongue. It looked like being an uphill struggle, winning Sergeant Digby's confidence.

"But normally you would have been—ah—fighting, is that right?"

"Yes, sir."

"And you're an officer in Orme's regiment?"

5. Roundhead Army will muster on Barford Village Green by not later than 2.45. Order of march will be: Allen's Regiment, Clarke's Regiment, Bradley's Regiment, Orme's Regiment, Cox's Regiment, Seager's Regiment, Wheeler's Regiment, Edward's Regiment, Ratcliffe's Regiment. Ms Anderson will assemble Angels of Mercy...

"Yes, sir."

Audley wondered what Ms Anderson would make of Ms Fitzgibbon on Saturday.

Unimportant. What was important was that Ratcliffe's Regiment—Charlie Ratcliffe's Regiment—was last in line of march, and therefore on the extreme left wing of the coming battle. Which, knowing Charlie Ratcliffe, was the appropriate place for them ... but which also put them farthest away from where James Ratcliffe had met his killer.

"And where exactly was James Ratcliffe?"

Sergeant Digby pointed upstream. "About twenty yards from here, sir. I'll show you."

The trailing blackberry shoots and young hawthorn growth were fighting with the vigorous crop of stinging nettles at the actual scene of the crime. Death left no mark on the ground for one man, recently despatched, any more than it had for hundreds who had been once cut down all around. For a time the nettles would rule here, but by next spring the bushes would again be dominant, and within a year or two this spot would be indistinguishable from any other along the Swine Brook.

The Sergeant led the way to the edge of the stream.

"He was down there, tucked in right against the bank," he said simply. "Out of sight, practically."

In the central gap the banks had been trampled down to the water's edge, but here there were miniature cliffs two or three feet high.

"There was a narrow opening to the brook here," explained Digby. "On this side, anyway—on the other it was solid brambles, four or five feet high."

"What was he actually doing here—James Ratcliffe?" asked Audley.

"He was in charge of two of the burning wagons. There were four wagons in all—old things we hired from the farmers—"

"To burn?"

"They weren't actually burnt. They were loaded with smoke-canisters, and it was the job of the special effects section to set them off at intervals."

"So James Ratcliffe was in the special effects section?"

"Yes, sir . . . and he was also chairman of the Safety Committee, sir." Sergeant Digby closed his mouth on the last word as though he wanted to make sure no other words escaped custody.

Audley nodded patiently. "And just what does the special effects section do . . . when it's not making smoke without fire?"

Digby struggled momentarily with the question, deciding finally that there was no way it could be answered with a straight yes-or-no. "They set off small explosive charges mostly. Anything that involves any sort of danger, too."

"Such as?"

Digby shrugged. "Falling off things. Falling into water . . . that type of thing. They put up their ideas to the Safety Committee first, of course."

Audley saw suddenly that the sergeant was being pulled several different ways at once. As a good copper he didn't want

124

to be unco-operative with a superior officer, even though in this instance the superior officer was a Home Office interloper. But as a uniform man attached to the CID and to Superintendent Weston, who was also his future boss as well as his immediate one, he resented the interloper's presence.

But there was nothing unusual about that professional tug-of-war; what distorted the pull was a third force exerted by his loyalty to the Double R Society, at least so far as he didn't want the interloper to get the wrong ideas about its operations.

"I see." He nodded gravely, stifling the temptation to observe jocularly that James Ratcliffe's final 'special effect' had been the most spectacular of all. "But this time he was just in charge of —ah—making smoke, eh?"

Digby gazed at him mournfully. "No, sir."

"No?"

"He was also one of the special casualties." Digby swallowed.

Understatement of the day. But rather than say that Audley managed a mild questioning grunt.

"The special effects are laid on to . . . interest the spectators." Digby nerved himself to the required explanation with an obvious effort. "On this occasion Jim Ratcliffe led our attack—the Roundhead attack, that is—on the Royalist line right in front of the crowd—"

7. *The battle will commence at 3.15 sharp.*
   (i) Roundhead vanguard fired on by Royalists blocking line of advance along Old Road . . .

   . . . (viii) General assault by Roundheads with whole force except vanguard (still engaging road block force). Death of Colonel Flowerdew (Roundhead commander) . . .

Audley frowned. "I didn't know there was a Roundhead attack. I thought the Royalists simply charged, and that was that."

"Oh, that was in the original battle—the real one." Digby's voice lost its official flatness and became at once more animated. "We didn't set out to reproduce it accurately, it wouldn't have been possible because—well, it was one big cavalry charge, and we've only got six horsemen."

"And it would have been over too quickly."

"It would. And it would have been dull for the crowd, too. It isn't that we don't try to be accurate when we can, as far as it's possible without horsemen. But this was a case where we had to give people something for their money—"

"And there's nothing like 'the push of the pike' for that, eh?" Audley decided that a non-patronising smile would be in order. "So—Jim Ratcliffe led the attack. And became a 'special casualty'?"

"That's right, sir. He played the part of Colonel Flowerdew, who was hit by a cannon ball—he really was hit, in the real battle. We simply moved him up closer to the crowd so they could see what happened."

"When what happened?"

"When—he was hit by a cannon ball."

Audley lifted an eyebrow. "And that, I take it, was a special effect—being hit by a cannon ball? I can see that it would be!"

Digby grinned. "Only a *small* cannon ball. Not from a Saker or a Drake, but a Fawconet or even arabinet—a three-quarter pounder, say."

"Oh, sure." Audley grinned back, happy to have found this easy way through the sergeant's armour. "Just a very little one. But it wouldn't have a very little effect—special effect, I mean."

Digby's grin evaporated, as though he'd remembered suddenly that the discussion was not academic. "No. Blood everywhere. The crowd really goes for that, sir."

Very true, thought Audley. For crowds there was nothing like blood for money.

"So how do you give it to them, then?"

"There are a number of different ways." Digby shrugged. "The one we use is the simplest and safest. The casualty wears a loose linen tunic—white for the best effect—and white breeches too if possible. Anything that'll show the blood, anyway.... And under it are fixed several contraceptives—condoms—full of red dye and a bit of air to make them easier to burst. Actually, we've tried using balloons, but condoms are better."

But condoms are better: *You Can Rely on Durex.* Although this was one reliability test the family planners certainly hadn't thought of.

Only Digby was deadly serious now. And more, there was something in his manner which told Audley that it would be a mistake to burst out laughing.

Burst?

"How do you burst them?"

Digby shook his head. "There are some pretty dangerous ways of doing that. I heard of one fellow using explosive caps on a thick leather pad. But we use drawing pins in special gloves: the moment the cannon goes off—and you have to be not less than twenty yards away diagonally from it—you strike the chest hard with the palm of one hand and the back of the other hand." He stared at Audley with peculiar intensity. "It usually works well enough."

"But not this time?"

Digby continued to stare at him. "Then—you haven't read my report, sir?" He blinked. "I mean—my statement in evidence?"

Audley shook his head.

"I see." The young sergeant paused. "Well . . . it worked . . . well enough—"

Well enough.

Audley stared out of his study window into the darkness, listening with one corner of his mind to the small dry rasp of the dead leaves on the terrace outside.

Suddenly his nerves tautened at the unnatural sound: there shouldn't be dead leaves moving like that in the gentle night breeze of summer. He half-rose from his chair before his brain relaxed the tension as instantly as it had arisen. The great elm across the lawn there was dying out of season, shedding its leaves for the last time like ten million other elms across the length of England which had been murdered by the invading Dutch elm fungus.

He subsided back into the chair, the knot in his stomach slowly untying itself. Whatever Matthew Fattorini might say, this wasn't the sort of job where the sound of dead leaves rustling in the darkness might not be what it seemed.

Well enough?

Such a beautiful, simple, professional killing, it had been. A pure, almost contemptuous best-laid scheme.

Colonel Flowerdew had died there according to plan on the hillside above the Swine Brook, deluged in contraceptive blood to the admiring "oohs" and "aahs" of the crowd.

And Colonel Flowerdew had been carried away, back down the hillside, to where the wounded and dying lay.

And Colonel Flowerdew had then become James Ratcliffe, ready for his next special effect—

(ix) Royalist cannonade resumes. Roundhead wagons set ablaze.

Snugged down in his small gap in the bushes beside the stream he had set off the smoke canisters on schedule, one by one.

(x) Roundhead vanguard begins to retreat.

But now there came an unplanned addition to the Swine Brook Field Scenario—

Enter one murderer.

Identity unknown. Believed professional. Long gone now. Route—in full view of seven thousand witnesses?

"He came down the stream, sir," said Sergeant Digby. "He couldn't risk coming upstream, because I was there, for one. And nobody came past me until the rout started."

(xiii) Collapse of Roundhead defence—

"And too many people would have seen him—it's surprising what people see. Whereas if he came down the stream—" Digby pointed.

Audley followed the line of the finger, past the fresh growth of the cropped section of bushes, to where the uncut bushes raged in their unrestricted summer tangle. The stream issued out of a green-shadowed tunnel, walled and roofed with leaves and branches. The open fields on either side were parched and dry, and open to prying eyes, the well-grazed summer grass of the meadow on one hand and the evenly-cropped wheat stubble on the other; but the Swine Brook itself ran in a secret place of its own making, nourishing the deep rooted things which shielded it from the sun.

He caught the old familiar stream-smell of cool, damp earth and rotting vegetation, and the smell carried him back to his

128

own childhood. He had explored streams like this a lifetime ago, searching for the shy things that lived and grew and died in hiding along the water's edge; the memory of soft wet moss under his fingers and smooth squidgy mud between his toes was there with the smell, long forgotten but never forgettable.... And the memory of the solitary little boy who had preferred such dark passages between the woodlands not only for the mysteries they concealed but also because of the invisibility they gave him.

Invisibility. No matter there were seven thousand pairs of eyes or seventy thousand on the ridge above, it would still have been easy for the killer to have stolen up on Jim Ratcliffe unnoticed.

"—somebody came down the stream, anyway. The mud was disturbed all the way to the farm bridge a quarter of a mile upstream, in the spinney there." Digby pointed again. "Couldn't make out the footprints, of course. Or anything else, except they were recent when we examined them. But someone came down and then went back again, and there's a road just the other side of the trees there. So it would have been easy, coming and going."

Easy?

"How did Ratcliffe die?"

For an instant the young sergeant frowned—no doubt Audley's ignorance of the simplest basic facts of the crime was still confusing him. Then he straightened his expression into formal blankness again. "One blow on the back of the neck, sir. What the newspapers call 'a karate chop' now, but what used to be called a rabbit-punch." He paused. "Easy again—if you know how to do it."

Easy?

This time Audley's eye was caught by the wheat stubble.

Another memory there, but one much closer to the surface, for he could never pass a harvested field without half-recalling this one... a memory half-golden, because time edged all youthful memories with gold, but dark also because time never quite succeeded in erasing the blurred recollection of unhappiness.

Not a child any more, nor even a snotty schoolboy though

still at school, but a gauche youth ... still lonely and introverted —the concept of the mixed-up teenager hadn't existed then because no one had yet coined the word 'teenager': it had not been his brains which had saved him in that cruel society, but his accidental prowess on the rugger field.

Tackle him low, Audley!

No, that was the wrong memory leading him up the wrong cul-de-sac—it was the school harvest camp he wanted, the endless boring stooking of the sheaves in the National Interest.

And one particular memory, obscene and humiliating—

It had been just such a corn field in the first year of the war. They had stopped stooking as the binder had come to the final cut in the centre of the field, fanning out in readiness for the rabbits trapped in the last of the standing wheat to make their break—and in the mad exhilarating chase he had driven one big buck right back into the cutting blades—

Kill it then, man!

One front paw gone, the other horribly mangled, the thing had suddenly come alive, the hind legs kicking with the strength of desperation.

Kill it, Audley—go on, man—kill it!

He had seen it done half a dozen times by the tractor driver, the grizzled man with the patch on his lung and the ten children. It had been a casual, matter-of-fact action: hold the hind legs and strike down with the edge of the stiffened hand.

Rabbit-punch.

Easy.

Four times he had tried, his own increasing desperation rising to match the rabbit's, but failing to master it. Blood had spattered his trousers—why can't you die, rabbit?

Then the tractor driver had snatched it from him—

Give us 'un, then, for Lord's sake.

One quick professional chop. Then, for final measure, the man had stretched the twitching thing, legs in one hand, neck in the other. He could still hear that stretching sound, the small creaking noise.

Well, 'tis a good 'un, any road. You'm let the other best 'uns go.

* * *

From that dark memory to the banks of the Swine Brook, and now to the darkness beyond the study window, was a journey across years and hours time-travelled in a fraction of a second. . . . But he hadn't returned empty handed.

There was the short answer to Weston's off-the-record certainty and young Digby's word for it.

Not easy.

Because it wasn't so easy to kill a rabbit with one blow, and a man was bigger game and another game altogether. It wasn't simply that they had eliminated all the costumed battlefield actors who'd been playing at killing—he could afford to take that for granted now, the hundreds of statements checked and cross-checked. This was a killing, and more than that, a neat and tidy killing, which was another thing and a very different thing. Because for all the popular claptrap, not one person in a thousand could guarantee to do that with one blow. That guarantee was the hallmark of the professional.

It had been Digby's qualification that mattered—

Easy—if you know how to do it.

"I see. He came down the stream—that's the hypothesis. And he hit Jim Ratcliffe once—that's the forensic fact?"

"Yes, sir."

"And Ratcliffe was crouching in his gap in the bushes beside the stream—here?"

"Yes, sir."

"Behind the smoke he was most conveniently making. . . . And then?"

Digby pointed. "Ratcliffe was struck down *here*, sir. Then his body was rolled over the bank—" he pointed again "—*there*."

"Hypothesis?"

"Fact." Digby took two steps. "And he was found in the water—there. Fact."

Audley peered over the edge of the bank. The motion of the water was imperceptible, it was like a millpond. At this point, where the Swine Brook flowed out of its tunnel in a gentle curve, the stream had formed a shallow pool behind a miniature dam built with fallen branches and plugged with the accumulated detritus lodged in them by the winter floods. Over the years those same floods had carved the overhang at his feet, through which the feathery roots of the bushes trailed in a curtain towards the surface of the water. In its original state, with the tangle of thorn and bramble all around, this would have been a fine and private place to tuck a body, no doubt about that.

"Ratcliffe was lying right under the overhang, sir." Digby seemed to have read his thoughts. "I didn't actually see him until I was standing right on the edge, where you are now exactly."

No need to elaborate on that. Rolled over and then tucked in out of sight. No one who had fallen, or been pushed or knocked, would ever have come to rest so tidily, virtually out of sight in the shallows. That had been the killer's risk, but one taken coolly to minimise the greater risk of quick discovery and maximise the chance of a trouble-free getaway. And a small risk at that, because only Sergeant Digby's trained eye would have spotted the dividing line between horrid accident and suspicious circumstance. And only Sergeant Digby, of all people, would then have fortified his suspicions with established police procedure—

Protect the scene of the crime.

Much more likely, even if the body had been discovered sooner rather than later, would have been these destructive moments of chaos which usually attended presumed accidents. People milling around in panic or ghoulish curiosity, moving the body, trampling the place flat and obliterating any shred of evidence or circumstance that there might be. With only a little luck here on Swine Brook Field—with a battle going on nearby and seven thousand spectators poised to stampede down the hillside—there wouldn't have been any scene of the crime left by the time any sort of trained observer reached the spot. And then, with just a little more luck, there might not have been any crime, just an unfortunate but comprehensible accident of the sort discerning coppers like Weston had foreseen.

But a little luck had gone the other way for once, in the presence of Sergeant Henry Digby.

And doubly the other way....

Audley frowned. "Why did you come here and look, Sergeant?"

"I beg your pardon, sir?"

Audley realised that he had been staring down into the still pool so long that the Sergeant had moved away from him. "I'm sorry. . . . You were on station down there—" he pointed towards the clump of willow trees "—and then you came up here to look for Ratcliffe. Why did you do that?"

Digby stared at him for a moment. "But it wasn't to look for Ratcliffe, sir. It was because of the dye—"

Such a curious thing, utterly unforeseeable, had made the best-laid scheme go agley. In less fatal circumstances a joke, and even now a piece of the blackest comedy.

The durability of Durex contraceptives.

It seemed likely, thought Audley, that James Ratcliffe had practical experience of their resistance, for he had taped no less than eight of them to his body, four at the front and four at the back, when the explosion of any one in each place would have been sufficiently effective to simulate death by cannonball.

Would have—and had been. For he had been carried out of the battle with most of them still intact, still loaded with air and red dye, and it had taken the spikes of the hawthorns and brambles against which he had fallen and over which he had been rolled to puncture the rest of them.

Dye on the ground, where he had fallen.

Dye on the edge of the bank, where he had been rolled.

And most of all dye in the Swine Brook itself, the tell-tale stain of which had eventually carried its message downstream to Sergeant Digby, who of all people happened to be the one best trained and disposed to read it.

"It was because of the dye—coming down from above where I was putting it in. So I knew somebody was playing silly buggers upstream from where I was."

"Why should that matter?"

"If it was the same stuff I was putting into the water it didn't matter, because that was non-toxic. But there are dyes and dyes. If there was some idiot adding a toxic chemical to the water there could be hell to pay downstream, where farm animals drank from it—it could have cost the society a fortune in damages. That's why I went to find out double-quick."

"I see. So you came to this gap first and found Ratcliffe in the water straight off?"

"Not straight off, sir. But I saw traces of the dye on the ground, where the contraceptives had burst. And the whole pool was red by then."

Blood everywhere. And not a drop spilt.

"That must have given you a nasty shock."

"It gave me a shock when I looked over the edge of the bank and found Jim Ratcliffe, I can tell you, sir."

Audley nodded. "In what you rightly took to be suspicious circumstances?"

The sergeant lifted his hands in an oddly uncharacteristic gesture of doubt. "Well, sir . . . it wasn't quite as cut and dried as that. I had to make sure as far as I could that he was dead first. There's—there's a routine for this sort of situation."

"Of course." Audley watched the young man closely. "Yet your suspicions were aroused very quickly, were they not?"

Digby's jaw tightened. "Yes, sir."

"Because of the way the body was tucked in under the bank, and the blobs of dye on the ground where he had fallen—and so on?"

"Yes, sir." A muscle in the young man's cheek twitched nervously. "I believed there was a possibility of foul play."

"And not . . . an accidental blow with the butt of a pike, say. During the rout?"

Digby steadied. "The body was in the stream before that."

"But that would have been . . . only a matter of minutes. How can you be so sure?"

Without a word Digby bent down and plucked a handful of dry grass from the edge of the pool. Then he leant over and dropped the handful into the water under the overhang.

"Watch, sir," he said simply.

Audley watched. For a few moments he thought the grass was stationary. Then, almost imperceptibly, it began to move upstream: here, in the still pool above the natural dam of winter debris there was a lazy backcurrent. Whatever entered it was

134

carried in a slow circle, round and round, until it sank or was caught by the band of accumulated scum at the lip of the dam.

Digby followed his glance and pointed. "The stream doesn't go over the top there, you can see—there isn't much water coming down, with the drought we've had, and there wasn't then either. It just seeps through underneath."

Audley eyed the drifting grass, substituting for it in his imagination the thread of dye which would have unwound from Ratcliffe's body in the sluggish movement of the water. And as it unwound it would have spread until the stain filled the pool ... and only then would it begin to sink to find the chinks in the dam ...

Not just sharp, but bloody sharp. Almost too bloody sharp to be true, was Sergeant Digby.

"How long did it take to reach you, then?"

"Not less than fifteen minutes." There was no sign of doubt and nervousness now. "And fifteen minutes before I found the body the rout hadn't started. Nobody broke ranks before the final attack, either—I know, because I was watching. And that was the way it was planned, too."

"Planned?"

"That's right. The first two attacks, the dead and wounded were carried back to the stream. But after that they lay where they fell—for effect ..." Digby trailed off, momentarily embarrassed.

Audley studied him for a few seconds, then turned back towards the pool. "And you took one look, and smelt a rat—because of the time factor ... that's what it amounts to, does it?"

The muscle twitched again. "You could say that, sir—yes."

"I am saying that, Sergeant. If it had been after the rout you might have put it down to accident, but before the rout you weren't so sure—is *that* it?"

"I couldn't see how it had happened when it did happen, yes sir."

"Good." Audley lifted his gaze back to the sergeant. "Well then, Sergeant, I'd be obliged if you'd tell me how the devil you knew there was a time factor at all?"

"Sir?" Digby frowned at him.

Audley hardened his expression. "How did you know so much about the behaviour of the stream?"

Digby relaxed abruptly. "Oh—that."

"That, yes."

"Because we don't leave anything to chance, sir." Digby smiled at him innocently. "When we stage a battle we do it properly.... So I gave the dye a trial run a week before, to find the best place for it, and I tried this pool first because the gap here was more sheltered than the one downstream. But it took too long—and it spread the dye too much." He pointed downstream. "What we needed was for the water to be good and red where Black Thomas was due to drink it, and still pink when it reached the road bridge where the crowd could see it. So in the end we decided on the big willow as the best place."

"We?"

"The Special Effects Section ... sir," amended the sergeant politely.

Good boy, thought Audley. If you have to kick the top brass, always kick them politely.

"I see. And everyone knew about this, I take it?"

"It's in the battle scenario, sir—Appendix F." Digby nodded. "Everyone has to know exactly what's happening, otherwise things are bound to go wrong. We've learnt that by bitter experience. So you see—"

Audley smiled into the stillness of his study, remembering the sergeant's meticulous account of the battle of Swine Brook Field with admiration.

Such a curious mixture, that account had been. Mostly it was still the formal recollection of a policeman trained to give evidence, but every now and then the youthful Civil War buff shone through, illuminating a sombre landscape of fact with shafts of enthusiasm.

He thought of Digby lying in the narrow bed in the spare room at the end of the passage, which had once been his own childhood bedroom, and realised without surprise that the thought was already edged with something close to affection.

It was hard to think of the boy as a police sergeant. If he had married young he could have had a son that age, and Digby could have occupied that bed as of right. To have a sharp son like that to put him in his place would be rather agreeable....

He was growing old, and the measure of his years was that he was already beginning to relive his youth through those who still had the whole exciting game to play ... and who could still do all the things he had somehow missed doing.

Neither Faith nor Superintendent Weston needed to worry: he would keep an eye on young Henry Digby. A protective eye.

And the irony now was that in that very responsibility lay the key to the murder of James Ratcliffe on Swine Brook Field, which Weston and Digby himself had both missed.

The red dye—the tell-tale red dye—had been an unforeseen accident. But Henry Digby's presence twenty yards from the killing had been a well-known fact. A fact well known to Charlie Ratcliffe.

A fact Charlie Ratcliffe could not afford to overlook: Sergeant Digby of the Mid-Wessex Police Force.

He stared down at the four names which he had written on his blotter.

VIII

On the corner of Easingbridge Village Green nearest
the Ploughman's Arms public house a yellow-coated musketeer
was vomiting up his heart and a quantity of beer, oblivious of
his admiring audience of small children. Two of his comrades,
obviously in little better condition, lay stretched out on the grass
nearby, their muskets and bandoliers at their side. And from the
pub itself came the sound of drunken, but nonetheless distinct
singing—

> *Oh, landlord have you a daughter fair?*
> *Parlez-vous, parlez-vous!*
> *Oh, landlord have you a daughter fair,*
> *With lily-white tits and golden hair?*
> *Inky-pinky parlez-vous.*

Audley manoeuvred the 2200 into a vacant slot in the pub
forecourt, reflecting as he did so that if the song was anachron-
istic ("Three German Officers crossed the Rhine", which as he
recalled was its first line, if not its title, could hardly be earlier
than 1914), the condition of the singers was no doubt historically impeccable: from the position of the village on the western
slope of the Easing valley, with the river between the Royalists
and Oliver Cromwell's advancing raiders, the cavaliers must
have been stoned out of their minds to let their enemies round
them up so easily in broad daylight back in 1644. Mere in-
competence couldn't stretch that far, only booze would answer
the case.

He switched off the engine and picked up the leaflet which
had been thrust through his window at the traffic jam by the
bridge. It was crudely printed, but the map on one side told its
story simply and directly: Cromwell, the cunning sod, had
feinted at the bridge to draw the Royalists' attention directly
across the river while actually sending the greater part of his
brigade up river to cross by a convenient ford. Once across the

138

river, his men had swept down on the enemy's flank; whereupon the attackers at the bridge had advanced in earnest and had turned the Royalist defeat into a rout.

It all looked nice and clear-cut; suspiciously so, indeed. But the reality had probably been very different, he thought, remembering what Captain (alias Sergeant) Henry Digby had told him that very morning. This had actually been the future dictator's very first truly independent command, the raid to stop the King transferring his artillery from the Severn Valley to Oxford. If he had fluffed it, the odds were that he might not have been given his chance as Fairfax's second-in-command in the coming campaign—the Naseby campaign which made his reputation as a cavalry general.

By the time he'd reached the Easing valley he'd already fought two successful actions, smashing three of the Earl of Northampton's regiments in Oxfordshire and then bluffing the Bletchingdon House garrison into surrender. But he still had everything to play for, and it would all have gone for nothing if those Royalist pickets at the upstream ford had been made of sterner stuff.

He stared down at the crumpled paper in his hand, at the black arrow which marked the line of the approach march, the river crossing and the flank attack. So that was how it had been done.

Old Cow Ford.

It wasn't even a proper name—more likely it had been just 'the old cow ford near Easingbridge'. But that was where history had been made—and changed—nevertheless.

Sweating, muddy horses and sweating, swearing men filing through the thick woods above the valley; jingling harness drowned by the distant sound of musket fire and cannon downstream, and maybe also diverting the attention of the Royalist pickets—"The buggers'll be catching it down by the bridge. Better them than us, though"; and then the terrible long cavalry swords drawn, the straight basket-hilted swords of the New Model Army ...

And then General Cromwell's men were across the Old Cow Ford. And General Cromwell was on his way to the Cotswolds

—and to Naseby, and the Palace of Westminster and the conquest of three kingdoms.

Colonel Sir Edward Whitelocke, foolishly believing a false report that Cromwell had been defeated and slain by Lord Goring, allowed his men to partake of a great quantity of fresh-brewed ale, so that on the morrow they were in no condition to withstand the onset of the Ironsides, when they came upon them untimely—

The black and white of the pamphlet registered. So he'd been literally and absolutely spot on with his first guess: in executing his flank attack (which, if it was well-advised, was still no great military innovation), God's Chosen Instrument of Vengeance owed more to the stupidity of his adversary than to Divine Providence, which usually received the credit for Crowning Mercies in those far-off days. Though perhaps the presence of that 'great quantity of fresh-brewed ale' was in the nature of Divine Providence at that, constituting as it did a temptation which no British soldiers—and above all no English cavaliers of the seventeenth century—could be expected to resist.

But no matter. If there were such things as omens, it was a good omen that his instincts were working. And perhaps even a good omen twice over: Colonel Sir Edward Whitelocke had joined the great company of defeated commanders because he had thought himself in the clear, had relaxed his guard, and then had been stampeded into the wrong counter-action.

And that, more or less, was the battle scenario for the defeat of Charlie Ratcliffe at this instant.

A crash of broken glass within the Ploughman's Arms, followed by a loud cheer, roused him from his military reflections just as a dark shadow loomed in the corner of his eye outside the car.

"Are you all right, sir?"

The dark shadow was a large policeman.

"Perfectly, thank you. Why shouldn't I be?"

The policeman sniffed suspiciously. "That's not for me to say, sir. But I've been watching you for the last four or five minutes and—"

There was another loud crash from the Ploughman, and a further outbreak of cheering which blended into the unforgettable strains of "The Ball of Kirriemuir". The policeman, who was young and fresh-faced and astonishingly like Sergeant Digby, lifted his nose from the car window and gave the pub a long, hard look as though calculating the breaking-strength of its structure under internal pressure.

The distraction gave Audley a moment to gather his wits. He had been sitting hunched down, slumped as though asleep, outside a pub where a great quantity of ale, fresh-brewed or otherwise, was being consumed—slumped in a car.

He was therefore about to be breathalysed.

"You should be worrying about them, not me, officer." He smiled up at the young constable.

"Sir?" The candid eyes fastened on him again.

"I said—you should be worrying about them."

"They aren't in charge of cars, sir."

Trust the police to get their priorities exactly right. Good on you, copper!

"Of course." He passed up his identification card. "I'm on official business, officer ... and, for the record, I haven't had anything to drink, either."

The eyes scanned the card, checked the face against the photograph, scanned the card again.

"Thank you, sir." There was no change in the voice as the card came back through the window; a potential offender against section umpteen of the Road Traffic Act was no different, until breathalysed, from one of Her Majesty's servants on his lawful occasion. "Can I be of assistance in any way?"

"I'm looking for Bridge House—Air Vice-Marshal Rushworth."

"Just on down the road, sir. The big stone place directly overlooking the bridge—you can't miss it."

"I see—thank you, officer." Audley reached for the ignition.

"But you'd do better to leave your car here, sir. I'll keep an eye on it. The yard at Bridge House is full of horses."

"Full of—horses?"

The constable nodded, deadpan. "That's right, sir. The Royalist cavalry—it's their headquarters. But it's only a step from here."

Audley couldn't prevent himself from looking across the

gleaming new cellulose of the car bonnet towards the Ploughman, from which some of the more esoteric verses of 'Kirriemuir' were now issuing.

The young constable caught the look. "That's all right, sir. Your car won't come to any harm. I shall be here until they close."

I shall be here. A pub full of well-oiled soldiery, armed *cap-à-pied*, but *I shall be here.*

The constable grinned. "It's just high spirits—they don't make any real trouble. It'd be more than their lives are worth if they did, their own people 'ud court martial 'em double quick. And with me out here..." He shook his head. "No trouble at all."

"And no one drunk in charge of a horse?"

"Cavalry don't drink, sir—they're very strict about that."

"And the infantry?"

"No car keys. They collect all the keys and label 'em the night before, and the general has 'em under lock and key. *And* they put up a £50 bond with the publicans, for broken glasses and such like ... so the only thing they've got to worry about is running out of beer." He shook his head again. "Much better to let them let off steam. And they'll all be sweating off the beer this afternoon, anyway."

Air Vice-Marshal Rushworth was a tall, very thin, stooping old man, with washed-out blue eyes and short, untidy grey hair that stood up at the back as though he had allowed it to dry in the wrong position and had forgotten to brush it.

As soon as he had established to his own satisfaction that Audley was who he claimed to be he gestured him into the long, shadowy hall of Bridge House with curious jerky movements of a hand the fingers of which were crooked into a permanent arthritic claw, fussy imprecise movements which made it difficult to imagine that the same hand, strong and supple with youth, had once wrestled a bomb-laden Lancaster into the air.

"Up the stairs, up the stairs ... right to the top, right to the top—door in front of you, straight in front of you, white door, brass handle—waiting for you there. Ringside view, too."

Audley wasn't sure what "ringside view" meant, but that would no doubt reveal itself beyond the white door. In the meantime he had the young constable's courteous example to guide him.

"It's extremely good of you to give us house-room, Air Marshal." He paused with one foot on the bottom stair. "We're very grateful."

With an effort the Air Vice-Marshal straightened up and looked Audley in the eye. "No need to be. Been thanked already—by a pretty girl too, what's more. And I expect Tommy will send me a proper bread-and-butter letter on expensive notepaper in his own good time ... which reminds me: there's a plate of sandwiches up there if you haven't had any lunch, granddaughter cut them. And a few bottles of beer ... but you tell Tommy it isn't necessary—save the cost of a stamp, and God knows they cost enough now. ... No need at all, glad to be of service for a change. Besides, makes life more exciting— battle outside and cloak and dagger inside—real cloak and dagger too, by golly." He cackled briefly at whatever the joke was and then waved the claw again upwards. "Don't keep them waiting—up you go. Right to the top, remember—white door straight in front of you."

Audley fled up the stairs. The Brigadier's christian name was Thomas, yet he had never in his life heard anyone refer to him as 'Tommy'. Even Sir Frederick, in moments of rare camaraderie, had never gone further than 'Tom', but presumably the Air Marshal dated from some unimaginable time when the Brigadier was a pink and scrubbed subaltern. Always supposing it had been the Brigadier who had pulled the string and opened this particular white door with the brass handle. But whoever it was, it was a piece of 'old boy' expertise such as Audley loved and admired. Good for Tommy, whoever he was!

Bridge House was lovely, the more so as he climbed: up from the coolness of the hall to the light of the first-floor landing, white doors everywhere and sunshine streaming in through the tall windows. For a moment he felt quite euphoric, with the warmth and the whiteness and the good omens—and the intelligence that Brigadier Stocker had once been 'young Tommy' to everyone, and still was to someone.

143

Then the shallowness of the euphoria steadied him. Arrogance was his besetting sin, he knew, because those who loved him were always warning him against it—arrogance that was fathered on pride by boredom. But arrogance had never betrayed him, all the same; it had been his passion for secrecy which had come closest to doing that, half a dozen years or more back, in the aftermath of the June War. And if that was another great sin it was at least the occupational sin of his work—and he had paid for it in full over the years since then.

But what threatened him now was smug self-satisfaction, which wasn't so much a decent, God-fearing sin as a mean little weakness. His battle hadn't even started, and he was already trying Cromwell's hat for size when he ought to be worrying about his feet fitting Colonel Sir Edward Whitelocke's boots.

White door, brass handle.

It was the playroom—and the children were playing in it.

Children in fancy dress, under the disapproving eye of their tutor.

Grown-up children.

What hit him first was their beauty: they were both beautiful as they never had been before.

Paul Mitchell was a good-looking young man, he had always known that, though without remarking on it. But Paul Mitchell the cavalier, in loose light-rust tunic and dark-rust breeches, with exquisite cobwebs of white lace cascading over his shoulders, at his wrists and even falling over the tops of his soft-leather calf-length boots, wide yellow taffeta scarf at his waist and broad-brimmed hat, ostrich-plumed, on his flowing hair—this Paul Mitchell took his breath away.

This Paul Mitchell was beautiful.

And Frances—

Where Mitchell was a blaze of colour and elegance, all velvet and lace and embroidery, Frances Fitzgibbon was total severity, starched white cap and collar, cut square and sharp, and a voluminous black gown censoring every curve beneath it.

And yet Frances too was beautiful now; and also in a new way which suited her as the old way had never done.

144

Which suited her—

That was it, of course: they were not dressed up at all, any more than they were children at all—for all that Mitchell sat astride a huge old Victorian rocking-horse and Frances knelt before a marvellous Victorian dolls' house. They were changed —even their expressions were different: they stared at him with the heavy-lidded calm of Van Dyck's portraits—but they had changed from strangers into themselves as they really ought to have been.

Panache for Mitchell.

Purity for Frances.

Mitchell rose effortlessly from the rocking-horse, checking its movement with a long-fingered hand. It was the first time Audley had ever noticed how long those fingers were.

"Steady there, Champion—steady," Mitchell commanded. "Well, my lord, how do you like us?"

Before Audley could reply Mitchell swept off the broad-brimmed hat with an exaggerated figure-of-eight movement, ending with its plume brushing the floor as he completed the elaborate ceremony of a seventeenth-century bow.

"Where be thy manners, my lady?" he hissed out of the corner of his mouth at Frances. "Show the Lord General proper respect, I pray you."

Well—*fiddlesticks* would be her quick answer to that, thought Audley. There was no nonsense about Frances Fitzgibbon.

Frances looked at him doubtfully for one fraction of a second only, then lowered her eyes modestly and sank into a deep curtsey, her black skirts billowing up around her.

"My lord—forgive me. I bid you welcome."

So . . . but if they were playing games, damn it—and they would never know how unsettling their games were after that eerie first impression—then it would be as well for him not to lose his temper straight off.

"Thou hast my forgiveness, child." He bowed to her.

Mitchell straightened up, squinting at him in the sunlight. "I pray you, my lord, to be not short with us. We do but—ah—practise those strange usages which thy command hath thrust

145

upon us. By our words thou must needs know the problems that beset us in this enterprise."

"Aye." Frances had the grace to blush, and that was at least something to hold on to. "We, being persuaded in the love of Christ that thou hast ordered us rightly, have purposed to the utmost to serve you in our places and our callings. But thou needest not reply to us in like manner."

" 'To serve *thee*'," corrected Mitchell. "You is wrong."

"But they do say *you*."

"Only in the plural, at least colloquially." Mitchell shook his head emphatically. "But that bit about 'the love of Christ' was good—absolutely right for you—thee." He turned to Audley. "The bloody trouble is, I don't know how to swear any more. I just don't know how to say 'Fuck off' in these clothes—I'm darn sure they said it somehow, and I've already wanted to say it a couple of times. But I'm a trooper—and I don't know how to swear like a trooper."

"They weren't singing like seventeenth-century troopers when I last heard them," said Audley. "It was strictly twentieth-century stuff, ex-British Army."

Mitchell nodded agreement. "Ah—they make an exception with the songs. It's the spirit that counts there, not the words."

"Same with us," said Frances. "It's Hymns Ancient and Modern."

"And political," said Audley.

"That's right—" she gave him a quick glance "—but you know about that?"

"Not nearly enough yet. So tell me more." What had ever made him think she looked sexy? As a puritan maiden she was not every man's mistress, but every man's daughter.

"Well, I've only had one evening of it. As far as I can see there are three regiments to the far left—the others call them 'the Angry Brigade'—but I haven't found anyone making bombs yet. It's just talk."

"What sort of talk?"

"Oh, the usual stuff, but all in seventeenth-century language." Frances fished in a small leather bag, producing a mini-recorder. "I went to a camp-fire service last night, down by the river—on our side of it. And there was one chap sounding off—

listen—" She held the recorder to Audley's ear, clicking the button with her thumb as she did so.

Crackle—crackle—crackle—

"I couldn't get as close as I'd have liked—"

"Yes, I tell you all, good people ... the liberties of this land have been lost since the coming in of William the Conqueror ... and that, ever since, the People of God have lived under tyranny and oppression worse than that of our forefathers under the Egyptians. But now the time of deliverance is at hand; God will bring His people out of this slavery, and restore them to their freedom in enjoying the fruits and benefits of the earth ..."

Crackle—crackle—crackle—

The voice was high and nasal—an American voice.... A New England voice.

"That's the American—Davenport—isn't it?"

"That's right. Bob Davenport—Preacher Davenport, they call him."

"... to make it fruitful for the use of man. And the time will surely be—I tell you, my comrades—my brothers, I tell you all —when all men shall willingly come in and give up their lands and estates, and submit to this community of goods."

Frances clicked the button off. "That's about as much as I could get of that. But it was all much the same—new stuff in old bottles." She gestured from herself to Mitchell. "Dressed up like us."

Like them? Well, she was half-right there.

"Not new stuff." Audley shook his head. "That's the genuine article, word for word—pure seventeenth-century revolutionary communism. It's the Thoughts of Gerald Winstanley—'Digger' Winstanley. His big idea was that you can only achieve a political revolution through a social revolution, not vice versa."

Mitchell laughed. "I can't see Oliver Cromwell going on that much, any more than we would have done."

We? Mitchell was certainly identifying with his fellow cavaliers, no doubt about that.

"He didn't," replied Audley. "They put him down damn quick.... What else have you got on Davenport, Frances?"

She shrugged. "Not a lot. He puts over his stuff as though it just came into his head. And he's strictly non-violent—he'll

147

preach all day, and help the wounded out of the battle too, but he won't carry a pike."

"The word is 'trail'—'trail a pike'," murmured Mitchell. "So Davenport is one of our possibles, then?"

"He is, oddly enough."

Frances frowned. "How did you come up with him? He doesn't seem quite the type for subversion ... in so far as there is a type."

"You may well be right. It's just a hunch I'm starting on, there's no evidence to back it yet so far as I know."

"What sort of hunch?"

"Maybe hunch isn't the right word—assumption might be better. An assumption of what precautions I would have taken if I'd hired someone to knock off James Ratcliffe the way it was done at Swine Brook Field."

He had them both with him in the twentieth-century now: the Van Dyke aura was fading visibly.

"Go on, David," said Mitchell.

"It's nothing very special. As a matter of fact, the police thought of it too and checked it out as far as they could.... The killer obviously had very exact inside information about the place and the timing. So he obviously had precise information about the people as well."

"Charlie Ratcliffe did, you mean," said Mitchell.

"What people?" asked Frances

"Henry Digby, for one," said Mitchell quickly.

Trust Mitchell for that, thought Audley. And trust him also to sit on it until he was good and ready.

"Henry Digby—exactly." He nodded. "If I was going to kill a man just twenty yards from a young police sergeant in front of thousands of people I should want to make very sure he was minding his own business."

Mitchell nodded. "Very true. I should want him tied hand and foot for choice."

"I'm with you there," said Frances.

"Well ... I've gone over Digby's evidence twice, and there are just four people who attracted his attention at the material time—or distracted his attention, as the case may be. He was

148

talking to two of the mock casualties, Philip Oates and David Bishop." He looked questioningly at Frances.

"Don't know them." She shook her head. "The names don't ring any bells, anyway, not among the Angry Brigade people I've heard of yet."

"They wouldn't be in the Angry Brigade. I don't know what the Roundhead Wing would call them, but according to Digby they were Labour Party moderates from the way they spoke."

"Ah—well, they'd probably be Militiamen. Sort of . . . well, moderate English Presbyterians. Meaning good Parliamentarians, but they don't want to get rid of the monarchy—would that be about right?"

"Spot on, exactly. And they hadn't much time for the Ironsides either, Digby said."

"That would be them." Frances nodded vigorously. "Militia regiments—there are half a dozen of them."

Mitchell sniffed disparagingly. "I'll never get the hang of your motley lot, Frances dear. In our army, we're all good King's men, and we're nearly all Church of England, and we're all good Conservatives. And that's that."

Frances smiled sweetly at him. "It's just a rumour about the Fascists, then?"

"Slander, more like. Got a few Monday Club supporters— quite good chaps. And some Roman Catholics, of course. Also good chaps. But nothing really weird, like your Tower of Babel. . . . Which, as I say, I don't really care to understand at all."

She lifted a black and white shoulder. "Well, you must be dim, Paul *dear*. Parliamentarian Presbyterian equals Labour Party—plus one or two Church of England left-wingers, who are Social Democrats. Then there are the Independents—they're the Communists—"

The light dawned on Audley in a blaze of understanding. Oliver Cromwell had metamorphosed into Vladimir Il'ich Lenin, none other. And that meant—

"—the Communist Party, anyway. And all the rest are the non-conformists: the Anabaptists and the Fifth Monarchy men and the Diggers and the Levellers and so on—they're the

149

Trotskyites and the Marxist-Leninists and the Maoists and the Revolutionary Workers." She turned towards Audley. "I don't know really how they number off with each other yet—they can't possibly fit each other historically—but that's more or less how they go."

No, they could hardly fit exactly, thought Audley. History never repeated itself so neatly; technically Cromwell's own Independents had included all the rag tag and bobtail of the religious sects that the Puritan revolution produced like fleas on a mangy dog—

Fleas on a mangy dog . . . He closed his eyes for an instant as the words struck a chord in his memory, and was back in Cambridge half a lifetime before in Highsmith's sitting room—

". . . like fleas on a mangy dog. But if you learn them, my dear David, you may at least impress the examiners even if you never impress anyone else. Baptists and Anabaptists; Brownists and Barrowists; Anti-Trinitarians and Anti-Sabbatarians—they're all listed in Masson's *Life of Milton*—Antinomians and Famulists; Divorcers and Seekers; Soul-Sleepers and Millenaries; Sceptics and Atheists; Ranters and Quakers—how the Quakers got into such company heaven alone knows, but at least they managed to get out of it; and the Muggletonians—I've really never been able to establish what they believed. And then there was Cromwell himself, but he took an agreeably pragmatic view of everyone other than Episcopalians and Catholics: 'If they be willing faithfully to serve the State, that satisfies'. And if not —when the Levellers tried to subvert the Army, for example—he clapped them straight into the Tower of London. . . . Or shot them. 'You have no other way to deal with these men but to break them, or they will break you'—for which devastatingly simple pronouncement the University of Oxford promptly conferred on him an honorary Doctorate of Civil Law, my dear David. . . ."

"David!"

Audley woke with a start to find them both staring at him: "I'm sorry. I was just thinking. . . ."

"There were these two Militiamen," prompted Mitchell. "They

distracted Digby while James Ratcliffe was having his neck broken."

"Distracted, possibly. They certainly talked to him, and one of them even restrained him, or tried to. Philip Oates and David Bishop."

"Do you want me to look them over?" asked Frances.

"Just keep an eye open for them. Colonel Butler is running a full check on them for me at the moment. And on Robert Davenport too."

"Where does he come in?"

"He was also on the spot at the right time. He preached a sermon on the wrath of God and the wickedness of the Royalists."

"He's always doing that."

"Yes—but apparently this was a particularly good sermon. Digby couldn't resist listening to it."

"Which was what Davenport intended him to do, you mean?"

Audley spread his hands. "It's another possibility."

Mitchell nodded. "And the fourth distractor?"

"Ah, the fourth is a long shot—and one of yours, too."

"Mine? You don't mean he's a Cavalier? A Royalist gentleman?"

"He is indeed. And not just any Royalist gentleman, either. Have you met Major John Lumley yet, Paul?"

"Major John—? You're kidding!"

"Alias Black Thomas Monson of Swine Brook Field—not at all."

"You're still kidding. Never in a thousand years," Mitchell shook his head vehemently, "not in a million years, either. Not John Lumley."

"A long shot, I admit. But as Black Thomas he made a special point of telling Digby to keep on pouring his red dye into the stream. And Digby says that simply wasn't necessary."

"So he was just making sure Digby did his job, then."

"Precisely. And if I was Charlie Ratcliffe's contract man that's the one thing I'd require of my employer: to ensure that Digby went on doing his job while I did mine. So Lumley stays on the list until we can prove otherwise."

"A waste of time." Mitchell's tone was obstinate. "Oates and

Bishop—maybe. Davenport—probably, from the way he talks. But John Lumley—never."

"What makes you so sure?" asked Frances.

"I also happen to have met the man himself and I know how his mind works. And it would never work on behalf of Charlie Ratcliffe, not ever."

"Maybe." Lumley was the longest shot of the four, but in the circumstances the more suspects he had, the better. "You may well be right, Paul. And if you are, then he'll emerge whiter than white from Colonel Butler's inquiries, and I shall be perfectly happy to accept his verdict."

"And if not?" said Frances.

"Until I hear from Butler in a few minutes' time that's academic. They may all be clean . . . they may all be dirty. But at the moment they are all suspect and we're going to lean on all of them and see what happens. That will be when you must keep your eyes skinned."

"Hmm . . ." Frances frowned slightly. "Talking of keeping our eyes skinned . . . there are several rather equivocal non-Roundhead types who've been loitering around the camp from the minute we arrived yesterday evening. And asking questions too, evidently."

"That's right. They've been lent to us by—some of our friends."

"Well, they're not exactly treading with fairy feet."

"They aren't meant to be. They're just softening up the targets."

"Which include Charlie Ratcliffe, I trust." There was a faint echo of his anger in Mitchell's voice, as though the slur cast on Major Lumley constituted a large addition to Charlie Ratcliffe's overdue account.

"Don't fret, Paul. We've been leaning on Ratcliffe since early yesterday morning."

"How?"

"He's been trying to raise money—and quite a lot of it, too—on the strength of his golden expectations," Audley began.

Frances stirred at that, her long skirts rustling. "That wouldn't be for the new printing press of his own he wants for *The Red Rat*, would it?"

"That—among other things." Audley looked at her with interest. "Where did you hear that?"

"Oh, it's all over the camp. And what's more, the word is that his old printer has got wind of it, so he's dunning Ratcliffe for all the money he owes, and Charlie's running round in circles." She stared back at Audley shrewdly. "You wouldn't be behind that, by any chance?"

Mitchell laughed softly. "What—queer a chap's credit, and then stir up his creditors with nasty malicious rumours? Do you really think David would do a thing like that? Perish the thought!"

No one could fault Brigadier Stocker for speed as well as judgement, reflected Audley. The word was not only out, but it was moving in directions they hadn't expected, like the smell of Stalky's dead pussy-cat under the ceiling joists.

"Yes . . . well, he *is* finding money tighter all of a sudden," he admitted. "That is, tighter than a young man with great expectations ought to find it." He turned towards Mitchell. "Which brings us to your gold, Paul."

The cavalier face twisted. "And don't I wish it was! Two million, two and a half million, I could rub along on that. It makes you weep."

"Finders keepers, losers weepers," murmured Frances.

"Finders is right. And as for weepers . . . yes, I should think the King of Spain must have dropped a tear or two when the *Concepcion* never showed up."

The sound of a distant drum, a brief, brittle tattoo beaten by a single drummer, echoed through the open dormer window from across the valley. Audley could see small figures with tall pikes assembling in the gap where the road down to the bridge cut through the skyline. Someone was waving a flag with the sweeping theatrical gestures of a Tyrone Guthrie production.

"Nothing to worry about," Mitchell reassured him. "The war doesn't start until three o'clock. In fact it can't start without me anyway—I'm galloping back with the news of Cromwell's approach."

"Well, what's all the fuss up there for?" Audley pointed.

"They don't trust each other," said Frances.

Audley frowned. "What d'you mean?"

"She's right—we don't trust each other." Mitchell leant out of the window, staring downwards to the left. "Here . . . look down there by the bridge."

He drew back to let Audley take his place. The line of the little river was thick with trees and even from the high window the heavy foliage of summer concealed whatever might be happening beneath them. But in a gap between two immense chestnuts he could see the bridge itself, and the cluster of Royalists who guarded it, heavily armed with muskets and beer tankards.

He turned back, still frowning. "I still don't understand."

Frances made a face. "I told you, David—they're weird. They have these strict rules, and on one level the whole thing's a childish game. But . . . I don't know . . . on another level it isn't a game at all. I get the feeling that what they'd really like is to play it for real, with real pikes and real guns. And that one day that's what it will be."

Audley nodded slowly. "I see. And the side that starts first wins—hence the pickets on guard?"

"I don't know. They would say that it's just a convention—and it gives the crowds a kick to see that they're taking precautions against a surprise attack. . . . But it's more than that. It's not simply that they don't trust each other. They don't *like* each other."

Audley's eyes were drawn to the window again as another drummer started drumming, this time from the Royalist lines. He was beginning to understand the full implications of Superintendent Weston's unease: under the cloak of seventeenth-century history the Double R Society seemed to have managed to break the rule that politics must never put on a uniform. To haul any of these people up in court, where they could always take refuge behind their historical knowledge in their ludicrous seventeenth-century language, would make the law a laughing-stock. But here they were, drilled and organised on the divisive basis of late twentieth-century politics nevertheless.

But that was Weston's problem. Or, if there really was anything in it, he could pass it on himself to the Minister as an addendum to his final report; there might well be something for the lawyers to get their sharp little teeth into in those political questions the membership committees had put to these children of his. In the meantime he had other fish to fry.

He looked at Mitchell. "Tell me about Ratcliffe's gold, Paul."

Mitchell relaxed into a frayed old cane chair beside the rocking-horse. "Not Ratcliffe's gold, David. The King of Spain's gold, for my money—the property of His Most Catholic Majesty King Philip IV."

"Spanish gold?"

"Oh, no. Not Spanish gold—American gold. Or, to be strictly fair, Spanish-American gold. The gold of the fabled Indies."

"You mean there's scientific proof for that?"

"I do—and there is. The BM let one of their metallurgists loose on it, and he had himself a field day. I can't honestly say I understand all his jargon, but the burden of it is that you can fingerprint gold like everything else. Some of the differences you can see with the naked eye. Apparently it ranges from deep gold-yellow to yellowish-white if there's a high silver content. But the real scientific clincher is the minute traces of other metals—all sorts of weird and wonderful elements are present in its natural state, according to where it was mined. Even with the modern stuff there are ways and means of narrowing down the source, like whether it comes from the Urals or South Africa. And with pre-1850 gold, when refining techniques weren't so sophisticated, it's even easier."

"And this is pre-1850."

"Oh, sure. The comparison tests don't pin down the age more precisely than that, but it's definitely Spanish-American, mostly from Peru and Colombia, with a bit of Mexican from Sonora and Chihuahua probably."

"Any stamps on it?"

"Stamps?" For a moment Mitchell looked mystified. "Oh— die-stamps or whatever ... no. But then the ingots are pretty crude, not even to any standard weight, which suggests that it was melted down again to remove whatever official marks there were on it originally."

"By Edward Parrott, you mean?"

Mitchell shrugged. "Edward or Nathaniel, your guess is as good as mine. But Edward for choice, I suppose. It isn't at all difficult to melt gold, but he wouldn't have had much time to

155

do it in '43 and I doubt whether Spanish royal mint marks would have worried him very much, either, come to that.... So more likely it was Edward." Mitchell's white teeth showed under his moustache for a second. "A very warm man, Sir Edward. He knew his gold was hot, so he heated it up again— if you'll pardon the puns."

And a very warm young man, Paul Mitchell, too. There wouldn't be much by now that he didn't know about 1643, his insatiable curiosity would have seen to that.

"But then, again, it could have been Nathaniel who did the re-heat," went on Mitchell. "I've talked to a chap who was a vet in the Army in Burma in '45—1945, that is. He actually knew more about mules than horses and ponies, but his estimate of how much a Dartmoor pony can carry for any length of time comes to the average weight of any eight of Charlie Ratcliffe's ingots, almost exactly. Which is a thought, you know.... Not that it accounts for Charlie's brilliant original detective work, of course."

"And have you got any leads on that?"

"A little." Mitchell's tone was smugly casual. "You know the BBC's doing a TV programme on it?"

"In 'The Testimony of the Spade' series, yes. BBC Two."

"Ah, well I'm told things have hotted up now. It's re-scheduled for peak viewing on BBC One. They've got a Cambridge Don by the name of Nayler as link man." Mitchell looked sidelong at Audley. "You wouldn't know him by any chance, David?"

Too casual by half, that question.

"He was up at the same time as I was."

And too casual by half, that reply, damn him!

"I rather thought so."

"Have you spoken to him, then?"

"Have I spoken to him?" Mitchell's lip curled and suddenly he was all seventeenth-century again. "Professor Bloody Nayler was my tutor for one brief—mercifully brief—period. Even if I crawled to him—which I don't intend to do—he wouldn't give me the time of day." Amusement slowly displaced cold anger. "I'm relieved to see that you dislike him as much as I do. But

156

why the hell didn't you drown him in the Cam when he was a puppy?"

"Get to the point, Paul."

"The point?" The glint of amusement went off abruptly. "The point is that other people dislike him equally. So a girl I know in the BBC was quite happy to show me his draft script —and talk about what's not in it yet."

"And what is . . . not in it?"

Mitchell sat forward. "Nobody knows—yet. But Ratcliffe and Nayler have cooked up a deal between them, that's for certain. What's in the script at the moment is their joint version of how the gold got to Standingham—Nayler's constructed most of that and Ratcliffe is going to give him the credit for being a clever fellow. But that's all just scene-setting for the big stuff, which is going to be filmed *in situ* next Saturday, when they re-enact the storming of Standingham Castle. Charlie's going to explain, blow by blow, what a clever fellow *he* was, and Nayler's going to stand on the sidelines and say 'Here! Here!' and 'I told you so' at intervals. But that's all under wraps at the moment— the producer doesn't like it, but he knows he's on to a hot news story so there's nothing he can do about it with Charlie and Nayler ganging up on him."

"But surely they know what happened during the siege— and at the storming?" said Frances. "I mean, I've heard people talking about it in camp already."

"They know the facts about the siege and the storming, sure. But not about the gold and how it was hidden." Mitchell swung back to Audley quickly. "It wasn't hidden in the house, that they do know. It was out in the grounds somewhere, apparently right out in the open. And he did go straight to it, like the papers say; he dug pretty deep before he hit on it, according to information received. The place was like a ploughed field when he'd finished."

Audley nodded. "But how does all this help us?"

"It doesn't, at least not yet. But my little BBC girl had one very interesting bit of scuttlebutt—in fact she thinks she knows how Charlie got on to the gold. Or at least how he was so sure it was there when everyone else said no. Because she did the routine research on Charlie himself—there's going to be some scene-setting stuff about his Maoist-Leninist revolutionary background, he's insisted on that. This is gold for the people, is his line—not gold for Charlie Ratcliffe. And he's going to spend it in the service of the people."

"Well, it makes a change from booze and women and fast cars," conceded Frances. "Except the people to Charlie are likely to be revolutionary people, I suppose. The Marxist heavenly host."

"Too right! But the point is that one bit of Charlie's background has been edited out of the record, ostensibly by Nayler because the script was running too long. But my girl says Nayler passed it and Charlie cut it out himself. And it's the exact bit of Charlie's past I've been looking for all along—the moment when he first met his long-lost ancestor Nathaniel Parrott. Which was a case of like meeting like, I suspect; there's no surviving portrait of Nathaniel, but if there was I've a hunch it'd be a dead ringer of Charlie Ratcliffe looking down on us."

That was very possible, thought Audley. Families erupted with genius, and then slept for centuries, as the Churchills had done between the first Duke and the appearance of Jenny's Randolph and her young Winston; no doubt they could do the same with the more uncomfortable qualities shared by Nathaniel Parrott and Charles Neville Steyning-Ratcliffe.

"I don't know what you're driving at now, Paul," said Frances.

"No?" Mitchell glanced quickly at Audley. "You disappoint me, Frances."

It wasn't Frances who disappointed him, of course: it was that he had failed to get the same response from teacher. With someone less self-confident than Mitchell a bit of that sort of encouragement might have been in order, but it would do no harm to let him see that he'd have to get up earlier in the morning to catch David Audley in bed.

"What he's driving at is that Charlie Ratcliffe's interest in his ancestral treasure—and in the English Civil War—is of rather more recent vintage than he suggested to the Press. Is that it, Paul?"

"More or less." Mitchell nodded cheerfully enough. "It's all in the Ratcliffe file, Frances—David's quite right, it's not much of a dossier, but it does have a few facts. Including that he didn't join the Double R Society until about a year ago. And, come to that, he didn't read history at college either, it was sociology."

"Surprise, surprise," murmured Frances.

"No surprise, I agree. But it all adds up to a little terminological inexactitude—he was lying through his goddamn teeth. If he was so taken with the war he could have joined the Sealed Knot eight or nine years ago, never mind the Double R lot."

Frances shrugged. "So he was busy being a flea in the establishment's ear."

"Telling soldiers in Ulster how to desert, and all that jazz?" Mitchell echoed her scornfully. "You think so?"

The drummers sounding the changing of the guard on the ridge and at the bridge had long finished, and for a moment only silence came in through the window. So obviously Mitchell didn't know absolutely everything about everybody, thought Audley; he certainly didn't know the circumstances of Frances Fitzgibbon's widowhood and recruitment.

"And all that jazz, yes," said Frances evenly.

"But it was a little lie, Frances dear. And it was a little *unnecessary* lie on the face of it. Because I've been talking to some people who know him—the last two-three years he's been working on a post-graduate thesis on the Paris troubles of '68—and the thing that comes over is that he never talked about the Civil War until about a year ago. Or about his family either, come to that. He was plain Charlie Ratcliffe until then, but then he started to let slip his real name was Steyning-Ratcliffe—and that's also when he joined the Double R Society."

"All right." Frances spread her hands. "So that's when he was bitten by the Civil War bug."

"Then why didn't he admit it? I mean, he should have said 'Until a year ago I'd forgotten all about the family treasure legend and I didn't know Cromwell from a hole in the road'. But instead he said 'I've been studying the period for many years, I've always been fascinated with its political parallels with our own revolutionary struggles'. And that just wasn't true."

"And what was true?" said Audley.

159

Mitchell looked at him triumphantly. "What was true was that about eighteen months ago he ran out of bread—he's on an LEA research grant, which doesn't go very far these days. So when he dropped out of circulation for a time no one thought twice about it. In any case, he's always going over to Paris to do research and gab with his revolutionary friends there. But my little BBC girl just happened to find out what he was really doing. Quite by chance, actually, because one of her unemployed graduate friends was in on the same job . . . which was sorting the archives of the Earl of Dawlish and packing 'em up ready for the Historical Manuscripts Commission to catalogue and calendar."

"The Earl of where?" Frances sounded disbelieving.

"Dawlish. It's down the south coast somewhere, near Torquay."

Frances shook her head. "I've never heard of the Earl of Dawlish."

"You wouldn't have done, because the title's been extinct since 1944. The archives have been given to the HMC by the Honourable Mrs Somebody Someone, the last earl's niece."

"So what do they reveal?" asked Audley. "Get to the point, man."

"Yes . . . well, the point is that the Earldom of Dawlish was created in 1690 by William III for services rendered by a certain George Dangerfield, who'd helped to raise the West Country against James II in 1688—"

Frances took a deep breath. "But—"

"Who in turn happened to be the grandson of a certain John Dangerfield—wait for it, Frances—who was the boon companion and crony of Captain Sir Edward Parrott, our Nathaniel's piratical father. How's that for size, then?" Mitchell smiled at them both. "And what is even more to the point is that John Dangerfield corresponded regularly with John Pym in Westminster. There are copies of letters he wrote to Pym in 1642 and 1643 in the archives, which means that he had a courier of some kind who was prepared to run the gauntlet through Royalist country."

For a moment no one spoke, then Frances said: "But he didn't write about the gold."

Mitchell's face creased with sudden irritation. "Aw—come on, Frances! What d'you want, a miracle? Look at the way it fits in—" he raised a hand with the little finger extended "—*one*—Charlie Ratcliffe, who isn't interested in Civil Wars or family history, gets a job sorting seventeenth-century documents; *two*—" a second finger came up "—the documents he sorts belong to a neighbour of his gold-robbing ancestors, the Parrotts; *three*—Charlie is suddenly in love with history and ancestor worship; *four*—Cousin James dies; *five*—Charlie starts looking for gold, and finds it; *six*—" the second thumb came up "—Charlie quietly suppresses all reference to *one*." He seized his little finger again. "Which means if there was evidence of the gold's existence, then Charlie's got it."

Audley rubbed his chin. "It would only be just that—evidence of its existence."

"Oh, sure. Nathaniel couldn't have known he'd have to hide it *en route*. But you wanted to know why Charlie was so sure there was gold to be found, and I reckon I've given you a pretty damn convincing sequence of possibilities. Everybody who ever looked for that gold could only hope that it wasn't a legend. But Charlie—he knew it was there somewhere. And I'd guess that Nayler knew it too."

Audley looked quickly at Mitchell. Not only a warm young man, but a hot one was Paul Mitchell. Because that was probably the key to Charlie Ratcliffe's achievement: the faith which moved this mountain was no relative of pious conviction, it was a positive certainty based on inside information. And that, at the moment, was also what made Paul Mitchell formidable too: he still believed with that same positive certainty that he had the inside information about himself.

And doubly hot, because the final conclusion of that sequence of possibilities of his—the seventh finger conclusion—had to be the correct one. Indeed, it was the logical extension of that midnight brainwave which had disturbed Faith: only something of quite extraordinary importance could have caused the Royalist and Roundhead generals to detach men from their field armies at the start of a desperate campaign, the campaign which had ended with the relief of Gloucester and the battle of

Newbury, to intervene in an unimportant castle siege which was little better than a private feud.

It was just possible, in fairness, that the Royalists were reacting to a Roundhead intrusion into their territory: a quick cavalry dash was the sort of risk Prince Rupert would have relished. But the solid Parliamentary commanders of 1643 would never have countenanced such a move for precisely that reason. For them there had to be a certainty, and for certainty there had to be—again—inside information.

Which meant that there must have been communication between Colonel Nathaniel Parrott in North Devon and John Pym in Westminster. And what better for that than John Dangerfield's own private courier?

"David—" Frances interrupted his train of thought.

And the irony was that almost all the details of this tapestry of events had been known long before Charlie Ratcliffe had chanced on the proof of it. It had all been there fossilised in history, like the bones of the dinosaurs, waiting for somebody to treat it not as a curious and amusing footnote, but as a rock-hard fact.

"There's someone outside, David," said Frances.

Audley's train of thought halted abruptly. He had half-noticed a mouse-like scuffling on the landing, but had dismissed it as the ordinary sound of the house; now, as he roused himself, the scuffling nerved itself into a sharp little knuckle-tap on the door.

"Come in," said Audley.

The door-knob shivered, then turned slowly. Mitchell came up out of his chair with uncharacteristic clumsiness, catching Champion's galloping leg on his sleeve and setting the horse rearing and plunging wildly on its stand. As the door began to open—and to open with the same terrifying slowness with which the door-knob had turned—he reached across for the hilt of his sword, for all the world like the young D'Artagnan surprised by the Cardinal's guard with the Queen's emeralds in his pocket. Incredibly, he even started to draw the blade; Audley's hold on reality went spinning as his attention was held by the mad grin of the rocking-horse and the madder sight of cold steel.

Then the sword-hand froze—and relaxed.

In the open doorway were two exquisite children, the seventeenth-century owners of the playroom, the boy an exact miniature of Paul in red taffeta and the girl a tiny blonde mite enveloped in apple-green watered silk.

The sword rasped back into its scabbard. It was an insane world, thought Audley—an insane, wicked, self-destructive world. And he had just witnessed (and, from the pounding of his heart, taken part in) one of its more horror-comic moments.

"Ahah!" The forced jollity of Mitchell's voice betrayed the same insanity. "Mistress Henrietta Rushworth and Master Nigel Rushworth—well met, once again."

The little boy's eyes shifted from Mitchell to Audley, and Audley's own eyes dropped to the plain buff-coloured envelope the child held to his chest.

"Mistress Henrietta and Master Nigel are going to watch the battle this afternoon," explained Mitchell. "Isn't that right?"

"Everyone's dressed up," said Mistress Henrietta breathlessly. "Even Grandpa's going to dress up."

"Is that so?" said Audley. "Do you like dressing up?"

Mistress Henrietta nodded solemnly. "Why aren't you dressed up?"

"I didn't have time—and I haven't a costume." *But I am dressed up really. It's the four of you who are in your real clothes.* "I shall dress up next time."

"Next time." Mistress Henrietta gave him a comforting nod.

"Next time." Audley nodded back.

"Nigel's got something for you," said Henrietta, reaching out for the envelope as she spoke. "The man gave it to Grandpa."

Nigel quickly lifted the envelope above her reach, though without attempting to offer it to Audley.

"What man?"

"The man with red hair and a red face," said Mistress Henrietta graphically. "He's waiting for you downstairs—*Nigel!*"

Nigel solved his problem by taking a step forward and handing over the envelope.

"Thank you, Nigel. Will you tell the man I shall be down in a moment?"

Nigel nodded, took a step back and dug Mistress Henrietta in the ribs with his elbow.

163

"Lay off!" said Mistress Henrietta angrily.

Blushing to the roots of his hair, Master Nigel bent over and whispered in her ear urgently.

"Oh!" Mistress Henrietta's gaze shifted from Audley to Mitchell. Then, as her brother straightened up, she searched in the leather bag which hung from her wrist and triumphantly produced a handful of rather crushed parsley. "For you," she said, holding it out to Mitchell.

Mitchell accepted the gift with one hand, and then swept off his plumed hat in the elaborate figure-of-eight bow with the other. "My lady ... and you, sir—" he looked down at Master Nigel "—remember what I told you—

> God for King Charles! To Pym and such carles
> The devil that prompts 'em their treasons parles!

—don't forget. And if they want to know where your father is, tell them he's riding with Prince Rupert, like every other true-hearted English gentleman."

Audley slid the photographs out of the envelope.

Robert Davenport—a lean, nondescript face sandwiched between the tall black hat and the plain white collar of the Puritan divine.

David Bishop—button nose and chubby cheeks, a baby-face made more for laughter than for the steel helmet perched incongruously above it.

Philip Oates—another ordinary Anglo-Saxon face, fair hair falling across eyes which stared in surprise directly into the camera.

John Lumley—those at least were memorable features, the arched nose and jutting chin framed by the black cavalier wig and beard: it had to be a disguise because that sort of expression went with short hair in the twentieth century, no matter what the fashions of the seventeenth might have decreed.

He watched as Frances and Mitchell swopped the prints between them, noting Mitchell's cheek muscles tighten with irritation as he came to Lumley's.

"Philip Oates knew he was being photographed," said Frances, holding up the snap.

"I hope they all knew they were being photographed," said Audley. "These are four people we're leaning on—I told you. Plus Charlie Ratcliffe himself. All five of them, they're going to hear their phones go 'click' when they lift the receiver. They're going to notice cars parked across the street from where they live—the same cars that were parked across the road from where they work. Their friends are going to tell them that people have been asking questions about them. And the people they see aren't going to be the people who are doing the real watching, either. They're each getting the VIP treatment."

Frances frowned. "You mean ... Fail-Safe Surveillance?"

"For a week, yes."

"Even for a week, that's pretty expensive stuff." Frances's brow furrowed with the effort of the mental arithmetic she was doing. "I didn't know your budget stretched to that sort of thing just now."

Mitchell laughed suddenly. "Maybe we're expecting a profit for once. A ton of gold would pay a fairish dividend on the deal."

"Don't be silly, Paul."

"I'm not being silly, honeybunch. If David does pull this rabbit out of the hat not even the Tribune Group will be able to complain about the high cost of security—we could probably put in for a Queen's Award for Industry, I shouldn't wonder."

"But there's something not right about this." Frances shrugged him off simply by staring at Audley. "There are too many people getting involved, David. First there were just the three of us—or four, with that policeman of yours. But now there are five surveillance teams ... and they can't possibly operate at fail-safe level without four to a team. Plus a field controller and a technical services adviser for the electronics." She shook her head. "That's an awful lot of people, David."

"Plus the red-haired, red-faced gentleman," murmured Mitchell. "But of course we do have 'friends' helping us this time, according to David."

"Special Branch," said Frances, still watching Audley. "Special Branch doing the harassment bit—which they hate doing. And we hate making them do it ... So you can talk about us

165

leaning on Charlie Ratcliffe, but it feels more like someone's leaning on *us*."

Another bright one, thought Audley. But then Mitchell, the trained military historian, had enjoyed his part of the assignment, which was little more than doing what came naturally to him. Whereas Frances, who had cut her teeth on very different problems, would have little sympathy for her task, and none at all for dressing up like this. And that had spurred her on to question its nature.

But with such a bright one, doubt was a corrosive which had to be treated seriously. "There's a political angle to this, Frances," he said gently. "Sometimes the politicians require us to pick their chestnuts out of the fire, and we have to do it."

"Of course there's a political angle," said Mitchell dismissively. "Charlie Ratcliffe is a political animal. And the lunatic left is a political force—a disproportionate force too, even without a war-chest full of gold. We've got to take his goodies away from him, Frances. It's as simple as that."

"It isn't simple at all," snapped Frances.

"No, it isn't simple." Audley recognised the source of her doubt: it was the knowledge that there on the left, but for the grace of God, went Frances herself, in the ranks of Charlie Ratcliffe's regiment. "But it isn't improper either. If Ratcliffe had played straight to get his gold, we wouldn't touch him. But he didn't play straight, he played dirty. He had another human being killed—" he had to hold her here "—like a rabbit."

Kill it, Audley—go on, man—kill it!

"Yes—" Mitchell started to speak, but caught Audley's eye just in time. As though to stop up his mouth he started to munch the parsley which Mistress Henrietta had given him.

"Like a rabbit, Frances," Audley repeated. "And he didn't even have the guts to do his own killing. He hired someone."

He could feel her doubt weakening. In the end it was always a matter of trust and now she wanted to trust him, not knowing that he had won her by summoning up that old, dark memory of the harvest field.

She stared at him. "You're sure?"

No.

166

But that trust was a two-way thing, like the feudal bond he had almost accepted in the Minister's car.

"Yes."

No more doubt: it was gone like a shadow in the sunlight. Frances would serve now, consenting to whatever had to be done.

"So what next?" asked Mitchell through the parsley. "You really want me to lean on John Lumley?"

"I don't want you to do anything, either of you. Keep an eye open for them, but don't do anything. Just fight your battle today the way it's scripted. You're my Tenth Legion."

"More like Fifth Column. So what are we being reserved for, my lord?"

"The storming of Standingham Castle next Saturday."

Mitchell's eyes lit up. "Of course! Forgive me for being so dim, David—I'd got my parts mixed up."

"Your what?"

Mitchell laughed. "I was still doing my *Henry V* bit—your favourite play, as we all know, David—

To horse, you gallant princes! Straight to horse!"

"Don't be a pain, Paul," said Frances.

"You can't talk, Frances dear. You've been doing it far worse than me—

But if the cause be not good, the king himself hath a heavy reckoning to make..."

What a young snake the boy was, thought Audley ruefully.

"But now you know our cause is just, our quarrel honourable, you can safely shift from Agincourt to Elsinore, my lady." Mitchell was enjoying himself. "Because we're going to be Hamlet's Players in *The Murder of Gonzago*—

*the play's the thing
Wherein I'll catch the conscience of the king.*

"Bravo and good on you, David. We'll pronounce our lines trippingly, I promise you. Is there anything else you want?"

Yes, just one thing so far as Mitchell was concerned, thought

Audley fervently. But he would have to settle for something less drastic.

"Yes, there is one thing," he said heavily.

"Be my guest."

"I'd like to know why the hell you're eating parsley."

But that only stopped Mitchell for a fraction of a second. "Mistress Henrietta's gift? But of course—I asked her for it." Mitchell pointed to the corner of the playroom, to a small table laden with Air Vice-Marshal Rushworth's forgotten sandwiches and beer bottles. "The Royalist cavalry aren't allowed to drink today—a shocking anachronism, because they were pie-eyed back in '44. But I've had a beer and I can't afford to be dismissed the service until after I've stormed Standingham next week. Didn't your father ever tell you that parsley takes away the smell of booze, David?"

IX

COLONEL BUTLER WAS standing in a great bow window staring down at the bridge. In his hand he had a large cut-glass tumbler of heavily-watered whisky; Audley knew it was whisky, because Butler hated sherry and avoided beer, which put too much of a strain on his bladder; and he knew it was heavily watered, because Butler was on duty, and if there was a god to whom Butler knelt (other than the one who protected his three small daughters) it would be Mithras, the soldier's god of Duty.

The same sun which had bathed Paul Mitchell and Frances Fitzgibbon with seventeenth-century magic, the high midday sun, turned Butler's fiery red hair to a rich gold, but even in the sunlight Audley could see that there was grey in it now. Colonel Butler had started to grow grey in his country's service, which would probably have pleased Butler if anyone had dared say as much.

"Hullo, Jack," said Audley. "Good to see you."

"David." The effort of saying 'David' taxed Butler sorely. It had taken Jack Butler five years to make the great leap from 'Audley' to 'David', which he would have managed for his youngest and greenest subaltern in a few hours if he had remained with his Lancashire Riflemen. And by now he would have been commanding that regiment for sure; in fact, with Ulster the way it was he would have been commanding a good deal more than that, certainly more than five surveillance teams and a few Special Branch men. But Duty had got in the way of predictable promotion, and Jack Butler would never wear red tabs on his lapels now, he would live and die a colonel on the general list, seconded to special duty with an obscure department of the Ministry of Defence. And live and die quite happily, by Mithras!

But that didn't mean that he had to like calling David Audley 'David' when he didn't even approve of David Audley. It had been his god-daughter Catherine Audley who had finally led him to that, and even she hadn't been enough to make Butler glad to see her father.

"Politics, Jack."

"Politics. Aye, politics." Butler looked at his watch. "We haven't much time."

"No. Thanks for the photographs. I liked your messengers." Audley smiled. "The boy didn't say a word, the girl did all the talking."

"That would be her." Butler didn't smile back, but his face softened for half a second. "I'm not supposed to communicate with your inside people, that's why—not even supposed to know who they are. But I've seen the young woman Fitzgibbon on the ridge."

Audley nodded. "Looks the part, doesn't she?"

"It suits her, I'll say that. And I wouldn't have thought so."

"You wouldn't?" But he couldn't have Frances sold short. "More fool you, then. She's a damn good one."

That seemed to please Butler. "If you say so."

Which side would Butler have been on in 1643? thought Audley suddenly. That would be a pretty question to settle, with loyalty and duty and honour split right down the middle by common sense and those intellectual qualities which were hidden behind the archetypal red face.

But that wasn't today's problem, thank God!

"The other one's Paul Mitchell."

"Hah!" That was as close as Butler ever got to laughing.

"You think that amusing?"

Butler's face shut like a portcullis. "I think you've got two good ones then, that's what I think."

Audley was irritated at the anger he felt. "But you also think it's funny. Why?"

Butler looked at his watch again.

"Why?" Audley persisted.

Butler shrugged. "I think it's ... interesting that you don't like him."

"What d'you mean by that?"

This time Butler sighed, looking at Audley for a moment with his head on one side. "Let's say ... I think you ought to look

170

in the mirror sometime, and then look at Mitchell. But I'd prefer to bring you up to date, if you don't mind."

Audley swallowed. "Very well."

"The London end is going satisfactorily. There's a rumour a foot thick in the City that Ratcliffe's credit isn't so good any more. We haven't attempted to define it, but the way it's come back to us is that there's been a break in the murder investigation which implicates him and that there's a technicality in the treasure trove law which no one has thought of before."

"But we didn't start those rumours?"

Butler shook his head. "No. We just put you in at the top, that's all. They've done the rest themselves . . . with a little help from your friend Fattorini. He's been a tower of weakness in the market."

Audley smiled to himself at the thought of Matthew happily serving God and Mammon at the same time.

"And our five subjects?"

Butler took a sip of whisky. "Ratcliffe is a bit rattled. He was close to clinching a deal on a nice little second-hand offset press—the printer's about to go bust—and this has nearly scuppered it. We've helped someone else put in a cash bid for the same press backed with a government printing contract, too . . . he doesn't know about the contract, but he does know about the bid. And his old printer is baying for the money he owes."

"I'd heard about that."

Butler's lip drooped. "There's a nasty solicitor's letter in the post. He should have got it by now."

"So he should be running scared?"

"Not scared. I don't think this lad will scare easily. But angry —yes, I think he may well be angry. Because he's not stupid and he can put two and two together."

"But he can't prove anything?"

"Not a thing. And that's really what's making him angry: he isn't used to the other side playing dirty. But beyond that, he must assume that we're working on something real, and he can't possibly have any idea what it is."

That was true, certainly. Charlie Ratcliffe had too much at stake to assume they were bluffing, and with luck also too much to tempt him to play it cool in the hope of calling their bluff.

If he wasn't off balance yet he was no longer quite steady.

"Good. And the other four?"

Butler drew a deep breath. "It's really too early to say. If there's a guilty one then he's got the most reason to play innocent, and the innocent ones haven't had enough prodding to wonder what the devil's happening. Also, if the innocent ones are guilty of something we're not interested in—that can be a problem."

"But you've done some checking on them?"

"Oh yes, we've checked them. But first time round there's nothing anyone could put a finger on."

"There wouldn't be. And Mitchell swears Lumley is clean, for one."

Butler nodded, lips tightly compressed. "Yes, he would. He knows Lumley from the time before he was with us, when he was a research fellow at the Institute for Military Studies. And I'd be inclined to go along with him there, too. Lumley has the wrong profile for Ratcliffe's purposes. And also he's the one of the four that Ratcliffe has never met, so far as we can establish."

"But he has met the others?"

"Oh yes. That's about all he has done with Oates and Bishop —met them. They're not in his regiment, and they don't have his extreme brand of politics, but they're both postgraduate students at Wessex University, which is roughly what he is."

"Sociology?"

"No. They're both geographers, actually. One's doing a thesis on geology now, and the other's writing a book on meteorology. Ology is about the only thing they have in common that we can find, but it's early days yet."

Early days. But there were only seven days to the storming of Standingham Castle, and after that all days might be too late.

"And that leaves Robert Davenport."

"Ye-ess. . . ." Butler spread the word reflectively. "That does leave Robert Davenport."

" 'Preacher' Davenport."

"He certainly does his share of preaching—for a foreigner in a strange land."

"You sound as though you've doubts about Davenport, Jack."

"Not doubts—reservations." Butler shook his head. "Davenport is the obvious one, that's all ... and I don't like obvious ones, they worry me. He fits too well."

"How does he fit?"

"Right politics, for a start—or right *left* politics," Butler growled disapprovingly. "Left of left, never heard anything like it in my life. Nor has anyone else, I should think."

Audley smiled, thinking of poor Gerard Winstanley and his ragged band of Diggers, who had once tried to cultivate a tiny corner of common land in Christian brotherhood and humility. That had been much too strong for Oliver Cromwell's stomach too. "I don't know about that."

"You haven't heard him talk."

"Did he talk like that in the States?"

"We're working on that." Butler bridled at the question somewhat, and Audley knew exactly why: it would ordinarily have been the easiest thing in the world to ask the CIA about Davenport, but in this case that might amount to washing their own dirty political linen in an inquisitive neighbour's machine. And with Davenport's radical politics there was the added complication that American intelligence might already be well-established in his home territory, wherever it was, so that any British agent moving into it would have to act with the greatest caution. But caution made for slowness.

"He's a New Englander, from his voice. And he's well-educated—he knows his history," said Audley.

"We know that. What we don't know is what he's been doing since he left his state university nine years ago."

"What's he doing over here—we have to know that, for heaven's sake."

"Officially, just travelling for pleasure. He's supposed to have had a legacy, or an inheritance of some sort, and decided to do Europe on it. He hasn't got past England yet." Butler paused. "Been here eight months now, and clean as a whistle. But he's still the obvious one—and we're working on him."

The years had mellowed Butler thought Audley.

"But ... I'll tell you one thing ..." Butler spoke slowly, as though he wanted the words to sink in deeply "... we're not really working on Ratcliffe himself. We're pushing him, but we're not investigating him. That's specifically outside the brief."

"Uh-huh?" And saying as much was also outside the brief, at a guess, thought Audley. It was a glorious defect of Butler's that his loyalties, even his overriding loyalty to Queen and Country, were still limited by his ideas of fair play.

"You know, eh?" Butler spelt out his warning with a shrug.

"I've been fairly explicitly warned off," Audley nodded. "And the file on Ratcliffe is an edited one, too—which means that they already have a shrewd idea what Charlie intends to do when he's able to do it. So this is in the nature of a spoiling operation." He smiled at Butler in sudden gratitude; fair play wasn't friendship, but among equals it was the next best thing, and possibly a better thing at that. "But thanks, Jack."

Butler shied away from the smile as though it were a snake in his path, half turning towards the window and putting his nose back into the tumbler. As he did so there came a shout of command from outside and the same brittle drumming which had marked the change of the guard on the bridge fifteen minutes earlier.

"Well, if you want anything else from me you'd better make it quick," said Butler. "Your man's arrived."

Audley peered over his shoulder down at the bridge. The Royalist musketeers had formed up in a line alongside one parapet, complete with drummer and standard bearer, all standing rigidly to attention. From the other side of the bridge a trumpet pealed out and a Roundhead trooper rode into view, less gorgeous than the knot of cavalier officers who had gathered at the Royalist end, but much more warlike in his lobster-tailed steel helmet, polished breast-plate and leather buff-coat. For a moment or two he fought with his horse, which clearly disapproved of the trumpet call, but having mastered it rose in his stirrups and lifted a white flag of truce high above his head.

"You're getting the full treatment," observed Butler.

One of the cavalier officers advanced a few steps and doffed his plumed hat, holding it across his chest. The Roundhead dismounted and advanced on foot across the bridge to meet him. The cavalier, still bareheaded, gave a small bow and the Roundhead lifted his gloved hand in salute—presumably his helmet was rather more difficult to remove. Then, after a few minutes of conversation, each returned to his own side.

174

"Just like a film," said Audley.

"Aye. And us in the one-and-ninepennies," said Butler.

"That dates you, Jack—the one-and-ninepennies."

The trumpet pealed again and a new figure appeared from the Roundhead side; like the troopers, he wore a steel breast-plate and a buff-coat, but these were topped by a wide lace collar and a large, stiff-brimmed black hat.

"Except I was always in the one-and-threepennies," murmured Butler. "But there he is, anyway: the Parliamentary Labour candidate for Mid-Wessex ... alias Oliver Cromwell for today. Which isn't altogether inappropriate, I suppose."

The black-hatted Roundhead paused for a second in the centre of the bridge. The Royalist drummer beat a fierce little ruffle and the King's flag came down in salute. Once more the cavalier officer advanced to meet his enemies, but this time he wore his hat—and this time when he swept it off he bowed much lower.

"What's he like?" asked Audley.

"William Strode?" Butler sniffed. "He'll never sit for this seat, I tell you. It's rock-solid Conservative, no matter how moderate he tries to be they'll never elect him here."

"But he will sit for somewhere, sometime?"

"Oh aye. When he's done his time losing they'll give him a winner. If your Minister stays in power, that is."

Audley ignored the jibe; Butler's contempt for politics, left, right or centre, was always apt to make him irascible. "He's a genuine moderate, then?"

Butler sniffed again. "Aye."

"Security rating?"

"Clean as a whistle. He'll not be one of Charlie Ratcliffe's friends, that you can rely on."

That was altogether very convenient, thought Audley. The way the moderate left viewed the far left was like the old orthodox Christians had felt about heretics: whereas pagans just didn't know any better, not having had the True Faith revealed to them, heretics were the devil's Fifth Column in their own ranks. ... Which hatred the heretics returned with compound interest, because they also knew that the only historical difference between orthodoxy and heresy was the final winning or losing.

He nodded at Butler. "So maybe we can do business with him."

"Not *we*—you. I'm damned if I'm going to horse-trade with politicians when I'm not even sure of the business I'm in. I'll do the donkey-work for you, but this time you do your own dirty work, David."

"Suit yourself, Jack." Audley smiled at Butler. The Colonel's political hang-up went much deeper than his military instincts, he reminded himself; in fact, despite all appearances, he had risen from the ranks and a cloth-cap background in which his subsequent career was regarded as an act of defiance, if not actual treason.

In close-up the Double R Society's version-for-the-day of the Grand Plotter and Contriver of all Mischiefs in England was something less impressive than the original, at least in appearance; even in his Roundhead General Staff uniform he was still a ratty little man, sharp-featured and bright-eyed.

The eyes fastened instantly on Audley, snapping him for future reference. So it wasn't going to be so easy after all: the prospective Labour candidate for Mid-Wessex was no fool and no beginner, those eyes indicated. The natural selection of political jungle warfare, which forced men like this one to watch their backs as well as their fronts, had made William Strode very wary.

"Mr—?" Strode didn't wait to be introduced.

"Audley."

"Mr Audley... Colonel Butler asked me this morning if I could come to see you now—here." The eyes flicked briefly towards Butler. "You both represent a branch of the security services?"

"That's correct."

"I can give you five minutes. In ten minutes' time I'm seeing the Royalist commander. You can have half that time, no more."

"I might want more than that, Mr Strode."

"It's all you can have."

Audley smiled his most unfriendly smile. "Then I shall have to be brief, won't I? Mr Strode, I want your help."

176

Strode said nothing for a few seconds, as though an appeal for aid hadn't been what he was expecting.

"Indeed?" he said finally. "Or?"

"Or—what?"

"Or what will you do if I don't choose to help you?" The gleam in Strode's eye was obstinate now. "After all, helping the internal security service isn't going to make me popular in my own party. If I help you I take a risk. It doesn't happen to be a risk I want to take."

"But I haven't told you what sort of help I want."

"You don't need to. I know the Roundhead Wing has some pretty far-out types in it—political extremists you people are bound to be interested in. But I intend to beat them my way without your help, Mr Audley. By the rule book and the ballot box, I shall beat them."

"Not Charlie Ratcliffe, you won't beat him that way." Audley shook his head.

"Charlie—?"

"That's right. Because Charlie isn't going to use the rule book and the ballot box. He's going to use the printing press. And he's going to do to you, Mr Strode—and people like you—what the South Africans are alleged to have done to the Liberal Party. And there's absolutely nothing you can do about him, Mr Strode. But there just may be something I can do—with your co-operation."

Strode stared at him. "You mean . . . you're just after Ratcliffe, no one else?"

"Ratcliffe—and whoever helped him murder James Ratcliffe."

Strode frowned. "You're re-opening the murder case?"

"It was never closed. Though, to be frank, I don't give a stuff who killed who—I already know that. But I want Ratcliffe to start worrying about it, so I want the word out that the police are pursuing a promising new line of inquiry. And I want that rumour to start at the very top—from you."

The cast of calculation was in Strode's eye now. "That's no problem. That's pure law-and-order."

"The next thing's no more difficult. . . . Will you be at Standingham next weekend?"

"Of course. I'm playing the part of Sir Edmund Steyning."

"With Charlie as Nathaniel Parrott?" Audley smiled. "It's all planned, is it?"

"It's the biggest show we've ever put on." Strode nodded, more cautiously this time. "The BBC is filming it for television, so we're aiming at a maximum muster."

"And it's all planned?"

Strode nodded again. "The advance party will be going down on Thursday to set the scene. Then there's a full-dress rehearsal on the Friday evening, and we'll stage the storming for the public on the Saturday and the Sunday. With any luck we'll have a turn out of at least eight hundred."

"Eight hundred and one now. I shall be attaching myself to your staff, Sir Edmund."

Strode frowned. "You can't fight if you aren't a member. I can't break our own rules."

"I don't want to fight. I want to be free to 'come and go and look and know'—put me down as a friend of yours, or a foreign observer, or whatever you like. But one way or another, Mr Strode, I want to be there to breathe down Charlie Ratcliffe's neck. I'm going to run him to hounds, and run him to ground —and then I'm going to dig him out and let him go again, and hunt him again—until he doesn't know whether it's April 1st or Christmas Day. And you're going to let me do it, with no questions asked and no answers given . . . which you'll do for the same reason that Oliver Cromwell came down on the Levellers: either we break them or they break us."

They stared at each other. The five minutes was long passed, thought Audley, but for this cause a Royalist general ought to be indulgent.

Strode blinked at last. "All right, Audley. . . . But not for that reason."

Audley shrugged. "Then whatever reason you like."

"I don't like—and neither should you." Strode shook his head. "It's because there'll always be someone like you, whoever wins. But if Charlie Ratcliffe has his way you won't have to ask me to help you—you'll be giving the orders. And I wouldn't like that."

Butler lingered at the door, one eye on the hall until Strode had gone.

"And now?" he said.

"And now—if they start cracking anywhere, Jack—then we're in with a chance."

"Aye. And if they don't?"

"Then we fail." Audley met the odds blandly. "This is bloody politics, man. We do our best, but we go by the rule book, like Mr Moderate William Strode. So at least we don't get our fingers burnt picking up someone else's chestnuts."

Butler grimaced at him. "You don't think we've got a hope, do you? You're just causing mischief, that's all."

Audley shrugged. "All right, then. Let's say: 'Mischief, do thy work', Jack. Maybe it will, at that."

"Aye." Butler looked out of the window, towards the cavaliers guarding the bridge. "But whose work will it do, I wonder?"

PART TWO:

How to be a bad winner

I

15. *Royalist Army regroups. Final exhortation by Lord Monson (to be relayed by loudspeaker to crowd). Pioneers will obtain fresh fascines.*
16. *Roundhead Army regroups. Regimental commanders to ensure that no personnel are within fifty (50) yards of glacis below Great Bastion (red flag markers).*
17. *4.40: Special Effects Section will fire simulated magazine explosion.*
18. *4.41: The Great Assault. Pioneers will...*

It had taken Audley four days to complete his report on the current state of the Central Intelligence Agency, which was three days less than he had allowed himself originally; and which, he reminded himself irritably, would have left him ten days buck-shee holiday with Faith and Cathy if he hadn't been conned, bullied and dragooned into messing around with politicians' chestnuts to absolutely no effect.

He looked up from the Double R Society's scenario for the storming of Standingham Castle to check the time by the grand-father clock beside his study door.

Absolutely no effect as of 10.15 a.m., Thursday August 28. Nobody had panicked, nobody had misbehaved, nobody had done anything that he ought not to have done. Nobody had done *anything*.

In a minute or two Faith would bring him a cup of coffee, and with luck she would kiss him, and since the heat of the day was yet to come he would kiss her back; and at 10.30 he would phone Jack Butler, and Jack would report that nothing had happened since 6 p.m. the previous evening, at considerable cost to the taxpayer.

He reached across his desk to check his assignment diary.

(Afterwards, when he looked at the diary, before he dropped it in his wastepaper basket, he would recall 10.15 a.m., Thursday,

183

August 28, with what he assumed must be the same bitterness as that with which some US Navy veterans must remember the last few minutes before 7.55 a.m., Sunday, December 7, 1941. By that time there was nothing they could do to stop the Japanese bombs and torpedoes, just as by that time there was nothing he could have done to stop Sergeant Henry Digby going down to the Ferryhill Industrial Estate in answer to a phone call the nature of which he never was able to establish. But those last minutes of peace of mind, before everything changed, were still the moments to regret.)

Faith came in with the coffee, still wearing her serene morning-after-last-night face, when everything had gone the way it ought to go, if not somewhat better.

(10.16 a.m. now: Sergeant Digby was turning into the Ferryhill estate, looking for the Wessex Electronics building. "I'm just going down to Ferryhill," he had told his mother, "to meet someone." He had seven minutes of life ahead of him then.)

But Faith didn't stay—

"Darling, I've got to fly—got to take Cathy down to the village to play with—"

No matter. Audley bent his head over the scenario. Tomorrow he would go down to Winchester, where Paul Mitchell would give him his costume for the afternoon, and report that nothing of interest had happened, and that the Tenth Legion was getting bored with inactivity.

He read the scenario again, and began to drowse over it, staring out at the dying elms beyond the lawn. He would have to hire someone to cut them down—they were too big for him— and then the bark, where the infection lay, would have to be stripped off. And that would be damned expensive, but he couldn't burn them where they fell; that would be wasteful as well as difficult. . . .

(It didn't matter now. The battleships were sinking and burning now, and the admiral had torn his epaulettes from his shoulders. Henry Digby was dead now.)

He started to think of the CIA. In a way, by carefully failing now, he was protecting the Department from that fate. If he'd really tried to screw Charlie Ratcliffe he would probably have ended up by causing a big scandal, which wouldn't have done

Counter-Intelligence any good at all—with all those far-left-wing MP's asking awkward questions in the House of Commons about the infringement of personal liberties. Even William Strode had suspected that he was a fascist beast in disguise.

He forgot all about phoning Jack Butler. It was no longer of any importance.

Just after the grandfather clock struck eleven Faith returned, bearing cakes which old Mrs Clark had baked for them, some of which she would pack up for the weekend expedition into seventeenth-century England.

It occurred to him that the best thing he could do would be to arrange for Charlie Ratcliffe to be part of the Special Effects Section's simulated magazine explosion, thus solving all problems. Which happy thought encouraged him to kiss her, which she mistook as an advanced farewell on account of his imminent departure for manoeuvres at Standingham Castle, and returned the hug with interest. And the late August sun shone on them both.

Then the phone rang.

Audley removed one hand from his wife and reached back across his desk for the receiver.

"Stop it, love—if you whisper into one ear I'll never hear anything in the other.... Hullo. Audley speaking."

For no particular reason he stared at the grandfather. The hands were on five past eleven.

Dr Audley, this is—

Superintendent Weston has asked me to—

I'm afraid I have to tell you that—

He was still staring at the clock. The minute hand always jerked forward so strongly that it marked each advance with a shiver.

"Are you there, sir?"

"Yes. When did this happen?"

10.23. Henry Digby had been dead for ... forty-three minutes *now.*

"Where?"

He listened.

"Where?" Time had stopped. "What was he doing there?"

185

Not in a position to say.

"Get me Superintendent Weston."

Superintendent Weston was busy. Of course he was busy.

"Don't argue with me. You don't think he told you to phone me out of courtesy, do you? Get him."

Hold the line.

"What's the matter, David? What's happened?" asked Faith.

"Henry Digby's dead."

"This time next year he'll be Inspector Digby CID."

"Well, you just make sure he is, that's all."

"So you be careful of him ... sir."

Faith was no longer touching him, she was looking at him in appalled anger. "What have you done, David?"

"I haven't done anything."

"You mean it was an accident? A road—" But she could read his face like a book. "But it wasn't an accident, was it? What have you *done*?"

He could only shake his head. "I don't understand. He wasn't doing anything dangerous. I deliberately didn't put him in harm's way."

"You said he'd have to take his chance." She was remembering the same conversation now. "You said that."

"That's what I said, not what I did." But he was already arguing with only half his mind; the other half was groping towards the immediate consequences.

"Well, you bloody well miscalculated, didn't you! Whatever you did." And already her anger was changing also, but into helplessness. "He was ... too young."

So he was, thought Audley, remembering Digby's threadbare dressing-gown. Too young, but no younger than half the names on the old hot war casualty lists—even older than some of those. Except that they had known the reason why, and Digby—

"What happened?"

He stared at her. "What happened?" He heard himself repeat the question with a curious detachment. Repeating questions was a stupid habit which had always irritated him.

186

"Or shouldn't I ask?" She was not far away from sympathy now, and anger was preferable to that; sympathy only emphasised the truth of her earlier reaction.

You've bloody well miscalculated!

"He was shot. It happened somewhere on the Ferryhill Industrial Estate." He spoke harshly. "And don't ask me what he was doing there, because I haven't the faintest bloody idea."

There was a click on the phone at his ear.

"Is that you, Audley?"

"Yes." Audley steeled himself for what was to come.

Yet nothing came: there was a vacuum between them as each waited for the other to speak. He had expected Weston to be tightly controlled in his reaction, but silence was a refinement which surprised him. It was pointless to be sorry, anyway: only Faith's question was left to him.

"What happened?"

"It was just bad luck, that's all."

"Bad luck?" The answer was even more surprising than the silence. It was the wrong answer the wrong tone of voice—the wrong everything. "What d'you mean—bad luck?"

"His being there just then." Weston paused. "Didn't they tell you?"

Audley just managed to stop himself repeating the question. If he did that once more it would become a habit. "No, they didn't."

He heard Weston speak to someone else—presumably the detective constable—but couldn't make out any of the words.

"I'm sorry, Audley." More indistinct words. "I'm sorry—I thought you had been told, but it seems they hadn't had the confirmation here until a minute or two back. It was the IRA." Weston paused. "I take it he wasn't investigating anything which had an Irish connection—for you?"

"Of course not." Sheer incredulity roughened Audley's reply.

"I didn't think so. Then that's what it was—sheer accident. He just happened to run into one of their bomb squads in the act of planting a bomb. He must have caught them planting it, and he tried to tackle them. And they shot him."

Steady. "You've had confirmation of that?"

"We had a phone call at 10.25—Irish accent and codeword.

187

They said there was a bomb outside Wessex Electronics and we had ten minutes to clear the place."

"And there was a bomb?"

"We've just defused it—the Army has. Ten pounds of gelignite and one of those damned American detonators—the ones they lost in Vietnam—that's what they think." Another pause. "Look, Audley—as you can imagine, I'm pretty pushed now. We've got a fighting chance of picking the bastards up—this is a largely rural area, outside the estate, not like Birmingham or London. So we've got it sealed off tight now . . . so I shall have to hang up on you, you understand?"

"Of course." Under the circumstances Weston had already shown remarkable courtesy in even coming to the phone. "Thank you for sparing the time. Goodbye then, Superintendent —and good hunting."

"Don't you worry about that. We'll get them." Weston was coldly businesslike. "I'm sorry about . . . your business. But there's nothing I can do about that at the moment. Goodbye, Audley."

"It was the IRA," said Audley.

"Oh," said Faith. "Oh . . . I'm sorry, David . . . I mean—I'm sorry."

She turned away.

Audley watched the door close.

Acceptance.

Just say *It was the IRA* and you receive acceptance. Anger and bitterness and helplessness and bafflement—and acceptance. Even from a total professional, with the evidence served up steaming on a plate, the acceptance was automatic. Except, to be fair, Weston was still in pursuit at this moment, and the unanswered questions had to wait in such circumstances.

Like—what the hell was Henry Digby doing on the Ferryhill Industrial Estate, way off course, at ten o'clock in the morning?

Audley picked up the phone again and dialled.

"Colonel Butler? Anything doing, Jack?"

Grunt. "Pretty quiet."

"Absolutely nothing you could put your finger on?"

"No. . . . Haven't had the morning reports yet, of course."

"You sound as though you've reservations about that."

Grunt. "Nothing tangible. We've pulled off the front men now, of course—did that on Tuesday midday, as I told you yesterday."

That was routine. The obvious watchers, having established their presence, had removed themselves, leaving the observation to more unobtrusive and sophisticated men and machines in the hope that fear or foolishness might now betray any guilty party into activity. It was a crude bit of psychology, but it was occasionally successful nevertheless.

"And?"

"Nothing. But the man Davenport worries me. He visited the American Embassy on Tuesday."

"No reason why he shouldn't. Did our inside man there know what he did there?"

"Apparently not. But it wouldn't surprise me at all if he wasn't getting ready to run for it, that's all."

"Why d'you think that?"

"Hard to say.... He's been buying one or two little extras, paying one or two debts.... And I had Maitland search his flat."

"Maitland?" Audley lined up the technical support men in his mind and picked out a freckle-faced expert with hair even more ginger than Butler's. "Yes, I know him. A good man."

"He didn't find anything. But he had the strong impression that Davenport was expecting to be searched—the way things were left. And he said he couldn't guarantee that Davenport wouldn't know his place hadn't been turned over, if that was the case, because he couldn't leave every hair in its original position."

"I understand—which would make Davenport a pro."

Maitland—of course!

"Very well." Audley steadied his voice. Maitland had once a partner, a clever young trainee who had got himself blown up while examining a booby-trapped car.... "You'd better put a watch on the ports and airports, Jack. If Davenport moves—if any of them move—pick 'em up and hold 'em."

"For what?"

"Suppression of Terrorism Act. No lawyers and no phone

189

calls until I've seen them. And see that their bags aren't searched, too."

Jenkins, that was the boy's name. He'd been the younger brother of a friend of Hugh Roskill's. And it had been Butler himself who had brought the news of his death—to this very house, four or five years back. . . .

"And you meet me at the Steyning Arms at Standingham tonight, Jack. As arranged."

Jenkins.

The Jenkins Gambit, he had called it, because Jenkins himself had been the booby-trappers' target: the best way to kill a food taster is by poisoning his master's dish—then it looks like an occupational hazard.

And, by the same token, the best way to murder a policeman was to kill him in the execution of his duty, where sudden death was an occupational hazard which good coppers could be relied on to accept.

And Digby had been a good copper.

Audley stared at the grandfather clock.

And now Digby was a dead copper.

The thought of Digby dead was a physical pain. He would never see Digby again. He would never introduce Frances Fitzgibbon to Digby, that little match-making dream of Faith's —a crazy dream, but no bad dream—was gone like smoke on a summer's day. He had only known the boy for a few hours, and the boy had felt nothing for him but curiosity, yet the sense of loss was none the less bitter for that. It was boys—and men— like Digby who held the sky suspended; taken for granted in life, and mourned only briefly in the headlines in death, more out of public piety than from conviction.

Henry Digby was dead, and he would rot and putrefy, and long before he was dust he would be forgotten. Even Audley himself, who might be as guilty as the killer, would soon relegate him to a dull ache of conscience, and then a mere regret, and at the last a hazy memory of one job that hadn't gone according to plan years ago.

Faith was in the doorway, beside the grandfather clock.

"It's been on the news, David—the twelve o'clock news."

He looked at her stupidly. "About Digby?"

"They didn't mention him by name. They said a policeman had been shot and killed, and that the army had defused a bomb—" She stopped.

"Yes?" He could see that there was more.

"But there was another bomb that went off—a car bomb. Two other people have been killed."

"Yes?"

"They think they were in the car. They're not sure, but they think so. And the police think they may have been the bombers themselves."

There was a nuance of satisfaction in her voice. No one was more resolute against the death penalty than Faith, but when God Himself jogged the hand on the bomb she was as blood-thirsty as any *sans-culotte* in her approval of the execution.

Now only the clock was staring at him.

Thesis: it had been Watson's "pure bad luck", with Digby going down to the estate to his death for some simple innocent reason. Bad luck with an Irish accent, and an IRA codeword and an IRA bomb to prove it, begorrah.

The minute hand moved.

Antithesis: bombs and brogues proved nothing, and pass-words and codewords were known; and any killer with the price of a phone call could have lured Henry Digby to meet his bullet, anywhere, any time—and who better than Charlie Ratcliffe, who had hired death once already? Charlie, whom they'd been driving towards action, driving with cold delibera-tion towards the belief that there was something very wrong with his beautiful golden plan.

And now the car bomb.

Another minute.

Thesis: it had happened before and it would happen again, the bomber fragmented by his own bomb. Bombs were no respectors of persons, Weathermen, Irishmen, Palestinians, housewives on the way to the supermarket, golden lads and lasses. And, as he well knew, those American time pencils from Vietnam were notoriously unreliable.

Antithesis: killers killed to a pattern, and stripped of all their superficial differences this was Swine Brook Field all over again, by God! Because but for the accident of Digby's presence Swine Brook Field would have been a nice neat accident too. Sooner or later in the controlled violence of the Double R Society's battles someone might have caught the butt-end of a pike. And now *sooner or later* had caught both Sergeant Digby and his killers.

But if his thesis was right?

That was the temptation. All he had to do was to accept his own innocence, and he was in the clear. Without Digby's special knowledge he would be half-blind at Standingham this evening and tomorrow and on Saturday. He could do his best and fail, and no one would blame him very much. Some you won and some you lost, and Sir Frederick would be the first to admit that politics was the very devil.

It didn't even require any special effort. It wasn't as if Digby had been ferreting around in the area of James Ratcliffe's murder at Swine Brook Field, and that was the only crime which Charlie Ratcliffe had committed. He'd only been filling in on the details of the gold itself, where Charlie had been on safe ground—his very own ground, where nobody could touch him.

Unless—

Audley knew that if he pursued the alternative he would have no choice in the outcome. Once he lifted the phone and called Weston again and said *No. Screw bad luck. He was working for me and therefore he died for me—until you can prove otherwise* then Weston would never rest until that otherwise was established. It wouldn't be a matter of guilt or blame for Weston—it would be a matter of truth, and a matter of keeping faith.

No choice, anyway. He could have no more avoided the alternative than the clock's minute hand could have avoided ticking to the next sub-division of its hour. Only when the clock stopped would the hand stop.

The phone rang in the exact instant that he reached for it, almost as though it had been waiting for him to make up his mind.

Audley stared at it in a mixture of exasperation and relief. It

192

had to be Weston, he felt that with a strange calm certainty: it had to be Weston because the moment the heat of the hunt was off Weston would find the accident of Digby's presence on the Ferryhill Industrial Estate sticking in his throat, a question much too sharp to be swallowed. And if he had been unexpectedly quick in feeling its point it was no less true that Audley had been fatally slow in anticipating it: he could never bring himself to say 'I was just going to call you' now, even if there had been the least chance of it being believed. As it was, he had missed his chance by a matter of seconds.

But there was justice in that. The error was still his error, admitting it did not exonerate him of it. No anger or contempt of Weston's would ever hurt him as much as his own self-anger and self-contempt.

"Weston?" He was so certain that the question was unnecessary.

"What?"

Butler?

Audley blinked with surprise. But he'd only just been talking to Butler—

"Is that you, Audley?"

Butler.

"Yes. I'm sorry—I thought you were someone else." Audley realised that he had a fresh lease of life where Weston was concerned. "I'm expecting a call, Jack, so make it quick—whatever it is."

"I will indeed," Butler snapped. "You were right."

It was a comfort to have been right about something, after having been fatally wrong once already today, thought Audley.

"I was, was I?"

"Davenport. It came in just after you phoned."

"He's started to move?"

"He's moved. And he damn near moved too fast for us. It's a mercy we'd strengthened the surveillance on him or he might have managed it."

Audley half-smiled into the receiver at the typically Butlerian modesty. Butler had been right in his suspicions and Butler had strengthened the surveillance, but nothing would make him admit as much.

"What happened?"

"He'd established a route pattern to London over the past three days. But this morning he ditched his car in Staines and threw our tail. But our lad was smart—he switched the back-up straight to London Airport and put them on red alert there, it's only minutes from Staines, of course."

"And that paid off, I take it?"

Butler allowed himself a small grunt of satisfaction. "He had a flight bag waiting for him there, and a ticket to Holland. *And* a spare passport in the name of Donaldson." Butler paused. "Which he's used half a dozen times before in the past year. One trip to Holland, five trips to Paris."

Davenport.

The conflicting implications of what Butler was saying suddenly began to jostle Audley, elbowing each other like a crowd which had smelt smoke in the auditorium. Digby was dead and Davenport had run for cover—and that escape kit at the airport made him a pro for sure. But, more than that, if the deed and the action were connected, he ought not to be running, he ought to be playing it cool; and if they were *not* connected, then that shored up the good luck thesis, undermining his own conclusions about Digby's death. And yet, again, those trips to Paris...if they were Charlie Ratcliffe-orientated—

But why should a professional run? What did he think they could prove against him?

"What does he have to say for himself?"

"Precious little. He says his name's Donaldson, and he's an innocent American. And this isn't a police state, but he wants to phone his embassy just in case."

Well, that was playing it by the book. And for a man in Davenport/Donaldson's position that was the only way he could play it, guilty or innocent.

But for his captors the options were more varied. There was no problem in holding him; even without the passport they had the Suppression of Terrorism Act, and with the passport they could probably make a legitimate meal of him at their leisure. But leisure was something they didn't have—he knew that, and Butler knew it too. And, for a guess, Davenport/Donaldson knew it also: if the ticket waiting for him had been for

Holland, then he would look to be met there, or at least to announce his safe arrival. So the advantage they had in having taken him on the wing was a fragile one, and every moment wasted gave the enemy time to adjust his defences.

The old clock was still ticking and Butler was waiting for him to do what he was paid for: to out-think the clock.

And he still had to phone Weston, to admit what the Superintendent would never forgive, the squandering of a useful life. That wasn't a pleasant prospect, rendered no more endurable for that it couldn't be avoided.

What can't be cured must be endured.

What must be endured must be used—

"Jack . . . listen—this is what I want you to do—"

He waited while they searched for Weston. It occurred to him that he could still be entirely wrong, and he had already made mistakes enough to make that a fair bet for any honest bookmaker. And if he was wrong he would be raising the devil for himself now.

But that too was what they paid him for, to raise the devil.

"Audley?" Weston's voice was rough with accumulated tension.

And that was also part of the payment, the excitement of backing the judgement and taking the risk. It was a very odd sort of job satisfaction.

"I'm sorry to bother you again, Superintendent. You've got your men, then?" He paused deliberately. "But in pieces—is that right?"

"That's the way it looks." The words came with an effort.

"You're sure?"

For a moment Weston didn't answer, but when he did the roughness had been smoothed away. "No. It's too early to be sure of anything."

"But you have some evidence that the men in the car were the killers?"

"I can't say that yet, sir." The voice was hard as toughened steel now; Weston was thinking new thoughts and connecting up old facts with them. He would have thought them eventually,

195

but this way he was being pushed towards them. "I'll let you know in due course, Dr Audley."

"I'm afraid due course won't do, Superintendent."

"And I'm afraid it will have to do."

"No, it won't." Steel cuts oak—diamond cuts steel. "Look, Superintendent . . . I can make you answer me, but it will take time and effort. I don't mind making the effort, but I can't spare the time—neither of us can spare the time. So don't let's waste it while we've still got it, eh?"

That was spelling it out both ways, confirming Weston's new suspicions about Digby's death and Audley's executive authority at the same time. Only the velvet question mark at the end had been a concession that Weston too had an authority.

Weston drew one deep, audible breath. "Very well. It is too early to be sure—we've been at the scene of the explosion not very long and we haven't near finished there. But it looks as though they were switching vehicles, and the bomb went off as they were driving away."

"And the connection?"

"It was a small bomb. The man in the passenger's seat was actually holding it, it looks like—on his lap, probably." Weston paused grimly. "There was a sawn-off shotgun in the back of the car."

"Yes?"

For two seconds Weston was silent. "The man who shot Digby used a sawn-off shotgun," he said.

Audley held the receiver tightly and forced his eyes to remain open, knowing that if he closed them for even one fraction of an instant he would start seeing pictures. And this wasn't the time for pictures.

"So it's all wrapped up neatly?"

"We haven't established any identification yet."

But they would, thought Audley. They would. And a dingy room somewhere, with bomb-making materials and ammunition, and maybe an Armalite rifle or two. There was always an Armalite. Perhaps there'd be a bunch of shamrocks and a couple of tickets for the Holyhead-Dun Laoghaire boat-train for good measure, too.

"Is that what you wanted, Audley?" Weston broke the silence.

"Yes. I don't believe a word of it."

"You don't—?" The words trailed off into a growl.

"I mean—it's all true and it's all false."

Pause.

"I think you'd better explain that, Dr Audley."

"I will. Where can I meet you?"

"I shall be here at headquarters."

"But I'm not going to meet you there. We're not playing that sort of ball game any more. This is between the two of us first."

Longer pause.

"Very well. There's a park about a mile from here—"

Audley relaxed and listened.

II

THE ROAD THROUGH the park ran, at the point of the first rendezvous, between an avenue of horse-chestnut trees, which in season no doubt provided a supply of conkers for the patrons of the children's playground on the left, but which now shaded the spectators of the cricket match in progress on the sports ground to the right.

Audley threaded his way between the deck-chairs and picnic-spread rugs to where Butler stood in front of another new Princess. It rather looked as though the Department had bulk-bought the new model as a patriotic gesture towards British Leyland's ailing fortunes, he thought irrelevantly.

"Enjoying the game, Jack?"

Butler waited until the batsman had played the ball safely back to the bowler. "Aye." He gave Audley a quick glance, and then returned to the contemplation of the game. "He's in the car waiting for you."

"Has he said anything more?"

Again Butler waited for the sharp *snick* of the ball on the bat. There was a scatter of clapping from the spectators, though nothing appeared to have happened on the wicket. But then cricket at the level which people like Butler enjoyed it was an arcane pleasure in which a whole afternoon of unrelieved boredom to the uninitiated was an action-packed battle to those who knew what was going on.

"No," said Butler. "Except he asked where we were taking him."

"And you said 'To a cricket match'?"

Butler registered his displeasure by waiting for the delivery of another ball, the last of the over. "And then he demanded to phone his embassy," he concluded heavily.

"But he doesn't seem worried?"

"More angry than worried, I'd say. He won't crack easily."

"What makes you think so? He ran quickly enough."

For an answer Butler produced an American passport from his pocket and handed it to Audley.

Robert Donaldson. Born: Hartford, Connecticut ...

'Preacher' Davenport stared up at him.

"It's good." He thumbed through the pages. "It looks perfect."

"It is perfect—perfectly genuine."

"Uh-huh? And Robert Davenport's passport?"

"Just as good. Only the trips are different, nothing else."

"The Paris trips?"

"The Donaldson trips coincide with Charlie Ratcliffe's—while Davenport stayed at home."

Audley nodded slowly. So anyone checking up on Davenport's movements wouldn't equate him with Ratcliffe; Davenport was for public consumption, Donaldson for private comings and goings from different points of entry and exit. It was all nice and simple—and professional. And that was what Butler was telling him, just as the man Maitland had told Butler from his own equally professional observations.

It was a pity a hundred or so reliable witnesses put Preacher Davenport on the wrong side of Swine Brook Field at the right time, but that simply meant he wasn't that sort of professional. And although they had him dead to rights on his two passports, that was a minor grief on a much smaller scale beside the things they really wanted him for.

"And yet he ran," Audley frowned at the cricketers.

"Maybe he was ordered to run," said Butler. "Even if he didn't get cold feet himself, maybe his control did—the way we were pushing him. That's happened before now."

His control, thought Audley. There it was, staring him in the face again, what he had begun to suspect and fear ever since Digby's death: that they were playing in a different league from the one he had assumed they were in, and that Charlie Ratcliffe was something very different from the ruthless young political activist he had seemed to be.

It had been there all along, of course. There in the urgency of the Minister's voice; there in the doctored Ratcliffe file; there in the cool efficiency of James Ratcliffe's death; and there even in Frances Fitzgibbon's disquiet at the resources lavished on them for the asking.

It had been there, and he had seen it all and ignored it because it didn't fit his childish preconception of the case.

Butler was right, shrewd and perceptive as ever behind that red military face of his: the young American wasn't so much worried about his predicament as angry with it.

Audley stared at him across the confined interior of the car. He looked younger in the flesh than in any of his pictures, but not so lean; perhaps the leanness had been an illusion fostered by the Puritan costume he had affected as 'Preacher' Davenport, but there was something about the bone-structure of his face which suggested that the Preacher's face was the shape of the face to come in full maturity. And then it would truly be an Old Testament face to the very life.

"And just who the hell—" Donaldson began belligerently, and then stopped abruptly, breathing out the rest of his stored anger as a sigh of relief. "Well—am I glad to see you!"

Glad? Audley froze his own face to prevent it betraying his surprise. The last time he'd heard that voice it had been declaiming pure seventeenth-century revolution in the words of Gerard Winstanley out of Frances Fitzgibbon's mini-tape. It couldn't have nonplussed him more now if it had continued in the same vein.

"Mr Donaldson?" His opening gambit of polite disbelief already sounded irrelevant. "Or is it Master Davenport?"

The American grinned at him, the laughter lines in his face at odds with those etched by anxiety. "Davenport, Dr Audley— Bob Davenport. And I guess I can say I'm pleased to meet you. I've certainly heard a lot about you, sir."

Audley had no choice but to shake the hand offered to him. It had not been his intention to do anything remotely like that, but then it couldn't be said that this harsh interrogation was going exactly to plan.

"Indeed? Well, I wish I could say the same for you, Mr Davenport. So perhaps you could give me another name to reassure me—someone else's name."

Davenport nodded. "Sure. At the embassy here I think Colonel Morris would be your best bet—Colonel Howard

Morris. Or Mr Legrange at The Hague, he's my boss. But I think you know them both, so you can take your pick."

Audley swallowed the lump in his throat. With a couple of casual sentences the ex-Preacher had completely rearranged the pieces of the jigsaw—and in doing so had made them fit as they had never fitted before. The professionalism which Butler and Maitland had sensed, those suspicious trips to Paris in Charlie Ratcliffe's wake, the precipitate withdrawal to Holland when it looked as though his cover had been blown.... Even the fact that he was talking freely now when he'd maintained his innocence with everyone else—it all added up to the same coherent pattern.

But the emerging picture was not the one on the lid of the box.

"For choice Colonel Morris," Davenport concluded.

Of course. He could imagine the final briefing almost word for word: if things go wrong play it cool until you reach one of their senior men. If Audley's back from Washington try for him, he's the closest we've got to a friend over there, and he and Morris understand the real score—if they can cover for you, they will....

"I see. But your control is in Holland?"

"Yes, sir."

That was what had thrown Butler. At a pinch they might have been able to identify the CIA's men in Paris, or even Brussels, but the station in The Hague was small and unimportant, more a presence than an operational centre.

"Then you're out of your territory, Mr Davenport—and out of line. We have an agreement with your people about manpower. And also we have an agreement about keeping out of our domestic hair: Charlie Ratcliffe is our problem, not yours."

"Yes, sir." The young American nodded. "But as to your first point, we also have a 'hot pursuit' agreement with you, if I may remind you, sir—"

"You may." That 'sir' was beginning to make Audley feel old and schoolmasterish, especially when added to the 'heard a lot about you' line. It was one thing for the Minister to use those words, but quite another for this boy to echo them as though he was already a living legend from the past. "You may, but it won't wash. You've been over here for months, and you haven't been looking for Ratcliffe, you've been watching him. And even if you had been pursuing him he's still ours. He's domestic."

"No, sir—with respect."

"Damn the respect." This was what Audley had feared, that part of the jigsaw where Charlie Ratcliffe fitted in with the activities of the CIA. Because there could only be one reason for that—the reason which explained the professional precision of the killings of James Ratcliffe and Henry Digby. All he needed now was final confirmation of that mathematical certainty.

"Well ... I guess we may have stretched the agreement a piece." Davenport grinned apologetically. "But it was pursuit— it didn't start here ... for us, that is—it started when he made contact with this guy we'd been watching in Paris—"

"KGB?"

"Oh sure—and top brass too. But don't ask me who, because they didn't tell me—" Davenport qualified the admission before Audley could pounce on it "—they pulled me in to establish the next link in the operational chain."

"Because you weren't known here?"

"Or in Paris. They got too many of our men tagged over there. ... Plus I had the right educational profile. Early colonial history just happened to be my hobby—it's not such a jump from New England to Old England. The guys who emigrated and the guys who stayed and made the colonies, they weren't so different, you know."

For once history was no temptation to Audley. "Yes, I'm sure they weren't. But I'm a little more interested in a more modern history, Master Davenport."

Davenport looked suitably contrite—and very young.

Davenport, little Frances ... Mitchell ... even Charlie Ratcliffe —he was trapped in a world of young people who seemed to know better what they were about than he did.

Well, they would grow old in their turn.

All except Henry Digby, who would never grow old. He would simply be forgotten.

But not yet, by God, not yet!

"But my job was strictly informational, sir." The young American was looking at him uncertainly now: perhaps he'd misinterpreted the expression which the memory of Henry Digby had stamped on the living legend's face, glimpsing hatred and anger behind the mask.

Or perhaps he hadn't misinterpreted it altogether after all, thought Audley with a flash of self-knowledge. Because this was one time when vengeance was going to make duty a pleasure.

"Even after Swine Brook Field?"

"After the hit?" Davenport was more cautious now. "Well, that only made it more interesting."

"Who made the hit?"

"We don't know for sure." Davenport scratched his head. "But we think it must have been a guy named Tokaev. He works out of Paris, but he was out of circulation at the time—and he speaks English perfectly . . . with a slight Cockney accent, that is." He nodded. " 'Fact, we're pretty certain, really. It's his style."

"And you found that merely . . . interesting?"

"Not merely—very. We still didn't know what Ratcliffe was up to, his cover's goddamn good."

But they'd watched him for months nevertheless. The KGB Paris contact must have been top brass indeed for that.

"Not until the gold turned up, anyway," continued Davenport. "Then we knew, of course. With that sort of finance he can really get *The Rat* off the ground, and with the dirt they can feed him he can pick his targets. . . . But I guess you know all *that* better than we do." He gave Audley a rueful look. "When it comes to cover your boys are no slouches either: until you cracked down a week ago we didn't think you were on to him at all."

"Until the gold turned up," Audley repeated the words mechanically.

"Yeah." Davenport shook his head admiringly. "You've got to hand it to the bastards—that was goddamn smart. *Goddamn* smart."

The distant sound of clapping intruded into Audley's consciousness, as though the cricket crowd agreed with Davenport. Someone had scored or someone was out.

Someone had scored sure enough: the Russians—£2½ million in good clean honest untainted money, for no losses.

He nodded wisely at Davenport. "Yes, I have to agree with you there. And all good genuine seventeenth-century Spanish gold too. That threw us, I can tell you."

"Hah!" Davenport gave a short laugh. "Well, they've obviously still got enough of it to pick the genuine article out of stock. But then Krivitsky said at the time that when they unloaded the stuff at Odessa in '36 there was enough of it to cover Red Square from end to end, and he had that from one of the NKVD men who was on the quayside. And some of that gold must have been in store in Madrid for centuries."

Dear God! thought Audley despairingly—how could they have been so stupid, so short-memoried! The Spanish Civil War gold—the gold of the embattled republic which Azana and Prieto had despatched to Russia for safe keeping in October, 1936, and which had turned all subsequent Soviet aid to Spain into a profitable deal that would have brought a blush to any Capitalist cheek; the gold—the Spanish gold—which had been such a bonanza that Stalin had announced shortly after that new mines had been found in the Urals, the old blackguard!

The Spanish gold which hadn't been found at all in the crater behind the bastion, but which had been planted there.

There was the full design at last. And all the elaborate tapestry of history they had woven was a lie: Matthew Fattorini's honest facts about cargoes and voyages, Nayler's painstakingly assembled inferential evidence, Paul Mitchell's elegant research...even his own smug reconstruction of how Edmund Steyning and Nathaniel Parrott had schemed to conceal *their* gold—all that was a lie, a self-deception, an edifice built with moonbeams and shadows.

The reality—as recalled by the one-time Chief of Soviet Military Intelligence in the West for the benefit of the *Saturday Evening Post* before SMERSH had caught up with him in a Washington hotel—the reality was a convoy of lorries from Madrid to Cartagena, and then an old freighter with its name painted out steaming slowly from there to Odessa, and then the train to Moscow and the Kremlin vaults.

And then, forty years later, a fraction of the loot had travelled West again, to finance another risky but potentially profitable operation. . . .

Audley superimposed the reality on the lie and came to the instant conclusion that the lie was more convincing. If Spanish gold, the gold of King Philip's Americas, had to end up in the kitchen garden of a great house in England, it should more likely have come via the son of a Devon sea-dog than by the order of a nameless Russian bureaucrat in some dusty office in Dzerzhinsky Street.

But, by the same token, when the KGB could summon up a man who could twist English history to his own use—and even the CIA could conjure up an agent who knew the difference between New England and Old England—then the English themselves ought to be able to screw them both into the ground.

I elect myself for that job, decided Audley dispassionately. *And I shall break the rules to do it, if that's the only way it can be done.*

Davenport was looking at him with a mixture of hope and expectation in his expression—the hope of freedom and the expectation that the legend would justify his reputation. It would be wrong to disappoint him.

"Well, Master Davenport, you've messed us up properly—I can tell you that for free," he said.

Davenport's lip drooped. "Once I was out you would have been given everything we had."

"But you aren't out. And we thought you were Charlie Ratcliffe's action man, maybe. So who is—can you give us that?"

Davenport blinked. "Sure. If it's a trade, that is."

"Part of a trade. You're not in a good trading position, but I'm inclined to be generous. I wouldn't like to see Howard Morris sent back home on the next plane." Audley smiled.

"Okay. He has two guys to hold his hand."

"In his—ah—his regiment?"

"No. In one of the militia regiments."

Well, well!

"David Bishop and Philip Oates, I presume?"

Davenport looked crestfallen. "You know them already?"

"Confirmation is always helpful. No one else?"

"I don't think so. But they're good operators—very careful. I'd guess they have instructions not to let him do anything, which pisses him off some I suspect."

"He sees himself as a man of action, eh?"

Small shrug. "He's been playing things close to his chest ever since Swine Brook Field, doing what he's been told. But I think you've shaken him up a bit this last week, with what you've been doing."

"Doing nothing isn't to his taste, eh?"

"Right."

So the editor of *The Red Rat* was pining to be a power in the land, the well-informed scourge of the enemies of the Union of Soviet Socialist Republics.

"And where does Professor Stephen Nayler figure in this grand design?"

"Oh, he's just window-dressing. Give him a TV programme and he'll kiss anyone's ass." Davenport's contempt warmed Audley's heart. "He's a punk, but he's clean—we looked him over good."

That was almost the last loose end tied up, thought Audley. All he had to do now was to tie all the ends in a new knot somehow.

"Well, that almost makes the trade, Master Davenport," he said.

"I'm glad to hear it." Davenport breathed out. "I shall be sorry to miss Standingham though. That should be quite a show, and I've gotten to enjoy the Double R Society—there are a lot of good people in it."

Audley smiled. "Oh, but you're not going to miss it—almost a trade, I said. I'm going to lose your extra passport and forget the breaking of our agreements, but there are things I need you to do first... after I've phoned Colonel Morris and talked to one or two other people. Nothing very difficult, certainly nothing very dangerous. But I want you there on the battlefield, preaching the revolution. It wouldn't be the same without you now, would it?"

He skirted the crowd unobtrusively, weaving in and out of the cars parked under the trees and the picnic groups among them. It surprised him, how many people there were, often whole families, able and willing to spend a whole weekday afternoon watching a cricket match. A rugger crowd he could understand, that was a contest of mind and muscle he enjoyed himself; and a football crowd, that was a statistical fact to be accepted, so there had to be more in it than met his eye. But cricket, that was a pleasant surprise.

His pulse quickened as he spotted Weston's car in the shadow of the trees beyond the old bandstand, and then Weston himself standing very still in the angle of the steps and the wooden balustrade of the stand.

The Superintendent was, if not the only unpredictable factor left, the last of the tools he required to handle Charlie Ratcliffe at Standingham. At a pinch he could probably do without Weston, but then he would have to give Weston's task to someone from the Department, and that might enable someone within it to ask awkward questions afterwards. Whereas if he had Weston and Frances and Davenport all doing their own different things—the police, the Department and the CIA—it was an odds-on certainty that they would never be in a position to exchange notes, and would never therefore be in a position to understand what they had done between them.

Weston was looking at him now.... Well, to be honest with himself, they might each of them suspect. Frances possibly, Davenport probably, and Weston ... Weston, being Weston, for sure, but without proof—only Charlie Ratcliffe would be able to supply that, and that was the one thing Charlie would be in no position to do.

But that thought armed him now for what he had to say. It was better to have Weston doing something for him than to leave him to his own devices. After what had happened to Sergeant Digby and with what he might already suspect, a copper like Weston would never rest quiet and easy.

The look on Weston's face confirmed his fear. There was no

mistaking the policeman for any tinker, tailor, schoolmaster or country doctor now: advancing on that look he knew how Prince Rupert's cavalry had felt when they saw the sun glint on the swords of Cromwell's Ironsides.

"Weston."

"Audley." The courtesies were minimal. "You've got a lot of explaining to do, I'm thinking."

"No." Audley shook his head. "Not to you."

The jaw squared. "If not to me, then to my chief."

"Not to him either. Sergeant Digby died in the execution of his duty while questioning two suspected terrorists who subsequently blew themselves up by accident. That was nothing to do with me—now or ever. The case isn't closed for me because it was never open."

Weston stared at him in silence for a moment or two, then took a sheet of paper from his breast pocket.

"Read it." He held out the paper. "Read it, Audley."

Audley opened the sheet. It was close-typed on cheap official paper, the words cutting across the faint blue lines beneath.

'Right worshippfule Sir,
Whereas of late have I suceeded to thee Estate wherof mine Fathyr was seised there cameth into myne possessioun alsoe a certeyne quantitie of treasure the whych did my Faither take from a certeyn Papisticalle shippe. But wheras at thatte tyme for inasmuch as his Majestie hadde mayd treatie and peace with thee king of Spayne it beseemed to hime not opportune to advertise thee whych and he caused itte to be hydden and to noo manne tolde he of it bethynking himme that as tyme showld shewe himme when and uppon what occasion he sh'd makke it knowne but he feeling thee comyng nighe of Dethe did tell mee of it.
And as nowe thee Lorde, to whom bee al prayse, hathe shewn unto mee the waye of righteousness and that Parliement doth strive mightilie in Hisse cause ageynst the wrongdoyng and persecution of the righteous by thee evil counselours of his Majestie it seemeth too me that trewe Religion and thee cause of Parliement requireth of mee that I sh'd place this treasyre atte the disposal and use of thee Lord's true

208

*servents as so vast a tresure the whych I doe assure Your
excellencie nor never in the tyme of her late Grace did come
into thisse realm beying twoe thousande pounds weght of
golde.*

*But as certyn shyps thee whych adhere to thee cause of his
Majestie make uncertain thee passage twixt Devonshyr and
London it seemeth to mee it were not wise to sendyth so
grete an cargo by see tho' thatte were in othyr time thee
suryst route. Wherforre will I brynge it mineself bye lande
untoe yr Excellencie thatte it maye serve wel as maibe thee
cause of thee Lorde and hys Righteouse tö bee of use and
servyce suche as seemeth wel to y'rselfe.*

*Writ by mine owne hand thee fyrst daye of August, the yr
of thee Lorde 1643.'*

So this was Charlie Ratcliffe's ace in the hole, thought Audley.
A copy of a copy of a letter from Colonel Nathaniel Parrott to
John Pym ... unsigned and unaddressed, but that was of no great
matter in the circumstances. It might be a forgery or it might
not, though with the run of the Earl of Dawlish's papers and
the technical expertise of the KGB's draughtsmen that might
never be established. It might even be genuine.

But it would serve as *wel as maibe* to make his case: 2,000
pounds of Spanish-American gold had been lost, and 2,000
pounds of Spanish-American gold had been found.

He looked up at Weston. "A poor speller, but an interesting
writer. Where did you find it?"

"On Henry Digby."

"And what else did you find?"

"Nothing else."

"Well then—that's all there was, I suppose."

"Don't play games with me, Audley." Weston's voice was
cold, but well-controlled. He wouldn't be a man to let anger get
the better of him ever. "You know who he obtained this from,
I take it?"

"Professor Stephen Nayler at Cambridge, I'd guess. I told
him to have a word with the Professor."

"The letter doesn't surprise you, then?"

"Not very much. I'd expect something like that to surface

209

sooner or later. I couldn't get it out of Nayler, but I suppose Sergeant Digby had a more persuasive manner than I have."

"So he was investigating the gold, not the murder."

"He was following my orders—" Audley lifted a finger quickly "—which didn't take him anywhere near the Ferryhill Industrial Estate, Superintendent. He must have gone there on a private matter."

Weston stroked his chin. "You seem to have changed your tune in the last few hours."

"I can play lots of different tunes on the same instrument."

"Aye, I can believe that. But I preferred the first tune. It sounded truer to my ear."

"That could very well be. I could play it again if you made it worth my while—just so long as you don't think you can force me to, that's all. Because you can't, you know."

"You don't think so?"

"Not a chance. I may not look it, but I'm top brass, Superintendant. And not in the Home Office, either. And Henry Digby's killers are dead, too."

"But not their killers."

Audley shook his head. "I can't give you them ... any more than I can give you James Ratcliffe's killer."

Weston pursed his lips. "What can you give me, then?"

"First we have to make our deal, Superintendent."

Weston shook his head. "I don't make deals."

"Better hear the deal before you turn it down. It won't stretch your conscience, I give you my word on that."

"I can listen."

"Off the record—the way I listened to you beside the Swine Brook?"

"No. After Ferryhill the case is altered." Weston shook his head again.

"I can close your mouth with the Official Secrets Act, man."

"I wouldn't bet on it."

Good for Weston, Audley thought approvingly. So long as there were policemen like him there would be no police state in Britain.

He nodded. "Very well, I'll just have to trust you, won't I?"

"That's up to you."

210

"Of course.... But then, you see, after Ferryhill the case is altered for me too, Superintendent. Because Henry Digby was my man at the time. So I have a score to settle too."

Weston stared at him thoughtfully, then away across the open field beyond the bandstand towards the children's playground. Finally his eyes came back to Audley.

"Off the record, then," he said.

"Thank you." Audley paused. "I have no proof for what I'm going to tell you, and I doubt if I could get it now. But I think I'm guessing right—at last."

"I understand." Weston nodded slowly.

"James Ratcliffe was killed in June by a Russian agent—KGB Second Directorate, Second Division, Ninth Section. Probably a man by the name of Tokaev, operating out of Paris at the time."

Weston's jaw tightened. "You knew this when you spoke to me last week?"

"No." Audley drew a deep breath. "I thought this was a domestic political matter—which in a sense it still is. Charlie Ratcliffe is a nasty little muck-raking revolutionary, and a lot of useful people have skeletons of one sort or another in their closets. If he became rich suddenly he'd have the resources to cause a lot of trouble—that's what I thought I was dealing with. And the trouble with me was ... that it didn't interest me one bit."

"Why not? A job's a job, isn't it?"

"Not for me. I'm a counter-intelligence expert, not a bloody little political errand boy. Besides, I'm not at all sure that a little muck-raking isn't a good thing—if the Americans sometimes go too far we usually don't go far enough. We're a bit too damn good at sweeping secrets under the carpet ... I've had the brush in my hands more than once, so I should know."

"I see. So you just went through the motions, eh?"

"More or less. To be honest, I thought the Double R Society was more interesting than Ratcliffe himself. I didn't think I could prove anything against him—and I never dreamed he was hooked in with the Russians."

"But your ... superiors knew better—yet they didn't tell you?"

Audley shook his head. "Frankly—I just don't know. They may just have had a suspicion, with no proof, and they wanted to see what I came up with. They certainly edited Ratcliffe's file, but I thought that was to remove some of the political dirt he'd uncovered. Because I doubt whether even he dares to print everything he digs up."

"Aye, there's still a law of libel. So you didn't do anything, is that it?"

"Oh, I set about trying to cause trouble for Charlie, in case he could be stampeded—lots of thrashing about was what it amounted to, with us doing the thrashing. There was an outside chance that one of his accomplices might crack. But if no one did . . . well, you can't win 'em all."

Weston's lip curled. "Yes. . . . And Henry Digby?"

This was the bitterest part, the price of stupidity that someone else had paid.

Another deep breath. "At a guess I'd say you'll be able to establish the killers as Irishmen, and maybe as suspected members of a Provo splinter group. But that won't mean a thing."

"No?"

"The KGB has men in every guerrilla outfit. They used these two to hit Digby, and then turned them into evidence for you. And you haven't a hope in hell of proving it. It'll be another dead end."

The only thing Weston couldn't control was that muscle in his jaw. The lips and the eyes were steady, but the jaw betrayed him. "Why Digby? Why not you?"

"They knew about Digby. They don't know about me."

"I see. Like the old story of King David and Uriah the Hittite— you put him in the forefront of the battle. Off the record, Audley —I hope that helps you sleep at night."

"Digby doesn't help me sleep—you're right there. But I didn't get him in the forefront of the battle, I thought I was putting him in the rear rank. I sent him to do a little gentle research into how Charlie Ratcliffe found his gold."

"And that killed him?"

"Yes, I suppose you can say that it did. I think he went to

212

Professor Nayler, and the Professor told him how Charlie Ratcliffe had done it."

"We can check on that."

"It's perfectly innocent, what Nayler told him. But I'd guess Nayler also told Charlie about him, and that frightened him."

"Why should it do that—if it was innocent?"

"Because Digby had been investigating the murder, and now he was investigating the gold. *And* he was an expert on the Civil War in his own right. Nobody else had those three qualifications."

"Qualifications for what?"

"For working out that the gold wasn't the Standingham treasure at all—that it *couldn't* be the real thing."

Jaw, eyes and mouth this time: Weston wasn't hiding anything.

"What d'you mean—the real thing?"

"It's horribly simple, man. You want to know why I'll always have Henry Digby on my conscience? Not because I was wicked, but because I was stupid, that's why. Because I had all the information too, that's why. I saw where Charlie Ratcliffe found the treasure. I suspected Charlie Ratcliffe of murder, even though I didn't know the KGB did the job for him. And I also know that Oliver Cromwell was one hell of a smart man—" Audley thrust the copy of the alleged copy of Nathaniel Parrott's letter to John Pym under Weston's nose. "If he knew —and I mean *knew*—there was a ton of gold in Standingham he'd have found it. And I'm betting he did find it, like the experts always said."

Weston waved the letter to one side. "That's . . . theory. You don't kill men for theories like that. Never in a million years."

"Right. Exactly right." Nothing would make Henry Digby's death less than bitter. But this was the beginning of the expiation. "And that's why the gold isn't the real thing: because it was found in the wrong order."

Weston frowned. "Wrong order? What wrong order?"

"Man—he had James Ratcliffe killed before he could possibly have known the gold was there. He had to bring in a bulldozer and grub up a damn great stone monument and two fully-grown apple trees—and even then he had to dig down fifteen feet before

213

he reached it. So he couldn't possibly have known it was there to start with, it had to be just a theory. He couldn't have been *sure*."

Weston's frown deepened. "But . . . he could have used one of those metal detectors. All the treasure-hunting people have them now, we've had complaints from landowners about them tramping over likely sites using the things—"

"At fifteen feet?" Audley shook his head emphatically. "No way, Superintendent. There isn't a detector made that can sniff metal at that depth, most of them don't get below the surface topsoil. Even the very latest induction-balance units—or pulse induction ones, come to that—they can't manage more than five feet, and they're tricky to handle if there's damp around or the temperature's wrong. He'd have needed proper mining equipment, and he'd never have got through the paving round the monument without making one hell of a mess—which the old gardener would have seen. I tell you, no way."

Weston stared at him, still unwilling to commit himself.

"It had to be a theory," Audley met the stare. "And you've made the rule for that yourself: you don't kill men for theories. Not even the KGB kills men on the off chance. They don't like off-chances—they like certainties. And there was only one way they could make it a certainty: they could supply it themselves. And that's what they did."

Still Weston wouldn't speak. The psychology of a ton of raw gold was too heavy for him. And that, thought Audley, was the measure of the KGB's shrewdness: figures with pound signs and dollar signs were mere abstractions, meaningless as the paper on which they were printed. Spend a hundred million pounds on a dying industry, or ten million on tarting up an obsolete warship, or strike as much off for a trade union squabble, and no one saw tons of gold flushed down the lavatory. But slap a single sovereign on the counter and you could catch everyone's eye: that was money.

So now it was beyond this shrewd man's understanding, that ton of gold. Spanish gold, still the rightful property of the Spanish people, stolen twice from them—and stolen before that from the poor sweating Indians who had hacked it out of the ground; Russian gold, a small price to pay for sowing subversion between

214

the decks of America's biggest aircraft carrier, still moored unsinkably off Europe.

Charlie Ratcliffe's gold.

Weston surfaced with an effort of will. "It was planted."

"Right. First dig the hole—then add the gold. Because with one ton of gold Charlie Ratcliffe can spread tons of trouble. And with what the Russians can feed him, plus what they can arrange for him, that's good business for them. The First Division of the Second Directorate spends ten times as much every year, with not a tenth as much chance of being believed."

"I see . . . or I'm beginning to see." The measure of Weston's intelligence was the speed with which he was adjusting himself to the new mathematics. "So—you had a deal for me."

"Yes. I don't want you following up Digby's death the way you might have done—I want them to think they've got away with it this time."

"For how long?"

"Until after the storming of Standingham Castle, no longer. If I fail . . . then you can do your best to prove what I've told you."

Weston nodded. "That seems fair enough. So I agree."

"And I shall want your help at Standingham. With no questions asked."

Weston looked at him sidelong. "I won't break the law. Not even for Henry Digby."

"I wouldn't dream of asking you to. I just need you to soften someone up for me, that's all."

"I can do that any time."

"Just this time, is all I want."

"To what end?"

"The other end of the deal, you mean?" No smile this time. This was a matter of vengeance. "I'm going to try and give you Charlie Ratcliffe—on a plate."

"How?"

"History, Superintendent Weston. They used history against us—now we're going to use it against them."

III

TEN MINUTES, WESTON had said. Half a day, or maybe never, for a guilty man, but for an innocent one only ten minutes.

There was a moral in that somewhere.

Audley watched the empty road ahead and wondered what it was like to be leaned on by Superintendent Weston. Probably it would be like being leaned on by an elephant, a remorseless pressure made all the more irresistible by the certainty that resistance was in vain: either the beast would stop of its own accord or that would be the flattening end of everything.

A movement at the roadside caught his eye. Police Constable Cotton was emerging from the Police House for his evening tour, majestic in his tall helmet, his height emphasised by the cycle-clips which tapered his trousers to drainpipes. A dull ache of guilt stirred in Audley's soul as he watched the constable cycle away. Less than a week ago he had sat at this very spot with Henry Digby, and those few days had been the rest of Digby's life. But nothing would change that now, the death sentence for Digby and the life sentence for Audley; not even vengeance, if he could manage it, would reverse those verdicts.

He locked the car and strolled down towards the Steyning Arms. At the corner there was a new temporary signpost, a handsome little poster on gold paper bearing a red hand pointing up the road and a boldly-printed legend in black:

Standingham Castle
Civil War Siege 1643, 3 p.m.–5.30 p.m.
17th Century Fair, 11 a.m.–7 p.m.
Adults 30p; children 15p
Sat August 30 & Sun August 31

It wasn't the first of such signs he had noticed, there was a rash of them for miles around. Nor indeed was it the only sign of the approaching hostilities and festivities. Stacks of POLICE—

216

NO PARKING cones were dotted in readiness round the village, balanced by cruder posters directing motorists to roped-off fields which were obviously about to yield their owners unexpected cash crops.

Even outside the Steyning Arms itself the coming siege was evident in a fresh notice:

NO VACANT ROOMS
CAR PARK RESERVED STRICTLY
FOR PATRONS AND GUESTS ONLY

Audley pushed through the hotel entrance door and advanced towards the reception desk.

The girl sitting in the office behind the desk didn't bother to look up from her nail polishing. "We're all booked up until Monday," she said to her left hand in a bored little pre-recorded voice.

"I don't want a room. I believe you have a Professor Stephen Nayler staying here," said Audley.

"Eh?" She stared at him as if he had made a lewd suggestion.

"What number room is Professor Stephen Nayler in?" said Audley conversationally.

"Oh... Number 10, up the stairs and turn left—" she answered before she realised what she was saying, then frowned at herself for being so unnecessarily helpful. It was a happy thought that next day several hundred rapacious cavaliers would be descending on her. He hoped they would behave with proper attention to historical authenticity, as they had done at Easingbridge, only more so.

The deep murmur of Weston's voice behind the door of Number 10 was stilled by his knock, but for a moment no one answered. Then another voice, high and familiar, answered.

"Come!"

The room had been a small one with no one in it. With Nayler it had grown smaller and with Weston it had become smaller still. But with the large detective sergeant who had accompanied Weston—a man with a marvellously brutal bog-Irish face which looked as if it had been carved out of soft stone and then unwisely exposed to the elements for a century or two—it must have been claustrophobic for those ten long minutes.

And now, as Audley eased the door shut behind him, it was the Black Hole of Calcutta.

"Audley!" Surprise and relief were mingled fifty-fifty in the exclamation. And for sure the elephant was the right animal: Nayler's aura was the shape and consistency of a Shrove Tuesday pancake.

"Good evening, Professor." Audley reserved his sharpest look for Weston. "Superintendent Weston—what brings you here?"

"Sir." Weston straightened up deferentially. "We're pursuing inquiries into certain matters."

This was a new Weston, subtly altered: it was Weston playing himself on television, not as he really was, but as the viewers might imagine him.

"Well, I didn't think you were paying a social call." Role for role, Audley played back. "The 'certain matters' are Sergeant Digby, I take it."

"That's correct, Dr Audley."

Audley pointed towards Nayler. "And just what has Professor Nayler got to do with him, may I ask?"

"That's for us to decide, if you don't mind, sir."

"But I do mind. I mind very much." It occurred to Audley that he was overplaying more than Weston was, but there was no help for it. "I'm not having you trampling around in this matter like a bull in a china shop. And I'm not having distinguished scholars like Professor Nayler bullied like this, either."

Weston gave a half-strangled grunt, the sort of baffled noise which Jack Butler produced in moments of excessive official stupidity. The brutish sergeant's face was a picture of perplexed ferocity: nothing like this had ever happened to him.

"I'm sorry, Professor," Audley turned towards Nayler. "There seems to have been some misunderstanding somewhere down the line. These officers will be leaving now."

Nayler was having the same trouble as the sergeant in adjusting to events; for once words failed him.

"Well, sir ... we have our duty to do." Weston was retreating in good order with his face to the foe, but clearly retreating nevertheless. "I shall have to consult my superiors about this... Sergeant!"

The sergeant gave him an appalled look and backed unwillingly out of the door which Audley held open for him.

"You do that, Superintendent," said Audley. "And you'd better tell them they should consult the Home Office before they try this sort of tactics next time."

He closed the door on them and lent against it thankfully, watching Nayler through half-closed eyes as he did so. This was the moment when the casting of his next role would be decided: it was up to Nayler to reward his deliverer or to remember old enmities.

"What an extraordinary bizarre episode," said Nayler to no one in particular. "I wouldn't have thought it possible."

No sign of gratitude, thought Audley. The man was quickly adjusting his self-esteem again as though nothing had happened, putting Weston's visit out of his mind as though it had been no more real than a nightmare.

"Yes...." Nayler wrinkled his nose and compressed his lips. "Quite extraordinary. And now what do you want, Audley?"

No gratitude for sure. Time had dealt too kindly with the bastard: where better men had lost their figures and their hair, Nayler's lankiness had aged into an acceptable scholarly stoop to which his thick pepper-and-salt thatch added distinction. Only that petulant mouth and the words which came out of it were unchanged.

"Well, Audley?" Nayler raised an eyebrow interrogatively. "I haven't got all night."

The hard way, then. And it was going to be a rare pleasure.

"You haven't got any time at all." Audley came away from the door. "You're in trouble, Nayler."

"What?" Nayler frowned. "What?"

"I said you're in trouble. Big trouble."

"And I don't like your tone." The lips compressed tighter. "You are beginning to sound like those—those two thugs masquerading as policemen, Audley."

"Oh, I'm not the same as them, don't make that mistake."

"I don't intend to, I assure you. Now—say what you came to

say and get out." Nayler waved his hand in a jerky, insulting little gesture of dismissal. "I have work to do."

"Very well. I believe you spoke to Henry Digby recently."

"I spoke to the fellow—yes—if that's his name."

"It was his name. Sergeant Henry Digby. He's dead now."

"So I gather. But that's absolutely no concern of mine. I spoke to the fellow about purely academic matters."

Audley felt his blood pressure rising, heated and reheated by the repetition of *fellow*.

"You spoke to Sergeant Digby about Standingham and the gold." With an effort Audley kept his voice neutral. "Now... could you please tell me what you told him, Professor?"

Nayler gazed at Audley for a moment, old memories flickering in his eyes. "Frankly, Audley, I don't see why I should."

"I see." Audley nodded humbly. "Professor, I explained that I wasn't the same as the police—"

"You did indeed." Nayler came in before he could continue, his confidence now fully restored. "And in consequence I can think of no reason why I should give you even the time of day."

That was just about perfect, thought Audley. If Nayler had read the script for a classic hard-soft-hard interrogation pattern he couldn't have played his part better than that.

"No? Well here's a reason, then." Audley looked at his watch. "If you don't answer my question in one minute from now—" he looked up "—I will arrest you—and I have ample authority to do that—and I will take you to the nearest police station, where you will be held under the Prevention of Terrorism Act until such time as I may charge you under the Defence of the Realm Act, or alternatively with impeding the course of justice. And I will further personally ensure that you are thereafter held in custody as being a person consorting, or likely to consort, with known agents of a foreign power engaged in a conspiracy to endanger the safety and security of the realm."

The colour drained out of Nayler's face.

"Fifteen seconds to go." Audley reached inside his jacket. "Here is my warrant card, which is issued under the joint authority of the Ministry of Defence and the Home Office."

"A foreign power?" Nayler whispered the words as though

only hearing them from his own lips would make them real to him.

"Time's up. Professor Stephen Adrian Nayler, I arrest you—"

"No—this is ridiculous!" Nayler squeaked.

"That's one thing it isn't. Professor Stephen Adrian Nayler—"

"I didn't mean that!" The jerky wave was abject now, not insulting. "I mean—I didn't understand—I didn't realise this was a matter of national security, Audley."

"Why the hell did you think I got rid of the police, you fool?" said Audley contemptuously. "For old times' sake?"

"I... no... I don't know." Nayler licked his lips. There was no room left on his face for anything except fear now. "But I didn't—"

"Shut up. And sit down, Professor."

Nayler sat down as though strings holding him up had been cut.

The very completeness of his collapse steadied Audley. This was how it must be in the Lubianka when the KGB man spoke; or how it had been in Fresnes when the Gestapo ruled there—

Saditye, Professor!

Setzen Sie sich, Professor!

The comparison wasn't flattering, it was sickening—not even the thought of Henry Digby could quite take the sickness away.

"Audley—I had no idea..." Nayler trailed off helplessly.

Audley swallowed. "You talked to Sergeant Digby about Standingham?"

"Yes." Nayler nodded.

"Did you tell anyone else about your conversation?"

"Only young Ratcliffe—" Nayler stopped abruptly as the implication of what he had said became clear to him. "Only... Ratcliffe," he repeated in a whisper.

"Why him?"

"Why..." Nayler blinked. "Well... I was surprised—I was worried that someone had come so close to our hypothesis about the storming of the castle... as the sergeant had done. He paused. "I mean, some of these amateurs are extremely knowledgeable—and he was a member of the Double R Society.... But it was disquieting nevertheless."

"Disquieting? Why was it disquieting?"

221

"Because we didn't want our secret to be known before the re-enactment of the battle—and my television programme. That would have spoilt the whole thing, you see. There would have been no surprise then. In fact there was no real danger of it, because after I'd spoken to the sergeant he promised not to leak his ideas, but I thought Ratcliffe ought to know about it even though there was no danger any more."

"Except to the sergeant," murmured Audley.

"I beg your pardon?"

So that was how Digby had made Nayler talk, thought Audley. By accident or design he had provided himself with the right lever.

"It doesn't matter. So what was your secret, then?" And there was another painful truth: young Digby had fashioned his lever out of pure knowledge, whereas clever David Audley had required the crude blunt instrument of the State bully.

"Our hypothesis?" Nayler's voice was almost back to normal. "Yes... well, how much do you know about the Standingham affair, Audley?"

"I've read what the Reverend Horatio Musgrave wrote about it, that's all."

"Indeed? Well, that's quite a lot really. In fact you might say that most of the basic clues are there... like one of those children's puzzles with the faces hidden in the picture, you might say."

"I've also assumed that Ratcliffe took his gold out of the site of the old crater, from under the monument. Is that correct?"

Nayler nodded. "Absolutely correct. A sort of double bluff—that was quite clever of you in the circumstances."

Double bluff, certainly. But not nearly clever enough, Audley thought sadly. Not clever at all.

"Yes, well we see it—that is, Ratcliffe and I see it—as a story of treachery and murder, Audley. Treachery and murder in a good cause perhaps, but nonetheless treachery and murder... Colonel Nathaniel Parrott was a very ruthless man as well as a brave one. He couldn't get the gold out of Standingham, but he couldn't allow it to fall into Royalist hands—it might have changed the whole course of the war. So it wasn't enough to hide it, he had to make sure no one survived to tell the tale."

"Meaning—he set the explosion?"

"Correct. It's possible that he and Steyning planned the explosion together, of course. But if so then Parrott contrived it prematurely, while all those who were privy to the burial were in the powder magazine, including Steyning. Or maybe they were in the shot-casting shed, which was next door, it doesn't matter."

"I see. So that was the murder. Where does the treachery come in?"

"Ah, well you'll remember what Musgrave said—what was it?—'Parrott took to horse and essayed to escape (and who shall cry "faint heart" or "treachery" in such an extremity?) . . .'. Even Musgrave suspected that Parrott was just a little too ready to break out, you see. That reference to treachery is an old tradition in the story, too. And there was also the fact that the Royalist forces did seem to be ready and waiting to attack at exactly that point, where the great cannon was dismounted by the explosion."

"So they'd been tipped off in advance?"

"It does very much look like that. They'd never tried to attack from that side before."

"Because of the great cannon?"

"No, not really. Steyning was always firing it, but he never hit anything—'he vexed us not at all', one of the Royalists wrote. No, it was because the valley bottom is marshy there, and with the field of fire in that open country they wouldn't have had a chance of getting across the marshy ground without taking unacceptable losses. But in the confusion after the explosion—and with Parrott trying to break out on the other side—well, with the preparations they'd made they got across before the defenders could react."

Audley nodded. "But then Black Thomas double-crossed Parrott in turn."

Nayler shrugged. "That, or perhaps the break-out went wrong and he ran into some Royalists who hadn't received the word. . . . But either way it does give the story a nice ironic twist at the end."

"It certainly does. And Sergeant Digby had worked all this out?"

"Most of it. He is . . . that is to say, he was . . . a rather shrewd

223

young fellow—for a policeman. But he was really more interested in the gold, I must admit. He wanted to know exactly how Ratcliffe had found it, he was very insistent on my telling him that."

"So you told him?"

Nayler sighed. "Well, in the circumstances I thought it prudent to do so. That was the other half of our secret, of course."

"And what did you tell him?"

Nayler blinked and didn't answer directly. "Well ... yes, well that began when Ratcliffe came to see me first."

"When was that?"

"Oh—" Nayler lifted his hand vaguely "—some time ago."

"When?"

Nayler looked distinctly unhappy. "About a year ago, it would be."

About a year ago. Long before James Ratcliffe's death, but after the sorting of the Earl of Dawlish's archives for the Historical Manuscripts Commission. And for a bet Professor Nayler knew both those harsh little facts, but had chosen to overlook them in his partnership with Charlie Ratcliffe.

Nor was that the only thing he had chosen to overlook, thought Audley with a sudden flash of understanding. It hadn't been simply their old mutual dislike that had closed Nayler's mouth: it had been a good old-fashioned bad conscience about more recent events.

"Of course." He nodded. "And he brought a letter with him—a very old letter."

Whereas of late have I suceeded to thee Estate whereof mine Fathyr was seised ...

"You know, then?" Nayler looked at him sidelong. "But of course you will have seen the sergeant's copy."

"Yes, I have. But I would have known anyway. You'd never have mixed yourself up in this just on Ratcliffe's word, there had to be proof of some kind. Was it a genuine letter?"

"It was a genuine seventeenth-century copy of a letter."

"To John Pym from John Dangerfield?"

"To John Pym, certainly. But it wasn't signed—it was obviously the author's copy."

224

"Didn't you want to know where Ratcliffe obtained it?"

Nayler's face screwed up with embarrassment. "He said he'd been given it. But he made me promise to keep that a secret until he was ready to reveal it."

There was no point in picking that sore at the moment. Nayler knew well enough how ugly it looked.

"So you knew the gold was there, then?"

Nayler stared fixedly at the carpet. "No, Audley, to be honest—I didn't."

"You—didn't?"

Nayler looked up. "I believed it had been there. I didn't believe it was there until Ratcliffe actually found it." He sighed. "Oh, I worked out with Ratcliffe where it might have been, and how it might have got there. But I never believed it was there until he found it."

"Why not?"

"Because I thought Cromwell had found it in '53, that's why. It takes money to make a revolution, and he needed money to make his. Not to mention making war with everyone in sight. . . . He needed money—and he went to Standingham for it. 'He made great excavation in that place', that's what the record says. So I told Ratcliffe the odds were a hundred to one against him, letter or no letter. And I was wrong."

Audley shook his head. "I've got news for you, Professor. You weren't wrong."

Nayler stared at him, humility melting into surprise, surprise yielding to horror. "Oh, my God!" he said. "Oh—my—God."

This wasn't the face of the Gestapo victim, thought Audley; this was the proud man who saw himself a laughing-stock among his peers, and that made them both brothers under the skin.

He grinned at Nayler encouragingly. "You and me both, Nayler," he said. "Two high IQ's equal one big zero. Because I was wrong too."

The grin wasn't catching. "What are we going to do?" asked Nayler.

What indeed!

Audley thought of Superintendent Weston, who would do anything he was asked to do, short of breaking the laws by which he lived.

And then of Robert Davenport, who had all the resources of the CIA and would exchange most of them for getting himself and the agency off the hook.

And then of Frances Fitzgibbon and Paul Mitchell, who would do exactly what they were told, but would report back to someone what they had done.

And even of William Strode, officer commanding the Round-head Army, who would serve the cause of law and order in the cause of social democracy and a better prospective Parliamentary seat.

And now Professor Stephen Nayler, who probably thought he had most to lose—and certainly knew more about the storming of Standingham Castle than anyone else alive, Charlie Ratcliffe included.

And finally David Audley, who wasn't nearly as sharp as he'd thought he was—

No. Not finally David Audley.

Finally Sergeant Henry Digby, who was to be avenged.

He nodded at Professor Nayler. "I think we might manage something nasty between us," he said.

IV

Audley raised the perspective glass to his eye and watched Paul Mitchell guide his horse down the steep side of the earthworks which marked the line of the Old Castle across the valley.

Somebody had taught the boy to ride well, he thought enviously. But then whatever Paul Mitchell did, he did well, and whatever Jack Butler might think of the resemblance between the young bull and the old bull, Mitchell would go further up the ladder than Audley. Twenty years from now, barring wars and revolutions, he wouldn't be mere top brass, he'd be the boss-man; he had the cold heart for it.

But twenty years was twenty years away from today, and today he was a gorgeous messenger boy playing Cavaliers and Roundheads at the Double R Society's dress rehearsal of the storming of Standingham Castle, no less and no more.

Beside him on the rampart the Parliamentary banners stirred in the breath of the early evening breeze which had forsaken them during the hottest hours of the day; and below him, beyond the ditch and the glacis, the first of the regiments of the Parliamentary battle-line began to debouch from the trees on his right.

> *Who would true valour see,*
> *Let him come hither—*

"Not much of a marching song, but they're in good voice," said William Strode. "They make a brave show, think ye not?"

"Aye, Sir Matthew. I doubt not they shall give a good accounting of themselves this day," said Audley.

Away from across the valley, but still hidden and muted by the earthworks, an insistent drumming commenced—

Tarr-rumpa-tumpa-*tum*, tarr-rumpa-tumpa-*tum*, tarr-rumpa-tumpa-rumpa-tumpa-*tum-tum-tum* ...

Strode smiled at him and nodded approvingly. "That's very

good, Audley—you're learning. You just missed one thing, though."

Mitchell urged his horse into the marshy bottom of the valley, where the Willow Stream meandered sluggishly between barely defined banks which would have been bright with king-cups earlier in the year but which now carried little to betray its treacherous swampiness. It had come as a shock to the advance party that the openness of this approach to the Royalist stronghold was an illusion; they had found out the hard way why every attack but the last one had been delivered up the other side of the defences. And they had laboured mightily all the afternoon to lay corduroys of brushwood to give the assault columns access to the firm ground of the rampart ridge; as no doubt Black Thomas Monson's engineers had once had to do themselves. . . .

The horse plunged and high-stepped frantically for a minute or two in the ooze, sending Mitchell lurching from one side of the saddle to the other. But he held his seat admirably and with a final effort the animal heaved itself out to the boos and yells of the Parliamentary infantry, who had obviously been hoping for an early Royalist setback.

"What did I miss?" inquired Audley.

The drums sounded a final elaborate tattoo and then settled down to a steady marching beat—

Tum, tum, tum-tum-*tum.*

Tum, tum, tum-tum-*tum—*

Up on the skyline of the old earthwork, as though growing out of the ground, came the battle-flags of the enemy.

"You left out God," said Strode. " 'By God's grace' you should have added."

The breeze caught the flags, opening them gaily above the long lines of men who rose out of the earth beneath them: musketeers, pikemen, officers with drawn swords . . . bright sashes and scarves and the sunflash of polished steel helmet and breast-plate. The opposing hillside was transformed from the parched green of a hot August to a blaze of colour.

Tum, tum, tum-tum-*tum—*

"Of course," said Audley. " 'When I saw the enemy march in gallant order towards us, and we a company of poor ignorant men, I could not forbear but to cry out to God in praise for the assurance of victory, because God would, by those things that are not, bring to naught those things that are'—will that do?"

Strode laughed. "Bravo! Cromwell at Naseby—almost word for word. You have an excellent memory, Audley."

"Yes. Except that Cromwell's 'poor ignorant men' outnumbered the Royalists two to one, I seem to remember."

"Very true. Whereas we're due for a licking today—or tomorrow, to be exact," admitted Strode. "But it's a splendid showing, you must admit that. We've already got a turn-out of nearly seven hundred—and that's not counting the Angels and the Royalist camp-followers. And there'll be more by later this evening when the muster's complete, so I think we'll give everyone something to remember Standingham by—wouldn't you say?"

Mitchell had wheeled his horse at the foot of the ridge and had trotted to the extreme right of the Parliamentary line. Now he wheeled again and galloped the whole length of it insolently, to a barrage of boos and catcalls, until he was level with the corner bastion on which the Parliamentary standard flew.

"Yes, I think we might at that," agreed Audley.

With a flourish Mitchell produced a large white handkerchief above his head.

"Parley! Parley" he shouted.

Strode leaned over the top of the bastion to call to a mounted Roundhead—the same trooper, thought Audley, who had advanced across the bridge at Easingbridge.

"Galloper!" Strode's voice was properly military now. "I pray you approach that gentleman and bid him advance under truce, according to the customs and usages of war."

The galloper saluted and spurred forward, up the worn side of the counterscarp and down the glacis towards Mitchell.

Strode turned to the officer on his left, who was busy checking the typed scenario against a very twentieth-century stop-watch.

"How's the timing going, Johnny?" he asked.

"Four and a half minutes extra, crossing the stream. We shall have to allow for that—and it'll take their footmen longer too."

"Very good." Strode stared down at the two horsemen now approaching. "Gentlemen ... hats and helmets on, please. This is a full-dress rehearsal, remember."

229

Discipline was as tight in the Double R Society as Superintendent Weston could have wished, thought Audley bitterly as he adjusted the uncomfortable lobster-tailed helmet. Nobody had demurred when Strode had ordered full costume for the afternoon. The general was the general, and that was that; his officers made suggestions, but once an order was given it was obeyed to the letter.

In fact he had already made the interesting discovery that a heavy leather buff-coat, with or without breast-plate, wasn't quite as bad as he'd expected: once a man started to sweat in it (which was within two minutes of putting it on) it trapped the sweat and delayed the dehydration a thin shirt would have accelerated. So even though the salt tablets which the Angels of Mercy had brought round were necessary, the discomfort was endurable.

But the lobster-tailed helmet was purgatory, especially since the hinged face-bars (which refused to stay up in the raised position) made him feel as though he was looking out at the world through the bars of a prison window. Paul Mitchell could just as correctly have provided him with a black wide-brimmed hat like the one Strode was wearing—it was more than likely that Mitchell had deliberately chosen the helmet, therefore. But all he could do was thank heaven that it was the half-armoured Civil War and not the fully-armoured Wars of the Roses which had taken this generation's fancy.

The horsemen checked on the lip of the counterscarp, almost at the same height as the bastion. Mitchell quietened his horse with a caress and swept off his plumed hat.

"Sirs—I give you good day," he called across the ditch.

Sir Edmund Steyning's hat remained on his head.

"Sir—say thou what thou camest to say. And then get you gone to the place whence you are come," he called back in a loud, harsh voice obviously designed to carry to the battle-line.

"Sir—I will." Mitchell raised his voice to match Steyning's.

The drumming on the hillside had stopped and the murmur of conversation among the Roundheads hushed. Even the wind seemed to have caught the sense of occasion, dying down so that the flags dropped on their poles.

"I am sent—" the voice rose to a shout "—to summon you . . .

to deliver into the hands of the Lord General appointed by his Gracious Majesty...the House wherein you are, and your ammunition, with all things else therein...together with your persons, to be disposed of as the Lord General shall appoint... the same to receive fair quarter, save only those officers of quality who shall surrender to mercy.... Which, if you refuse to do, you are to expect the utmost extremity of war."

The twentieth-century had slipped away unnoticed, dying with the breeze. On this very ground the English had killed the English, and if that had been the original summons then killing had been the intention, for 'surrender to mercy' was only a hair's breadth away from 'no quarter'.

Audley felt the sweat cold inside his buff-coat. This was what Civil War meant; brother against brother, neighbour against neighbour, north against south, you against me.

Steyning took a pace forward, to the edge of the crumbling parapet, and pointed at the horseman. "Thy master hath shown himself to be—truly—the Beast of the Abomination...and thou art but the serpent's tongue that spits the venom." He paused. "I for my part shall abide by the Lord God, by true religion and by the just cause of Parliament unto my life's end."

The horseman turned in a full circle, sweeping his hat to cover the Parliamentary line.

"Then these men shall perish by thy means—as thou art prodigal of thy blood, so thou art prodigal of theirs. For God shall give you all into our hands, and we will not spare a man of you when we put you to the storm."

Steyning lent forward. "Then shall men say—'Your storm—your shame; our fall—our fame'. Depart, thou accursed!"

The horseman waved his plumed hat, jerked at his bridle and galloped back down the slope, the hooves throwing up gobbets of earth. As he passed between two of the Parliamentary regiments he let out a wild shrill cry—an obscene mixture of triumph and glee and menace.

Christ! thought Audley, shocked out of his trance: he had heard the famous Confederate yell in a peaceful English valley. But maybe it was no anachronism at that, for Prince Rupert's cavaliers and Jeb Stuart's cavalry had ridden the same path down history into legend.

"I hope the young bugger falls arse over tip," said one of Strode's officers vehemently. "He wasn't fooling then."

Audley watched Mitchell struggle through the mud, praying for that very disaster. But the man and the horse had both required only the one lesson.

"Quicker that time," said the stop-watch man, clicking the button with his thumb and noting the time on his scenario. "But I'll allow four extra minutes to be on the safe side."

A stocky young man in a loose white shirt, a curious tasselled forage cap on his head, appeared on the edge of the counterscarp where Mitchell had been. He swept off the cap and bowed to Strode.

"Sir. The ordnance awaits your pleasure," he said.

"Another five minutes," murmured the stop-watch man. "Their guns aren't in position yet."

Strode nodded. "Patiently, Master Rodgers. Do thou await our signal." He smiled again at Audley. "Billy Rodgers always likes to get off the first shot against the Malignants," he confided.

"We go down to the field now," prompted the stop-watch man.

"Gentlemen—" Strode gestured to the left and the right "—in God's name let us look to the ordering of the battle."

Audley lifted the lace at his wrist to check his illegal wrist-watch. It was time at last for him to look to the ordering of his own battle too.

He touched Strode's arm. "Mr Strode, I must speak to Charles Ratcliffe now—at once."

Strode ran his eye along the battle line. "He's down there on the right with his regiment, Dr Audley."

"But I must speak to him up here, alone." Audley pointed along the ramparts towards the Great Bastion. "There, say—on the redoubt by the big gun."

Strode frowned. "The bastion's off limits, Audley."

"I know. That means we won't be disturbed. It's vitally important I speak to him."

Strode looked from Audley to the battle line, then to the roped-off area of the redoubt, and finally back to Audley again. "Oh—very well, Audley. You've called your dogs off, so I owe you the other side of the bargain, I suppose. . . . *Galloper!*"

The Roundhead horseman, who had remained on the counterscarp in readiness for further orders, raised his hand in salute. "Sir!"

Strode pointed towards the right of the line. "I pray you, carry my compliments to Colonel Ratcliffe together with this strict order: I charge him to repair with the utmost despatch on this instant to the Great Bastion, there to receive of one of my officers further intelligence concerning my will and pleasure."

"Sir! The galloper wheeled away down the slope.

Strode turned back to Audley. "But don't keep him too long. He's in command of the right wing, and although we're not actually fighting today I do want him down there to see that angry brigade of his obeys orders—they're a damned quarrelsome lot."

Audley saluted. "I shalln't keep him long, sir. And then, by your leave, I shall strictly attend your grace once more upon the field of battle."

There was a puff of smoke and a bang from the ridge opposite. The first of the Royalist guns had been brought into action ahead of the scenario's schedule.

Audley put his telescope to his eye and focused on the Roundhead guns just in time to see Billy Rodgers shaking his fist first at the enemy, and then at his own general.

Tum, tum, tum-tum-*tum*—

The Royalist musketeers were advancing towards the stream, pacing themselves with their musket rests, their ammunition bandoliers dancing. Now the whole elaborate ritual of the seventeenth-century fire-fight was about to begin, with the rival sergeants intoning the long sequence of orders—'Blow off your coal', 'Cock your match', 'Guard, blow and open your pan' and so on—which preceded each volley, and which according to Strode was an enormous favourite with the watching crowds.

Now too there was movement in the Roundhead ranks as their musketeers detached themselves to the sound of drum-and-fife—

Tumpty-*tum,* tumpty-*tum,* tumpty-*tum*—

Charlie Ratcliffe was coming up the hillside, from the right.

Audley swept the telescope to the far left, where the militia regiments were lined up in the shadow of the trees, next to the guard ropes which would keep the spectators off the battlefield tomorrow.

Superintendent Weston was watching him like a hawk.

He snapped the telescope shut and started along the rampart towards the Great Bastion. He could just make out the top of the red powder-tent in the crater behind it.

Red for danger.

Tum, tum, tum-tum-*tum—*

Charlie Ratcliffe was there ahead of him, scrambling up the half-ruined rampart wall with the agility of a monkey and ducking under the restraining rope.

DANGER!
Authorised persons only
may proceed beyond this point

Under the broad-brimmed black hat the face was shadowy, but as Audley approached him he lifted it off and shook his fair hair free in the fitful breeze.

Fair hair, blue eyes, high colour—the English subaltern face *par excellence,* like a million others which stared out of group photographs on the walls of school studies and regimental messes, betraying nothing except self-confidence.

"What's all this then?"

"Master Ratcliffe? Master Charles Neville Steyning-Ratcliffe? Or should I say Colonel Ratcliffe?"

"Who are you?"

"Colonel Hog, you might call me, if I'm to call you Colonel Ratcliffe." Audley felt a trickle of perspiration run down the side of his face inside his cheek-guard. "Hog would be your seventeenth-century name for me."

"Hog?" The blue eyes were bright with intelligence, but just a shade too close together. "I see! 'Hog' in the seventeenth century, so presumably 'Pig' in the twentieth—is that it?"

"Very good! I can see we're going to understand each other very nicely. But I'm a special breed of Pig, just as you are an unusual variety of Rat. And we do have one or two very important things in common which should help us to understand each other."

"You don't say?" A good education had taught Charlie Ratcliffe the art of being insolent without trying. "Such as what?"

"Gold, for one thing."

Charlie Ratcliffe cocked his head on one side. "Do we have that in common? Well, that's news to me. I didn't think it was gold that pigs wallowed in, you know."

A sudden ragged volley of musketry burst out below them in the valley.

"Ah! Now the battle's starting," murmured Audley, looking at his watch. "And not more than five minutes behind schedule, too.... Yes, gold is one thing—see those fellows down there?" He took a casual step sideways and caught Ratcliffe's left arm in a tight grip just above the elbow. "I think it would be as well if we pretended to watch them."

Ratcliffe tried to move his arm, wincing as the grip bit. "You're hurting my arm," he said in a surprised voice.

"Yes, I know I am. But the pain will help to concentrate your mind on what I'm saying—please don't struggle, you'll only hurt yourself more."

Charlie Ratcliffe graduated quickly from surprise to incredulity. "You're a fucking madman—ouch!"

"No I'm not. But I am very strong, and if you don't relax and listen I'll cripple you." Audley pointed with the telescope in his free hand. "Now—see those pikemen with the blue flag? They make a brave show, don't they?" He increased the pressure. "Don't they?"

"Yes—bloody hell!—yes."

"Good. First gold, as I was saying. Then treason. Then murder. And then gold again. That's what we've got in common, Charlie lad."

"You're crazy."

"Next time you say that I'm going to hurt you a lot, Charlie. So just look to the front and listen. What I have to say is very much in your interest, I promise you that."

Charlie gritted his teeth. "You have to be joking."

"Joking is the very last thing I'm doing. I don't like you, lad —but I need your help. And you need mine—look to the front!"

Charlie made the start of a sound and the first twitch of a movement, and then thought better of both. It was beginning to occur to him that if this was madness he was dealing with there might be method in it.

"Your gold first. I know all about it, from A to Z. I know where it came from, and how it was planted—understand?"

"I don't know what you're talking about."

"Madrid-Cartagena-Tunis-Odessa-Moscow. . . . Standingham."

Ratcliffe still managed to register a proper mystification, but he couldn't control the muscles in his arm.

"I know how you set up Nayler, and I know about the Dawlish letter. And about the Paris meeting, and the other little side-trips—I know about them."

The muscles were like whipcord now, tensed under his hand so that he had to tighten his grip to hold them.

"And I know about Swine Brook Field—that was my old friend Tokaev I presume—and about the Ferryhill Industrial Estate . . . which was a very much better organised operation— the police haven't tumbled to it, I can tell you that. And you did me a good turn there too, getting rid of that nosey Special Branch man—I'm grateful for that."

The musketeers' fire-fight was reaching its climax, with the dead being carried away behind the clumps of pikemen to recover surreptitiously and rejoin their regiments as reinforcements. Death in the early stages of a Double R Society battle was clearly a tidy and economical business.

"But I'm not going to bore you with what you already know, lad. Your treason doesn't interest me any more—nor the murders you've ordered either. It's my treason that interests me now—and the next killing. And *my* gold."

Charlie Ratcliffe grunted derisively. "So it's your gold now, is it?" He shook his head.

"My gold—yes."

"Oh, no . . . I haven't the faintest idea what you're talking about with your treason and your killing, and all that— hogwash. . . . But when it comes to gold at least I can begin to understand you. And the answer is—go take a running jump at yourself, fuzz."

"You haven't heard the deal yet."

236

"I don't need to." Charlie's confidence was reasserting itself, despite the arm-grip. "I should have expected greedy fuzz—or whatever you are. Just because you've got a good imagination you think you can make things awkward for me, so I have to buy you off—is that it?"

"I've got a lot more than a good imagination."

"No way." Charlie shook his head. "Your bunch would like to smear me, I know that. But it takes proof to do that, and proof is what you haven't got. And the same goes for blackmail on the side—I'll enjoy giving you a paragraph or two all to yourself in my next issue, Colonel Hog. Not that it'll surprise anyone—crooked fuzz working for a crooked establishment."

"You think I'm bluffing?"

"I think I'd like you to let go of my bloody arm—you're hurting me almost as much as you're boring me."

Audley held the pressure steady. "That's because you don't listen, Charlie lad. That's one trouble with you—you talk, but you don't listen. And another trouble is ... you're not nearly as clever as you think you are."

"I have trouble figuring out how pigs think—if they do—*ouch!*"

"That's enough now. Just listen ... I have a deal for you and I have proof for you—and the proof is in the deal. *Listen!*"

His urgency transmitted itself at last. Charlie Ratcliffe stared fixedly into the valley, where the Roundhead musketeers were beginning to withdraw slowly towards their battle line. On the Royalist side, under the cover of their own guns, pioneers were carrying bundles of brushwood towards the marshy ground. The next phase of the battle was beginning.

"I don't want your Russian gold, Charlie—you can do whatever mischief you like with it, I don't give a damn. Because you did your seventeenth-century research just a bit too well, but not well enough, that's why—and I did it better."

Charlie moved uncontrollably, twisting against the pressure. "What the hell d'you mean by that?"

"I mean, lad—you can keep the Russian gold. *And I'll keep the Spanish gold.*" Audley released the arm abruptly as he spoke.

Charlie stared at him.

And stared.

Audley nodded slowly, letting himself smile at last. "That's right . . . I've found it." He paused to let the words sink in. "You see, Charlie, you worked it out—you and Professor Nayler worked it out between you." He paused again. "But the difference between us was that when you'd worked it out you didn't have to look for it, you just had to work out why it was where you intended to put it . . . which you did remarkably well. In fact you had me convinced it was the real thing.

"So when I . . . found out where your gold really came from I couldn't resist going back over your evidence again—to see if there was a hole in it somewhere—a weakness. And of course there was."

Charlie Ratcliffe frowned, and the frown seemed to loosen his tongue at last.

"A weakness—?"

"Oh yes . . . Nayler saw it too, only the gold blinded him to it—quite understandably. But that isn't the point. The point is —I came up with a different answer. The right answer."

Charlie's tongue had stuck once more: his lips moved, but no word escaped before they closed again.

"That's why I don't want your gold, Charlie. Because—you could say—I've already got your gold." Audley showed his teeth between the smile. "Which is really quite amusing, because there isn't a thing you can do about it. I mean . . . you can't find the same treasure twice, can you? That's something neither of us can afford now—too much gold would be as bad as none at all."

He turned away from Charlie, focusing the little telescope on the battle lines beneath them. With the help of the brushwood which had been trodden into the ooze earlier in the day the Royalist pioneers were making good progress with their causeway. Another five minutes, or ten at the outside, and the assault troops would be able to move.

"And that's where you come in, lad," he continued, casually running his eye along the Roundhead line. There was Robert Donaldson, Bible in hand, praying on his knees to the Lord of Hosts just behind the Roundhead guns; and there was little Frances among the band of Angels in the shadow of the trees on his left, watching him; and there, staring at him through his binoculars from his post just inside the wood, was Superintendent Weston.

"You see, we've each got our gold, but if we don't do something about it we're each going to lose it, I suspect."

"Why?" Charlie Ratcliffe's voice was thicker than it had been.

"Why?" Audley's eye ran back along the battlefield. The man had to be there somewhere, but he could no longer afford to wait for him. "See there—behind your cannon—like a black crow?"

"Why?"

"I'm trying to tell you. See that man in black down there?"

Charlie Ratcliffe glanced quickly towards the Roundhead guns, then back at Audley. "Bob Davenport, you mean?"

"Right—and wrong." Audley lowered the telescope, reaching under his buff-coat for his trouser pocket with his free hand. "Name of Donaldson. Operates out of the CIA's station in the Hague normally, but working with our people at the moment." He offered the telescope to Ratcliffe. "He's been watching you for months."

Charlie raised the telescope to his eye.

"And watching both of us today, but me particularly," continued Audley. "Agent Donaldson is just beginning to have his doubts about me, I rather think. . . . So please don't stare at him too hard."

Charlie lowered the telescope.

"One American passport, in the name of Donaldson." Audley passed the green book over for Charlie's inspection. "Lifted by me out of his flat yesterday afternoon. Check the picture . . . and the dates of the Channel crossings."

Charlie flipped the pages of the passport.

"So what?" he said harshly.

"So Agent Donaldson knows too much about you. And he suspects too much about me." Audley paused again. "And what is even worse he's on the way to suspecting too much about our gold."

"How d'you know?"

"Because I've been working with him. All he needs is one cosy talk with Professor Nayler and he'll have everything I've

239

got . . . which talk is scheduled for this evening To be precise—" Audley raised his lace cuff "—in exactly thirty-five minutes from now."

He took the passport from Charlie's hand. "So you see, Charlie, if our gold is to be preserved one of them has got to go. And for my money it's got to be Agent Donaldson. So you're going to kill him for me."

Charlie's mouth opened, but Audley forestalled him. "Oh, not you personally, lad. You must get one of those nursemaids of yours to do the dirty work for you—Oates or Bishop, I don't mind which. There's not the slightest risk involved, because I've pulled all our people off the three of you, as you may already have noticed. . . . All they have to do is to follow my instructions and it won't take a second—I set it all up for them last night."

The distinctive beat of the Royalist drums broke out again on the far hillside, but this time more fiercely—

Tum, tum, tum-tum-*tum*—

"Set up what?"

"A shocking accident." Audley nodded towards the red tent. "The Double R Society is about to have another tragedy."

"You're mad."

"No." Audley let the edge of desperation show. "If I was mad I'd risk doing it myself. It's because I'm sane that I'm determined to be in the clear. It's got to be one of your men who does it—we'll never have another chance like this. So it's now or never."

Tum, tum, tum-tum-*tum*—the columns of pikemen were beginning to assemble.

"Donaldson thinks he's meeting Nayler in the powder tent at half-past five exactly—when everyone's busy with the battle." Audley nodded. "And that's exactly where I intend to be—busy with the battle—when it happens."

"When what happens?"

"There's a First Aid box in the tent, right next to the black powder charge for tomorrow's explosion. Last night I put a fifteen-minute time pencil in the box—a grey plastic cylinder, to arm it all your man has to do is twist the head anti-clockwise and press it down. He'll know, anyway—it's standard CIA

240

issue." He smiled coldly at Charlie. "That was another thing I lifted from Donaldson's flat. . . . So that's all there is to it: twist and press at 5.15, and we both keep our gold. Or do nothing—and we both keep nothing. That's the deal."

He gave Charlie one last hard look to go with the ultimatum, and then turned away towards the parapet to examine the progress of the assault.

It was obvious at a glance why the Double R Society found it necessary to rehearse their major operations; the fire-fight had gone according to schedule, and the pioneers had wallowed in the mud to good effect, but the conversion of the lines of pike-men into columns was proving more difficult in practice than in theory.

Also, with the advance of the first regiments on to the newly-laid causeways, it was becoming apparent that the width of the column was greater than the width of the causeways.

As he watched, several of the outer files were jostled into the mire, where they quickly discovered that it was one thing to negotiate eight inches of mud unencumbered, but quite another to do so in full seventeenth-century battle order carrying a twelve-foot pike. Nothing could have more effectively illustrated why their ancestors hadn't attacked on this side of the defences until they were confident that treachery would even the odds.

He took a few paces towards the side of the bastion, where the remains of an embrasure still marked the spot from which old Edmund Steyning had intended that the defenders should enfilade any Royalists who might get as far as the ditch below the curtain wall. Not even Sebastian de Vauban could have sited it better, nor could Vauban have used the ground better to shape a peaceful manor house into a fortress. The old warrior had deserved a kinder fate than a kinsman's betrayal, no matter what the good cause.

He turned on his heel and faced Charlie, the great cannon between them now, with its flanking pyramids of weathered cannonballs.

"Time's up. Am I your partner? Or do I go back to Robert Donaldson and tell him the meeting's off?"

Charlie watched him intently, brushing nervously at a strand of fair hair which kept falling across his eyes. Audley conjured up the image of Henry Digby, and hardened his heart with the memory. "You still have a problem?"

"That would be one way of putting it." Charlie gave up trying to discipline the lock. "I find you . . . intriguing, as pigs go. But hardly believable."

"No?" Audley stepped forward and placed both hands on the cannon. Then he lent towards Charlie. "You find greed unbelievable—and you know the feel of gold? I find that even harder to believe."

Charlie shook his head. "Oh—not your greed, that I can accept. I can even understand why you're so pig-scared of your own side that you have to give yourself a perfect alibi."

"That's true—I admit it. But then I'm still risking my life for my gold. You only stand to lose your gold and spend a few years in jail."

"Your gold . . . your gold. . . ." Suddenly Charlie's expression hardened "Why should I believe in your gold? Why should I believe one single word you've said?"

"Why?" Audley drew a deep breath "Well, I'll tell you why. . . . Because your ancestor Edmund Steyning was an artillery expert by profession—a trained gunner."

"So what?"

Audley straightened up. "So he brought his biggest gun—*this* gun—" he slapped the cannon sharply with the palm of his hand "—and he put it in the one place where it would be absolutely useless."

Charlie frowned. "What d'you mean?"

"Isn't it obvious?" Audley pointed out across the valley towards the earth ramparts of the old castle on the far hillside. "Four hundred yards as the crow flies—that would be point-blank range for this gun. Even the smallest field-pieces could carry far further than that. . . . So it's wasted here—there wasn't anything to fire at anyway: this wasn't the vulnerable side, this wasn't where the Royalist siege works were, or their batteries."

"But this was where they attacked in the end—" Charlie answered automatically, as though he didn't know why he was arguing.

"A surprise attack. So how long d'you think it takes to load and fire this gun? Five minutes—ten minutes? Man, you'd be lucky to get ten shots an hour out of a monster like this—and even if you did you wouldn't hit anything."

"Why not?"

"Because it's too big to depress the angle of the barrel down the glacis. All he could do was fire straight ahead—" Audley pointed his finger across the valley "—and that's what Edmund Steyning did for a whole week: he fired point blank into a great bank of wet earth and *vexed* nobody. Except that he vexed Black Thomas Monson and Oliver Cromwell when they came to look for Nathaniel Parrott's ton of gold and found that it had vanished into thin air. And they didn't find it inside the castle defences because it wasn't inside any more—it was outside."

Charlie Ratcliffe was staring at the old castle as though hypnotised by its grassy banks.

Audley came round the rear of the cannon and stood at his shoulder. "The night before last I took an electronic metal probe and worked all along there," he murmured. "And after an hour it started to sing like a nightingale to me.... See that scar of earth spread in the middle there—about half-way along—like a big rabbit-hole? They're planted all around there, most of them, not more than three-foot deep, so far as I can make out ... I dug a couple out from there, anyway." He paused for a second. "Because I thought you might like to see a sample."

Charlie turned his head quickly. "A sample?"

"Call it a souvenir, if you prefer. Or even a present." Audley smiled. "I shall have enough for my modest needs, so I can spare you one—if not a present, say a down-payment?"

He lifted his sword-scabbard and jabbed hard at the topmost cannonball on the pyramid in front of them.

The ball quivered very slightly in its concrete socket.

"Forty-pounders—or something more, seeing that this one isn't like the others," said Audley. "I rolled the original one into the ditch."

He held the scabbard in both hands and ran the metal tip of it down the dirt encrusted surface. "A very proper token from

243

one traitor to another—in the best tradition, wouldn't you say?"

The scabbard-tip began to bite deeper into the encrustation as it travelled down the arc of the ball towards its widest circumference, until finally it dislodged a whole flake of dirt.

Under the dirt, bearing the bright new scratch of the scabbard-tip in its softness, lay pale gold.

EPILOGUE

A Skirmish near Westminster

SOMETIMES IT WAS better not to know a man too well, decided Audley. For just as inevitability took all the fun out of victory, so it removed the blessing of hope out of approaching disaster.

But there it was: Sir Frederick Clinton was standing under the John Singer Sargent portrait of Rear-Admiral Sir Reginald Hall, the greatest of all of his predecessors, with a glorious blaze of gladioli in the fireplace behind him and a welcoming smile on his lips, as he was accustomed to do before putting in the boot.

"David—good of you to drop in—sit down. . . . And how was Washington?"

Setzen Sie sich, Herr Audley!

"Too hot."

Like this office.

"Yes, you're a cold weather mortal, aren't you! Next time we'll have to find somewhere cooler for you. . . . But we've been having it quite warm here, you know, as a matter of fact."

Too many double meanings there for comfort.

"So I've gathered," said Audley.

Clinton sat down. "Well, I've been reading your reports—"

Plural.

"—the CIA one is most interesting." Clinton paused. "And the Ratcliffe one . . . that's interesting too. What you might call a satisfactory conclusion, fiscally speaking."

Obviously he was expected to fight to the end, thought Audley. He shrugged. "We were lucky."

"Ye-ess . . . I'm inclined to think you were."

Audley smiled back at him. "The Minister said I was lucky. He'll be glad to know I'm still on form." Put that one in your pipe, Fred, and see how it tastes. "It's a great virtue—luck."

"But not everyone would say you'd been virtuous."

"Not everyone would say I'd been given a fair chance. Little Tommy Stocker didn't exactly confide in me at the briefing."

247

Clinton shook his head. "Ah, now that's not quite fair. We hadn't the faintest idea Ratcliffe's gold wasn't genuine. And we had no proof of the Moscow connection either."

But a suspicion, Audley thought bitterly. And a suspicion would have made all the difference to Henry Digby.

"So this is another one we owe to the CIA, then?"

"Indirectly, you might say." Clinton had had almost enough of sparring now. "But then they did break the rules, didn't they."

"What rules?"

"Ye-ess, from you that's a good question, David." Clinton stirred the files in front of him to reveal a sheet of paper with a pencilled scrawl on it. "I've had a call from the Chief Constable of Mid-Wessex. It seems that you've annoyed one of his officers —a superintendent by the name of Weston."

Audley felt absurdly pleased. It made him feel better not to have put one over on the Superintendent too successfully.

"If I have, then I'm sorry, Fred. He's an extremely capable chap, Weston."

"He is?" Clinton raised an eyebrow. "Well, he thinks you're capable too—capable of anything. And this time he thinks you've got away with murder."

Audley enlarged his smile. "Yes . . . well, I often do, don't I? But I shall have to apologise to him."

"I think he means it literally. So he may not accept your apology."

"Literally? How on earth does he arrive at that conclusion?"

Clinton's smile was no longer even a memory. "Fortunately for you—not with any proof. Otherwise he would have charged you, his Chief says. But he maintains you did it, all the same, somehow or other." Clinton slid the paper back under one of the files and stared at Audley. "He'd just like to know how . . . and so would I, David."

Audley pointed. "You've got my report, Fred."

"So I have. And yet it doesn't say anything about murder in it, or not the one Weston's inquiring after." Clinton tapped the files. "And I've also received a special forensic report from the Mid-Wessex Force."

Audley nodded. "Well, you'll just have to choose the one

you like the better, won't you?" he said politely. "As Weston would say, it's proof that counts."

Clinton continued to stare at him. "Oh, but they don't conflict with each other at all. Yours has more . . . shall we say—theory in it. Plus all the information about the gold . . . But the section relating to the last fatality doesn't differ factually. Indeed, both reports come to the same conclusion."

"So the Chief Constable's call was unofficial, then."

"Entirely unofficial." Clinton opened the top file and turned its contents to a marked passage almost at the end. "So . . . let me see now . . . what it amounts to is that you both believe that Charles Neville Steyning-Ratcliffe blew himself up while tampering with—or perhaps setting—an explosive device . . . which according to you was probably intended as a trap for—who was it"

"Professor Stephen Nayler."

"That's right. Because Nayler knew too much about the gold —yes." Clinton nodded at the typed words. "And their forensic people have passed on various small objects and specimens to the Bomb Squad . . . which have been identified as parts of an American time pencil detonator—" He looked up. "—the standard CIA fifteen-minute device."

Audley nodded back. "There've been a lot of those around since Vietnam, Fred. Standard terrorist equipment now as well, they are."

"Quite so, David. And of course it was the same type as the one found on the Ferryhill Industrial Estate—which really clinches it, doesn't it?" Clinton paused. "But in any case you were in plain view, playing Cavaliers and Roundheads, for a good half an hour before the explosion. You never even went near the so-called 'Powder Tent'—as the Superintendent himself is the first to testify."

"Mrs Fitzgibbon will, too."

"I've no doubt she will. So you emerge without a stain on your character. . . . Which is just as well, because the Minister will want to see these files, and he would take an extremely dim view of our conniving at an assassination."

"So he made very clear to me, Fred. He just wanted me to make things happen."

"And you did, didn't you?" Clinton shut the file and sat back. "But you had quite a long conversation with Ratcliffe earlier. What exactly did you talk about?"

"It's in my report."

"Yes. You say you pushed him a bit with what you'd found out about him. But he must have known you couldn't prove anything?"

"I suggested to him that with Nayler's help we could probably prove quite a lot. I'm a good liar."

"I certainly wouldn't quarrel with *that* claim." Clinton put his hands on the edge of his desk and considered Audley in silence for a few moments. "So he decided to remove Nayler from the scene—that's what it amounts to, does it?"

"Obviously he intended to remove somebody. Nayler's the best bet."

"Ye-ess. . . . But don't you think it a bit odd that he should have tried to do it himself? He usually let the professionals make his hit for him."

Audley shrugged. "Maybe he didn't have time. Or maybe they just weren't available when he needed them." He looked inquiringly at Clinton. "Did he look for anyone?"

"Apparently not. He went back to his regiment after you'd talked to him, and then he ducked out again just before the explosion—they didn't miss him at the time." Clinton paused. "Funny though . . ."

"What?"

"Two of the people you suspected might have a hand in things—the men Oates and Bishop—they had a road accident just before the battle, on their way to Standingham. They ran into an American Air Force lorry—did you know that?"

"No." Audley shook his head. "Nothing serious I hope?"

"Concussion and fractures. And it was their fault, it seems. You didn't know about that?"

"Why should I? We never proved anything against them—or Colonel Butler didn't. And if Ratcliffe didn't look for them . . ." Audley spread his hands. "We'd pulled our people off them the day before, anyway. All except Frances—I told her to keep her eyes open for Oates and Bishop. And Paul Mitchell kept a sharp eye on Davenport all the time."

"I know.... So what it amounts to finally is that Charlie Ratcliffe tried to do something for himself for once, and made a balls-up of it."

"It looks that way," Audley agreed. "He should have stuck to revolutionary journalism. It's safer."

"Very well." Clinton leant forward and extracted the piece of paper from under the file again, tore it in two and dropped it into his wastepaper basket. "I accept your report."

"Thank you, Fred."

Now for it.

"And now, David, let's stop chasing around and get down to the real facts. Weston's a damn good copper, his chief says—and I'm an old copper of a sort too.... And you, as you have already admitted, are a liar."

"So what does that mean?"

Clinton pointed a finger. "It means that you came to some sort of arrangement with the CIA—with that young man you so promptly allowed to get away afterwards, Davenport or Donaldson, or whatever his name was. Which I don't like at all, but which I just might be ready to forgive, in the circumstances."

· "You would?"

"I *might*." Clinton's voice was suddenly cold. "But killing is another matter, David. If you're getting a taste for that as a quick way out of your difficulties then I have to know about it. Because you're no use to me like that."

"You really think I killed him, Fred?"

Clinton stared at him. "Weston said you were after blood—he says he recognises that now."

"I see." Audley nodded back slowly. That was fair enough on Clinton's part, because killing was as much an acquired taste as duelling, and there was only one way a successful duellist could reassure himself that he was still on the top line.

"The truth now, David."

What was the truth?

"All right. I didn't kill him, Fred. He killed himself."

"But you knew he'd kill himself?"

"I hoped he would. And I did my best to ensure he did."

"Then where's the difference?"

"The difference ... the difference is that it was up to him. If

251

he was willing to kill—then he died. If he wasn't—then he was home and dry. It was his choice."

"That's pretty shaky morality, David."

"Okay. So next time a terrorist blows himself up on his own bomb you weep your crocodile tears and I'll stick to my shaky morality, Fred." Audley made as if to get up. "Is that all, then?"

Clinton waved his hand irritably. "Sit down, man, sit down— if there was a fault it was mine, in letting you loose."

Audley sat down.

"How did he blow himself up?" asked Clinton.

Audley smiled. "With what they call a 'Judas'."

"Who call?"

"The CIA. When they lost all those fifteen-minute sabotage pencils in Vietnam they were pretty pissed off. And then one of their dirty tricks specialists thought of a simple way of getting even. They withdrew all the existing stocks and doctored 'em for instantaneous detonation, then they shipped them out to Vietnam again on the quiet to add to the other stocks. Which is why there have been so many terrorist accidents of late, I should guess."

"And you . . . acquired one from your friend Davenport?"

"Could be."

"But—you picked up that information in Washington?" Clinton's tone was hostile suddenly.

"I picked up a lot of information in Washington."

"And didn't report it?"

"I put in a separate technical report to the Equipment Section." Audley paused. "Yesterday."

They were now at the exact point of balance, he judged. It must be clear to Clinton that however improperly he had acted, nobody was in any position to prove otherwise, no matter what they might suspect. And if there was one thing that Clinton loved—although he would never have admitted it—it was low cunning.

All he had to do to keep his job was to throw a few more words into the balance.

And then, to his surprise, he realised that it wasn't the choice of words which mattered to him, but whether he wanted to say

252

them. Faith wouldn't mind if he didn't, she would be glad. But there was still Sergeant Digby's opinion to be consulted.

The sad truth was that he could no longer recall Sergeant Digby's features with absolute clarity, only the colour and texture of the boy's threadbare dressing-gown. He remembered thinking that he had once had a dressing-gown exactly like that, which had been threadbare in exactly the same places. You probably couldn't buy dressing-gowns like that any more, not of that durable quality. He should never have let Faith get rid of it—

"Tell me one thing, David—" Clinton was staring at him with unconcealed curiosity. "Tell me one thing—"

I've missed my opportunity, thought Audley. *Now he thinks I don't give a damn either way!*

"—as between friends—" Clinton's eyes were no longer angry. It was too late. The balance had tipped of its own accord.

"—how the devil did you con a smart fellow like Charlie Ratcliffe into doing a damn silly thing like that?"

When he'd finished Clinton sat silent for a few moments.

"A golden cannonball! God bless my soul!" His eyes narrowed. "A *solid* gold cannonball?"

"No, not solid gold. Just a thick coating of gold on lead—like a big toffee-apple, really."

"I see. But even that would have taken quite a lot of gold."

"It did."

"Not from the CIA, I trust."

"No. I have a ... friend who has a tame goldsmith."

"Matthew Fattorini?"

Audley ignored the question.

Clinton frowned suddenly. "But is it possible? I mean, is it ballistically possible? Wouldn't the gold have distorted in the barrel—and have blown the whole thing to kingdom come?" He paused, no longer really looking at Audley. "Though ... I suppose they did use lead bullets in muskets—even in rifled muskets ... and if the muzzle velocity was very low—" The eyes came back to Audley. "Is it possible?"

Well, well! thought Audley. *Even Fred Clinton.*

"Nobody knows." He shrugged. "Because nobody's ever tried. It would take a metallurgist who's been a gunner to tell you off

253

the cuff, and even he wouldn't know for sure. Charlie Ratcliffe was only a sociologist."

"But you didn't actually check—with a metal detector?" Clinton looked at him, his eyes narrowed again. "You just dug a hole at random?"

Audley stifled the rising temptation to laugh. "It isn't there, Fred. Cromwell got it."

"We shall have to look all the same." Clinton shook his head as though to clear it. "But he believed you, anyway."

"I wouldn't go so far as to say that. I'd guess he saw the possibilities, though."

"The possibilities?"

"Oh yes. . . . He saw that if I betrayed my own side—and the CIA as well—then I wouldn't have a friend in the world. And that would change me from a greedy pig into a sitting duck—for him and his friends. And the fact that I'd not asked him to do the job himself reassured him that he wasn't in danger."

"Except you'd made sure they wouldn't be there—Oates and Bishop—so he couldn't ask them to do it." Clinton frowned. "But he didn't try to ask them, did he? He didn't even look for them?"

"No. But taking them out of circulation was really just . . . insurance. I was relying on his doing it himself."

"How could you rely on that?"

Audley looked at him for a moment, then down at the files on the desk. " 'Information received', I suppose you might say."

"Information from whom?" Clinton was clearly puzzled.

"Oh, it's not in the record, Fred." Audley shook his head slowly. "It wasn't the sort of information that goes in records. It was much too subjective for that."

"But good all the same—obviously."

"But good . . . yes." Audley nodded. "You see, I talked to this—well, I guess you could call him an expert on human greed. . . . And he said that the possession of gold does things to people. He made it sound like a contagious disease."

"Contagious?"

"Infectious too—you showed a symptom or two yourself just now. But the contagious variety is the worst, and Charlie had got that badly. Because he'd handled the stuff . . . he'd felt the weight of it, and seen the beautiful colour of it. Which was why it didn't surprise him one bit that I was prepared to kill and betray for it—he recognised his own symptoms subconsciously."

"And twice the gold made him twice as greedy, you mean?"

"Maybe. But I don't think he would have seen it like that at all. Because what the Russians had given him was *their* gold. What I'd got—what I might be taking from his land right under his nose—that was *his gold*. And he couldn't bear the thought of it, it was worth almost any risk to stop that—and he couldn't bear the possibility that Oates or Bishop might say 'no' to the risk being taken. So he had to take it himself."

Clinton studied him. "You sound as though you were very sure of him."

"Not totally. But there was one thing I was sure of."

"And what was that?"

Audley's eye was caught for an instant by the rich colours of the flowers in the hearth. "I only met one man who'd actually seen Charlie Ratcliffe in action—who knew him as he was. . . . He was an old gardener who liked growing flowers—the gardener at Standingham Castle."

Clinton waited.

"He said Ratcliffe was a chancer. So I gave him his chance, Fred. That's all. And he took it."

AUTHOR'S NOTE

The Sealed Knot, the King's Army and the Roundhead Association, which are mentioned in passing in this story, are real organisations. The Double R Society and its members in no way resemble these admirable and innocent groups, except perhaps in such virtues as they may share. No comparison between the factual and the fictional is intended.

On the other hand, the story of Soviet Russia's acquisition of the gold of the Spanish Republic is a matter of history; as is also that of General Krivitsky, the one-time Chief of Soviet Military Intelligence in Western Europe, who escaped to tell the tale—and to die in suspicious circumstances in a Washington hotel in 1941.